Hunger and Thirst

'Love story, psychological thriller, highly literary horror –
Claire Fuller pulls off all three with this brilliant novel that is
familiar and frightening in equal measure. Most of all,
it's GREAT FUN. I absolutely loved it'
Kathleen MacMahon, author of *Nothing But Blue Sky*

'Gripping, haunting and deeply visceral, this book is a
beautiful nightmare that I just can't shake off'
Tobi Coventry, author of *He's the Devil*

'I was enthralled, rapt, utterly unable to put this book down.
Claire Fuller, a master of psychic suspense, has done it again'
Lindsay Hunter, author of *Hot Springs Drive*

'Harrowing and tender . . . the kind of book to clear
a weekend for, the kind of resonant nightmare
that lingers long after its end'
Hayden Casey, author of *A Harvest of Furies*

'I've read everything Claire Fuller has published. Her writing
is so emotional and intelligent in looking at the real struggles
that so many people go through. I'm really passionate about her
writing and so excited for this new book' Eric Karl Anderson,
My Most Anticipated Books of 2026 (YouTube)

'Utterly absorbing, genuinely unsettling . . . like all the most
terrifying horror films of the seventies and eighties,
and all the most scary ghost stories'
Jennie Godfrey, author of *The List of Suspicious Things*

'It frightened and enthralled me'
Alice Winn, author of *In Memoriam*

Hunger and Thirst

CLAIRE FULLER

FIG TREE
an imprint of
PENGUIN BOOKS

FIG TREE

UK | USA | Canada | Ireland | Australia
India | New Zealand | South Africa

Fig Tree is part of the Penguin Random House group of companies
whose addresses can be found at global.penguinrandomhouse.com

Penguin Random House UK,
One Embassy Gardens, 8 Viaduct Gardens, London SW11 7BW

penguin.co.uk

First published 2026

001

Typeset by Six Red Marbles UK, Thetford, Norfolk
Printed and bound in Great Britain by Clays Ltd, Elcograf S.p.A.

The authorized representative in the EEA is Penguin Random House Ireland,
Morrison Chambers, 32 Nassau Street, Dublin D02 YH68

A CIP catalogue record for this book is available from the British Library

HARDBACK ISBN: 978-0-241-75738-3
TRADE PAPERBACK ISBN: 978-0-241-75739-0

Penguin Random House is committed to a sustainable future
for our business, our readers and our planet. This book is made from
Forest Stewardship Council® certified paper.

For Stuart, Georgie, Dom, Helen, John, Sarah, Carol, Rhian, Denise, Melanie, Chris, Hilary, Robert, Eloise, Greg, Caroline, Paul J, Izabel, Julie, Samantha, Paul L, Julian, James, Rachel, Polly, Carinna, Andy, Louise, Clio, Peter, Beverley, Paula, Rich, Nicola, Heidi, Paul T, Tim and Lucille. W S A. Class of '89.

I

All everyone wants to know about is the murder and what we did with the body: armchair detectives, tabloid journalists, the curious and the ghoulish, speculating on what happened. After the documentary was broadcast, even a few art critics and reviewers circled back to the events that occurred in the late 1980s at the Underwood. The house was bulldozed years ago, but as I sit half-asleep and upright on my chair or sprawled out in a dream state, I see again the textured glass in the front door, find myself creeping down the L-shaped hallway or staring through the kitchen window to the garden, where the sofa squats in the long grass. Then my mind takes me outside and up on to the roof, where I balance on the highest point and gaze at the flowering candles of the horse chestnut – the tree miraculously alive once more. I spread my arms and tip my body forward, aware that behind me the garage waits.

The conspiracy theorists, internet trolls and Emma Zahini will not be happy with what I have to say, but nevertheless this is the truth. Now I have to prepare myself for whatever is coming, and must decide whether or not I let it in.

In 1987 I was a naive sixteen-year-old living in a halfway house inhabited by recovering alcoholics, ex-junkies labouring at keeping themselves clean and men recently released from prison. This troubled hotchpotch was no family, but it was the only place my social worker, Joy, could find for me at short notice. She'd got me a job as well, in the local art school's post room, hired via a 'Get Youth Back Into Work' scheme she'd managed to wangle me on to, although at sixteen I was below the eligible age and, since it was my first job, I wasn't going *back* into employment.

In the mornings, after sorting the post with my colleague Terry, I pushed my trolley through the art school's various departments: Film Studies, Painting, Photography and Print-making. I saved Sculpture until last so I could linger, inhaling the industrious smells of plaster, glue and sawdust, loitering by the noticeboard – a palimpsest of flyers for the Wednesday-night disco, guitar lessons with tear-off strips, film nights, lost keys and a found watch, a sign-up form for a trip to a forth-coming Jacob Epstein exhibition in London.

Of course, I wouldn't have used the word 'palimpsest' in those days. Like most teenagers, I believed I knew everything, but really all I had to go on was the shitty little corner of the world I'd experienced so far. Joy was always saying, 'Keep your head down, Ursula, stay out of trouble and you'll be fine.' She liked that I was a hard worker who didn't question too many things and didn't usually cause a drama, and it made her life easier that at least one of the children on her list hardly lifted her head to look around. My eye-opening understanding of the world came only a month or so after I walked through the Sculpture department that morning in early May.

I pushed my trolley with my good hand, and with my left – the forearm in plaster after a nasty break – I held up and read one of the visiting Sculpture tutor's regular postcards from Canada. Come on, who wouldn't read someone else's postcard given the opportunity?

The bear misses you. I miss you. How long till we can be a family of two again? (Three if you count the bear.) Eight weeks and five days.

All my love, Samuel

Samuel always wrote jokey messages like this, counting down the days, waiting for Ms Barker, sometimes talking about the house he was renovating for them. On the front of the postcard was an old photograph of two men, brothers maybe, one in a bowler hat, the other with a small brown bear. PET BEAR, BANFF, CANADIAN ROCKIES, the inscription read. My mother, Sadie, had called me Little Bear when she was in a good mood and I was behaving, and Ursula when I was not. When I was very young, I loved both names, but through puberty and beyond I was mortified by 'Ursula' and its meaning. The frizzy hair on my head was hard to tame, and the rest of it, my other body hair, something I mostly managed to ignore.

I slotted the postcard into Ms Barker's pigeonhole, deposited the other post for Sculpture, and stopped at the double doors to the second-year studio. They were always open, and I would often pause to look in, but that morning I left my trolley in the corridor and stepped inside. The studio was large and white, with a high ceiling and windows that faced north. There weren't any students in that early, but they had demarcated their workspaces with strips of masking tape stuck to the floor, and I went from one area to the next, examining the sculptures: an enormous horse welded from rusty lengths of metal; chunky sections of wood pegged together to make what looked like a giant's chair without a seat; a mountain of old boards nailed any which way; and a clay head covered in damp hessian that I unwrapped and prodded. I touched them all, inspected them, formed an opinion.

In the fifth space the student had left a half-finished wood carving about the size of an adult torso, and it lay in the middle of the marked-out area with chips of wood strewn about like dry potato peelings. I hefted the sculpture over with ease and considered what it was supposed to be, coming to the conclusion that the student was trying to carve some oversized intestines tangled around half-a-dozen ribs. Beside it lay the tools the student had been using: a squat mallet and several chisels, one of which I picked up and moved from hand to hand, trying to work out how it should be held before raising it above my head like the killer in the shower scene from *Psycho*, a film I'd watched many times.

'What do you think of the carving?' a voice said and, hoping I hadn't been seen, I put the chisel back on the floor. Ms Barker, tall and slender with long limbs and short hair cut high across her forehead like a helmet, crouched beside me, and I inhaled the citrus scent of her perfume. I waited for her to say something about the chisel or to ask what I was doing in the studio. My usual response when caught doing something I shouldn't was to launch an attack, a defence mechanism my current therapist tells me stems from a childhood lived in children's homes, a reaction that will either keep people away or provide me with a feeling of control; preferably both. She says I have rejection issues; they've all said the same. But Ms Barker was waiting patiently as though she valued my opinion, and I did have one, I'd just never been asked it before, about anything.

The intestines didn't contrast enough with the ribs; they looked like they were made of the same material, which of course they were.

'No comment?' she said. I remembered what the all-male post-room and maintenance teams said about her:

smutty things about how her use of 'Ms' must mean she was a lesbian, and who didn't like a little girl-on-girl action? Although she wouldn't have had any idea about the 'jokes' these men made, I didn't want her to think I was like them – stroppy and uncommunicative with lecturers and tutors, which was the men's own defence mechanism, if only they'd known – and so I said, about the sculpture, 'It's not hungry enough.'

I wasn't sure 'hungry' was the right word, but Ms Barker said, 'I think you might be right. It's not working hard enough, there's no desire in there.' I was proud that in a small way I'd impressed her. We stood, and then she took in the nylon jacket and skirt of the post-room uniform, saw the trolley she must have walked past. On her face was an expression of awkwardness that she'd mistaken me for a student. She muttered an excuse and hurried out into the corridor as if she was going to the Sculpture office. I followed and she made a show of seeing her postcard in the pigeonhole, giving a hoot of delight, and for an instant I hated her for the life she had that I didn't: a person who cared about her enough to write postcards from Canada. Beside the noticeboard, strips of yellow sunlight slid through the small oblong windows near the ceiling, and a cold rushing swept through my body, a sensation I'd had a thousand times before.

Perhaps these things aren't significant: the postcard from Canada, the life I didn't have, the way the light fell from the windows across the floor. Maybe they don't mean anything, but long after what happened that summer, and the consequences, which have lasted a lifetime, I have finally realized that some stories need to be told.

2

The estate management building was a maze of leaky rooms in a block across the road from the art school's main campus and had been due for demolition ten years previously. It housed the post room and the maintenance office, my boss Alan's cubbyhole, various other storerooms, as well as the staff room. This had a small kitchen unit where I boiled two kettles of water and, following the stained list on the wall, made a dozen cups of tea or instant coffee, with two sugars or three, milky or strong, handing them out as my colleagues arrived for tea break. A dozen mismatched armchairs gradually filled around a low table with several ashtrays, the local paper and that day's copy of the *Sun*. My colleagues argued about an article revealing that men had been receiving infected blood from the NHS. Jonesy from grounds maintenance said 'poofters' deserved what they got, and Sue from the main office said he was a 'homophobic wanker' and he was wrong, these were haemophiliacs, not AIDS victims. Jonesy said he didn't care who they were, they were all bloody pervs. Alan said, 'Steady on. Remember we're all family here.' Terry stared into his coffee.

When everyone had arrived, I sat too, lit a cigarette and picked up the newspaper and a pen from the table. I was rather good by then at managing mostly one-handed. Someone had been doing the crossword. Vince, from buildings maintenance, was sitting opposite me, and in the paper's margin I drew him: his brown hair in a bun on the back of his head – to keep it out of the machines he repaired, I'd heard him explain – his wide mouth, pointed Adam's apple and the beginnings of a moustache, which was harder to get right than I'd imagined. Good-looking, I supposed, in a laddish kind of way. Usually everybody ignored that I was drawing, but this day Vince reached across and snatched the paper from me.

'Is that what you think I look like?' He waved it around, showing it to Terry and Sue.

'Give it her back,' Sue said in a bored tone, picking at her fingernails.

I'd never spoken to Sue properly, although she was about my age. When I handed over the post in the main office or collected any that was to be sent, one of us might say, 'All right?' with a nod of the head. She was slight with a narrow face and nose, and fine hair that lay flat against her head so that it was possible to imagine the shape of her skull. Her eyes were pale, and her eyelashes and eyebrows almost white. She looked like Jodie Foster in *The Hotel New Hampshire*, and I imagined she would fight for you with her claws out, until she changed her mind.

'Give it back,' I said to Vince and snatched the paper from his hand. Bob, who worked with Vince, whistled and I sat down again, and when their attention moved on, I scribbled hard over Vince's face and slapped the newspaper back on the table.

Alan checked his watch and said, 'Drink up, lads,' and the men drank the last of their tea and stubbed out their cigarettes. 'You okay to finish up, Ursula?' he said as he always did, and followed them out.

'For Christ's sake.' Sue, still sitting, gave the table a shove with her shoe, making the dirty mugs jiggle. 'I've had enough of this place. Family, my arse.' She stubbed out her own cigarette, stood and rinsed her mug under the cold tap, placing it upside down on the drainer. 'You should refuse.'

'What?' It hadn't occurred to me that this was an option.

'Just don't wash up,' she said, and before I could reply she snapped, 'Oh, do what you like,' and left.

I took my arm from its sling, removed my jacket and put on a single rubber glove. It wasn't so bad washing up – I was the newest employee, and it seemed to me this must be how it worked. In Doughty House, the last children's home I'd lived in, there had been a washing-up rota, and if you missed your slot or complained, Uncle Jimmy, the house manager, would enforce a penalty – grounding you for a week, or something worse.

Alan stuck his head around the door. 'By the way, I heard from her upstairs.' He looked up to the ceiling and I looked too, as though we could see through it into Mrs Rooney's office. 'I gather your tête-à-tête went well. Looks like you'll be staying with the family.' He winked.

When I'd gone up the previous afternoon, Mrs Rooney hadn't seemed to be expecting me, although Alan said he'd booked in my appraisal. He'd said it was best done by a woman even though he was my boss, something about the females of the species understanding each other better. Mostly I'd sat at her desk, looking at the tangle of cables that trailed out of the backside of her personal computer as we waited for it to wake itself from a black sleep. She asked if I'd settled in and whether I was finding my way around. I told her I hadn't had any problems. She said I'd do well if I made sure I fitted in with the lads, didn't disturb the status quo and let them have their jokes. We'd finished our conversation by the time the computer whirred awake. She ended by suggesting I try to join in more, so that I wasn't considered stand-offish. I hadn't known this was how they saw me; I hadn't realized they saw me at all.

In the staff room, Alan said, 'How about going to the dinner on Friday night?'

I pulled a face.

'What's wrong with a nice dinner? You won't have to put up with me. It's only the young ones going.'

I shrugged. I didn't want to go, but like the washing-up, I didn't know I could refuse.

'Berni Inn, seven thirty. It's a send-off for that feather-brained girl, what's her name, Michelle from the Painting office. Getting married. God knows how.'

'I don't think –' I started.

'Are you busy on Friday night? Got better things to do?'

I didn't answer.

'Good, because I've put your name down.' And he was gone, along the corridor. 'Back to work, Ursula,' I heard him call.

Would any of what came after have happened if I'd stood up to Alan? If I'd said, *No, I don't want to go.* But to do that I would have had to be a different sixteen-year-old, more like Sue, less like myself, prone to hiding in a crowd despite my size and attempting to get along with authority. There are consequences for every action, of course, but some – the theft of a weapon, the howl of a wolf – have repercussions that end lives.

Emma Zahini contacted me about a year before her television documentary *Dark Descent* was broadcast. I knew who she was even though I don't watch much television; she had a reputation as a troublemaker, but her documentaries were watched by millions across the world. I thought my email address was private, but for someone like her – tenacious, unscrupulous, obsessed – it must have been easy to find. She wrote that she'd always been fascinated by the case. *Case.* I didn't like her choice of word, as though the things that had happened could be assigned a number and filed away. She said she was reaching out to me, and others, to see whether we could meet. Her excitement repelled me, how she might have been leering over the body and rubbing her hands. But it was the word 'others' that worried me; I was always going to say no to her request for an interview, but who amongst those involved might have said yes?

3

I thought I knew what a Berni Inn would be like from the adverts on the telly. The couples were always slim, good-looking and old; they ate their steaks with their mouths closed and talked quietly. They were nothing like our group. We were younger and noisier, twelve of us sitting at three tables that had been pushed together. At one end was Michelle, a helium balloon bobbing above her head with the words WE NEVER LIKED YOU ANYWAY taped over the original message. She was wearing a sash that read YOU ARE DEAD TO US.

I'd never been to a restaurant before. When I was seven, nearly eight, my foster parents, Dr and Mrs Hulse, would occasionally order a Chinese takeaway, and once Dr Hulse took me with him to collect it. I stood eye level with the counter, amazed at the number of dishes on the menu, which was pinned under glass, and wondering how the owners could make them all in the tiny kitchen I could see through the hatch. I was disappointed when Dr Hulse, as ever, ordered the set menu for three. We waited on the row of chairs against the front window for our food, and, twitchy with the smells of cooking, I snapped a leaf from the dusty cheese plant stuck in a dry pot. Dr Hulse, his bushy eyebrows pushing together like hairy fighting caterpillars, slapped my bare leg.

The cheapest steak on the Berni menu was sirloin, and it

came with chips, half a tomato, peas and some leafy fronds. I bent low over the meat and inhaled – a childhood habit I'd acquired from Sadie. She had an excellent sense of smell and often claimed she could 'smell a rat' or that there was 'something fishy' about where we were staying, and, wrinkling her nose, she'd make a game of packing our things into the car and taking off.

Vince, sitting opposite me, gawped, his mouth widening to a grin. He'd finished a pint of lager and was starting on a second. I'd ordered a glass of white wine, which was too sweet. I was sure I'd seen Vince sniffing the milk at work even when it was a fresh bottle, even if he had to press the foil top to open it. 'Find something in common and talk about that,' Joy would tell me when encouraging me to make friends. Did sniffing your food count?

Sue, sitting on my left, picked up her fork and serrated knife to nudge her meat away from the tomato. She'd ordered the steak too. I held mine with my fork upright and sawed through it with the knife, hindered by the greying plaster cast, which didn't allow my wrist to bend.

Michelle was shouting drunkenly, and Sue, tilting towards me, said, 'I'm never going to get married. No way.' I hadn't thought about it – in those days I wasn't a person who thought very far ahead; most evenings I didn't know what I would eat until I got home and looked in the cupboard at what tins I had. 'And why is she leaving her job? Like you can't be married and go to work. Probably up the duff. I'm never having kids either.' She ate a piece of steak. 'How are you planning on getting out of here?'

'Out of here?' I looked behind me to the restaurant door.

'Hilarious,' she said, as though I were joking. She waved her fork in a circle. 'The art school. The post room.'

Now, I know that the question *What are you going to be when you grow up?* is a standard, but in my sixteen years no one had asked it of me. Without us being aware, there was an assumption that the lives of us children raised by the state would follow a habitual course. We would flow downstream with the current; one or two of us might manage to cling to the bank and climb out, but the rest would end up in deep water, flounder and go under.

'You need to have an escape plan,' Sue said. 'I'm going to America to make movies. I'm applying for my passport as soon as I've got the photos done.' She chewed her meat. 'Want to go to America?'

'What?' I wasn't certain I'd heard correctly, that she'd invited me to go with her. I knew nothing about the place, except it was where they made most of the films I watched. Glamorous, unreal, not for people like me. 'To Hollywood?'

'Or wherever.'

Vince interrupted. 'You're better off at a Berni!' he shouted down the table, and gave a long rumbling belch accompanied by a clenched fist and a lowering arm. This sort of behaviour had been common around most of the children's home's dining tables and didn't trouble me. Michelle and her friends shrieked with laughter. Vince had released his hair from its bun, and it fell in waves to his shoulders. He reminded me of the actor from *Jesus Christ Superstar*.

'Vince thinks he's going to get some soon.' Sue was tilting closer. 'Watch this.' She licked her lips. 'Vincent?' She leaned across the table suggestively. Her oversized white T-shirt with its shiny blue lettering had slipped off one shoulder, revealing a bra strap. 'How's your fish?' She drew out the last word.

'Fish?' Vince said.

'You'd love a bit of fishy, wouldn't you?' The people around us laughed and she nodded towards his plate.

'This is scampi, not fish.' His words were slurred.

'Is it not fish, Vincent?'

The rest of us watched their back-and-forth.

'Right.' Vince picked up his glass.

'Right, Vincent,' she said, copying his intonation, laughing.

'You think you're so funny. It's Vince,' he said. 'Not Vincent, just Vince.'

'He thinks *Vince* is cool,' she said to me. 'Vincent believes he's going to have a bonk holiday soon.'

He stuck up two fingers. 'I believe I'm going to have another drink.' He drank half his pint, his Adam's apple going up and down like a piston, and he moved so his back was to her.

And as if she'd given up on him, her attention returned to me. 'What happened to your arm?'

'My arm?'

I wetted my lips with the wine. I'd never really taken to drinking, although there'd been plenty of opportunities to drink alcohol growing up. In one home a staff member sold it to the children for favours, and as far as I could see, the children drank to fit in with their peers, to blot out what they didn't want to remember, or to change their reality. But I could never drink enough to forget that, when I was sober again, my reality wouldn't have changed. Where to start about my arm? Maybe when I was seven and was stuck in a bathroom for three days. Or a month ago when I landed on a bedroom floor. 'A cry for help', Joy had called it, and it had been enough to persuade her I was serious about wanting to get out and have my own place, without chores and rotas, curfews and punishments. I thought I was an adult, and I wanted to be treated like one.

With my steak knife in my hand, I looked at the plaster cast covering my left arm from hand to elbow, blank except for a few doodles I'd done myself. 'I broke it.'

'Were you in a fight?'

'Something like that.' It wasn't a big secret; it was just that I didn't talk about my past and I never asked anyone about theirs.

Across the table, Vince saw the knife in my raised hand, and he pretended to press back the people sitting either side of him.

'Careful, she's got a knife!'

I jabbed it towards him, and Sue hooted with laughter and Vince fell about in mock fright, knocking over his empty glass as he put his hand to his throat as though I'd cut him. I lowered the knife and hacked off another piece of steak.

'You don't have to tell me if you don't want to,' Sue said.

'I fell off a bunk bed. Put my hands out –' I demonstrated. 'And snap!'

Something in Sue's mind whirled; I could see it in her eyes. 'Was there blood? Could you see bone?'

'The cast is meant to come off next month. I can't wait. It's so itchy.'

Across the table, Vince said, 'Good to see Ursula enjoying her meat.' He showed his teeth.

Sue picked up a chip and put half of it in her mouth, closing her lips around it. Vince and I goggled as she withdrew it, slowly. Her mouth opened and her tongue licked, and she bit down on the chip, breaking it in half and chomping the piece in her mouth with her lips parted, before chucking the rest of it on her plate.

He shook his head at her. His eyes were glassy with drink. She put her head back and laughed.

'Ursula doesn't call me Vincent,' he said, to draw me in. 'Do you, Ursula?' I wasn't sure I'd ever called him anything.

'Ignore him,' Sue said, turning away. She put some of the leafy stalks from her plate in her mouth. 'You should always eat your vegetables,' she said.

In the filthy shared kitchen in the halfway house, I cooked frozen peas because Joy said I had to eat something green with every meal. I kept my own washed-up plate and bowl in my bedroom because I knew that at least one of the other tenants washed his crockery by licking it. But these green leaves, the same as on my plate, I'd never had before. I resisted the urge to sniff them and instead, as Sue had done, I picked up a stalk with my fingers and crammed it into my mouth. Not all of it fitted, and when I bit down, my mouth was filled with peppery juice that made me gag.

'Are you okay?' Sue asked.

I pushed my chair back and blundered across the plush carpet of the restaurant, following the signs to the ladies', and into a cubicle where I spat into the toilet bowl and hung my head over the water, waiting to be sick. I sat on the floor with my shoulders against the wall and wondered what Mrs Rooney and Alan would say if I left. That I'd deserted the family. When I wasn't sick, I splashed my face with water at the sink and went back to my seat. Someone had crossed out the message on Michelle's helium balloon, replaced it with the word WILD and tied it to my chair. Vince had swapped places with Sue, and my plate, with what had been left of my steak, was gone, and the knife too; all the table had been cleared. The waitress handed out menus for dessert.

'What do you fancy?' Vince said, waving his about. The balloon bobbed over my head. 'Black Forest gateau? Ice cream sundae? The cheese and biscuits are only 50p. Look at her.' He pointed the menu at Sue, across from us. She was studying hers, biting her bottom lip. 'Has she told you that she's going to America? Well, that ain't gonna happen.' He tried on an American accent. It was poor. 'A girl like Sue doesn't get to go to Hollywood and direct movies.' He struggled to get a cigarette out of a packet and light it. 'They'd never let her in.' As he spoke, his body slanted sideways until I thought he might fall on me.

The waitress arrived at our end of the table and a couple of women ordered dessert. Sue asked for the gateau and Vince ordered cheese and biscuits. I wanted more. When it was my turn, I said, 'I'll have the steak.' The waitress gaped and Vince's laughter was crazed. He slapped his thigh and the table. 'Rare, please,' I said. 'No green leaves. No chips.'

'No green leaves, no chips,' he repeated, and held his mouth open as though waiting for applause.

'Don't be an idiot,' Sue said without looking up.

'It's fine,' I said. There was power in making Vince laugh, in having Sue want to stick up for me.

The waitress laid out pudding cutlery from a silver tray. People asked for coffee liqueurs and Vince ordered a brandy. The waitress brought me a fork and another steak knife.

This steak was better than the previous one, redder and juicier in the middle. I ate it while Vince jabbered away beside me, making quips, swilling his brandy and sniffing it, laughing. Sue joked with Terry, their heads together, and Vince placed squares of cheese on his crackers. I was the last to finish, and he'd grown bored of watching me eat. He called up the table to Michelle about how he'd like to cream her cracker, and she called back, 'Never in a million years!'

'You won't make me jealous,' Sue said, quietly, and he didn't respond, and I thought maybe he didn't hear.

As the plates and bowls were cleared for the final time, I slipped my second knife under the table. I don't know why I took it; perhaps I liked its power. The waitress didn't notice it was missing. Vince had the hiccups, and he tipped back the last of his brandy. The waitress was hovering with a small plastic folder.

'You can tell us.' Vince's voice carried across the emptying restaurant. 'No way you broke your arm falling off a bunk bed.'

I looked at Sue – she'd told him, while I was in the toilet. She didn't look at me.

Vince continued: 'Fell out of a tree more like! Were you brought up by monkeys or gorillas, or what? Did your mum and dad do it doggie?' He moved his hips backwards and forwards sitting in his chair. The table quietened. No one spoke and no one stopped him. 'It couldn't have been cows with all that steak you put away tonight.' Another hic. 'Must have been wolves.' He put his head back and howled. Two yips and a longer note, repeated. The waitress placed the folder in front of Michelle.

Only Vince was laughing, and I stood quickly and raised the knife and, holding the bottom of the balloon, I stabbed it.

'It was bears,' I said, and his laughter died. The pop was loud, and Sue covered her mouth with her hand and the balloon's silver insides fell to the floor.

'Put the knife down, Ursula,' Vince said.

I smiled, taking a step towards him, enjoying the sight of him listing until he was almost in his neighbour's lap, but I swerved, dropping the knife into my handbag – it might be useful at home, where the knives were blunt.

Sue stopped me at the restaurant door. '*Remember, we're all family here,*' she said in a good impersonation of Alan. She was trying to make me laugh. When I didn't, she said: 'You mustn't mind Vince, he gets a taste in and he can't stop. He'll feel bad about it tomorrow, and we can make him pay. You have to make them pay, it's the only way to get ahead.'

4

The next day, a Saturday, I lay on the sofa in the lounge rewatching a videotape of *The Stepford Wives*. The other tenants in the halfway house got up late at the weekend, and I didn't like the quiet. In each children's home, and I'd lived in seven, there'd always been noise and chaos – staff or children shouting or crying, small acts of violence against one another or some big enough for the police to be called. Noise and violence had been part of my life, and maybe I missed them.

I was drifting in and out of the film, thinking about Sadie and what kind of housewife she might have made if she had lived; certainly not one who liked ironing and discussing which brand of starch was preferable. One of my first memories was of waking inside her open guitar case with the scent of the dusty plush interior and seeing her foot tapping on the floor beside her chair. I don't remember the music, but if her foot was tapping, she must have been singing and playing guitar – 'Happiness Runs' or 'Those Were the Days' or the song she hated but everyone wanted: 'All Kinds of Everything'. If it was summer, we slept in her car, me across the back seat, Sadie on a bed she made in the front. She worked whatever jobs she could get with me in tow, or played in pubs, or busked on the street, dressing me in a dirndl and tying bells around my ankles so my dancing would earn us more money. A dancing bear. Once, when I asked whether my dad liked dancing, she'd hugged me and said, 'Don't give that man a single consideration. He was a one-night stand and we do not think of him.' For years I imagined him hairy, large-bodied and standing for a whole night on one leg.

In the house the doorbell rang, but I didn't get up. I was half listening to a muffled conversation and half watching the climax of the film when Joanna, the main character, has her worst fears realized. The front door closed. One of the tenants had let someone in. I sat up, dragging my eyes from the screen. Sue was in the doorway of the lounge. She'd never visited me before; no one came to the house to see me except Joy. I wondered how Sue had got my address, but she worked in the art school's main office so perhaps it was as simple as lifting my file from a cabinet.

'Who was that?' Her eyes were wide, and I tracked her gaze as she stared over her shoulder.

'Dave? Big beard?'

She shook her head, almost laughing. Her hands moved expressively downward and apart. 'Black man, posh, boxers.'

'John. He forgets to tie the belt of his dressing gown. He's harmless.' I sneaked a glance at the film, where Joanna's neighbour was pushing her trolley around the supermarket in her sun hat and white gloves.

'I love this film.' Sue sat beside me. 'You know when Joanna takes her photographs into the gallery to get that man's opinion?'

'Yeah?'

'I wish she wouldn't care so much about what he says. Stand up for herself a bit.'

'Right.'

'And you know when Joanna stabs Bobbie in the stomach with the kitchen knife?'

'Yeah?'

'Apparently, Joanna – Katharine Ross – couldn't face doing it even though Bobbie was wearing a false stomach. Forbes had to do it for her – it's his hand we see. Don't you think that's funny?'

'Who's Forbes?' I pulled my eyes from the television to look at her.

'Bryan Forbes? The director?'

We turned back to the film and watched to the end of the credits without speaking. When the screen was black, I ejected the videotape and snapped it into its box.

'Can I borrow it?' she asked.

'I have to return it tomorrow.'

'I'll watch it tonight and take it back for you.'

'I don't want to get a fine.'

'Don't you trust me?' She cocked her head and smiled, but I held on to the box. 'Forget it. I've watched it a zillion times already.' She scrutinized the room, taking in the sagging arm-chairs, the coffee splatter across the wallpaper, and the little table with its full ashtrays and beer cans, its dirty plates left by whichever tenant had been in here the night before.

'It's temporary,' I said. 'I'm looking for somewhere better.' It hadn't occurred to me until I said it that I could find another place to live. After I broke my arm, Joy had pre-sented the house and the room to me, and I'd accepted them without question.

Breaking my arm had been my first proper act of subver-sion. I was sitting on the edge of the top bunk in my friend's room in Doughty House, leaning forward and flicking through a magazine about clothes, music and boys that she'd swapped with me for a cigarette. The term 'friend' was a loose one in Doughty House. We were often moved without a chance to say goodbye or a way to keep in touch; friendships were fickle and based on what items or services you were able to offer. I had many of these relationships; sometimes they were over in a day or two, firing up intensely and burning themselves out in a fight or when one of us was relocated.

This girl was on the top bunk too, leaning against the wall, when she said, 'Why don't you shave that gross hair on your back?' And I realized my T-shirt was untucked from my jeans. I sat upright. 'While you're at it,' my so-called friend said, 'you should do something about that hair in your armpits and on the insides of your thighs.'

One moment I was reading about Rick Astley and banana-coloured dresses, and the next I was thumping a solid fist against the side of her face. She shoved me hard and fast with both feet, and at the same time I launched myself off the bunk with my left arm out. I'd had enough of her and Doughty House, and as I hit the floor I heard a crack, but was only winded until the searing pain outstripped my surprise. It's a short and simple story, not unusual for Doughty House. The girl looked over the edge of the bunk and started to scream.

In A&E the staff member who'd come with me phoned Joy, and when she arrived, uninhibited by the painkillers I'd been given, I said that after the operation to screw a metal plate into my bone was over, when my arm was in plaster and they let me out, I wasn't going back to Doughty House. I'd sleep in a car if I could find one unlocked. The next day Joy found me the room in the halfway house and gave me her home phone number.

'Emergencies only,' she'd said, and I'd tucked the piece of paper into my purse.

In the lounge, I asked Sue if she would like a cup of tea. Joy had got me into the practice of asking this whenever she came to see me. She always replied 'That would be lovely' in a sing-song voice that let me know there was a lesson in our question and answer.

'I'd kill for a coffee,' Sue said, and followed me to the kitchen. 'I'm so hungover.'

This room, after a Friday night, was in a worse state than normal; I could see it in Sue's face and hear it in the way the soles of her trainers stuck and unstuck to the lino as she walked. Foil containers with what looked like the remains of chow mein and egg fried rice lay across the counter, and the sink was piled with dirty plates. She sat on the edge of a kitchen chair in her jeans and baggy sweatshirt. I wanted to ask why she'd come round, but in my head the sentence sounded rude no matter how I rearranged it, and I worried that as soon as I asked her, the visit would be over. I made her a coffee using John's instant granules and someone else's milk. I made myself a black tea and we took our drinks upstairs.

'Oh, your room is –' She paused. 'Tiny!'

My bedroom was a narrow space created from half the landing, with a single bed and a sash window at the far end, murky with dirt.

'It's better than my old place.'

'The children's home?'

I was only a little surprised that she knew this was where I'd lived before; perhaps this too was in my work file.

'Didn't you have your own room there?' she asked.

'It never felt like mine.'

'But you had bunk beds. Why did you have bunk beds

if the room was yours?' She seemed to be trying to catch me out.

'I didn't have bunk beds. I jumped off the top of someone else's bunk, not mine.'

'I thought you said you fell?'

'Fell, jumped, same thing.'

She considered me for a moment. 'What happened to your parents?'

I closed my mouth and didn't answer; this was too much, but she seemed unfazed by my lack of response.

'Look at these,' she said admiringly, about the drawings I'd taped up of John and the men in the staff room. 'These are amazing. You should have an exhibition.'

I liked her praise, but I wasn't going to let her know it. 'I don't think so.'

'Draw me,' she said.

'I have to be in the mood.'

'Now. Oh, please now.' She heeled off her trainers and sat cross-legged on the bed, facing me. She was motionless. 'Like this?' she asked. She tilted her head against the wall. 'Or this?' She looked down.

I'd never drawn to order before or with someone watching; I wasn't sure I could do it. My drawings were on discarded pieces of paper I'd salvaged from the post-room waste bin, the margins of newspapers or whatever else I could find. I took a pen and an old envelope from my bag and rested it on a magazine, trying to keep the paper steady with my left hand.

'Is the coffee okay?' I asked.

'It's great,' she said. Her hands were wrapped around the mug in her lap.

'You can drink it. You can move about.'

She took a sip. 'It's definitely helping with the hangover.'

'I didn't think you were that drunk last night.'

'Not as bad as Vince. I bet he's feeling rough this morning, and he's got a football match today. He always feels guilty after he's been drinking, never plays his best after a night on the piss. Reckons they'll chuck him off the team soon.'

My pen hewed its way across the paper, carving out Sue's central parting and flat hair, and I wondered how we were going to make him pay for what he'd said the previous night. I drew the bones in her face and her sharp jaw, which came down to a chin like the stern of a tiny boat. Her top lip was thin and the bottom fuller, and her eyes lined imperfectly with blue eyeliner beneath eyebrows fine and light like her hair. Sometimes she looked at my drawing or my hand moving; now and again she looked me in the eye and I looked away.

'Oh my God.' She snagged her bottom lip with her teeth. 'I just remembered. You popped Michelle's balloon with your steak knife.' She put her head back and opened her mouth and laughed, and her face was transformed, suddenly alive and beautiful. I tried to capture it with my pen, but my shoulders started shaking and I giggled. We caught each other's eye and she collapsed sideways, coffee sloshing. I could see the pink of her gums, her red tongue and the back of her throat. 'And you ordered another steak.'

'Don't you ever get so ravenous you could eat everything and still not be full?' I was laughing too.

'Did you see Vince's face?' She was lying on the bed and had to put her coffee cup on the floor. 'And then you went for him too.'

'He deserved it.'

'Stop!' she said. 'Stop. I'm going to wet myself.' She rolled off the bed and on to the narrow strip of carpet, just missing her coffee. I lay on the bed in the opposite direction and finally we stopped laughing.

'I've never been drunk,' I said. 'I don't like the taste of alcohol.' I looked at her over the side of the bed.

'Probably good for you that you don't. Good for your liver or something. Vince can be pretty obnoxious when he's drunk.' She sat up, her arms around her knees. 'He was adopted when he was a baby. Why didn't anyone adopt you?'

Long after I learned what a one-night stand was and understood that my father most likely didn't know of my existence, I used to imagine him coming to save me. Hairy forearms hacking through thorny thickets, storming through doors and beating back the social workers and teachers to reach his daughter. He never came.

Sue's question was asked without malice, but I didn't like it. 'I don't know,' I said. 'Why didn't your parents give you up at birth for being nosy?'

She grinned. 'Fair point. What did you think of *The Stepford Wives*?' She didn't give me time to answer. 'I like that Joanna doesn't survive in the end. I'm tired of watching girls screaming and begging and getting attacked and still showing their tits. Or fighting back like a man would – why can't they fight back like a girl, like a woman?'

'Or do the killing.'

'Exactly!' She grabbed my arm and shook it. 'Do the killing like a woman. It makes me so angry that they don't.'

'Do you know anyone in Hollywood?'

'I'm writing the script for a short film. Nearly finished, I hope. But my camera has to be mended.'

I offered her a cigarette and we lit them. 'What's your film about?'

She waved her hand. 'I'm not ready to say. Let's see your

27

drawing.' I held it out. 'That's good,' she said. 'You should do something with your art.'

I thought she was going to ask to keep it, but she took my arm in its plaster cast and the pen and drew an approximation of my face – round with an excess of frizzy hair, which that morning I'd forgotten to try to tame. She drew small circles for my eyes, far apart. It wasn't a good drawing even when I attempted to look at it the right way up, but I told her it was great and she took my arm again and drew a heart around my face with an arrow going in one temple and out the other side, an *S* at the top and a *U* at the bottom.

We talked more about the art school and our favourite films. She told me that the next day she was having Sunday lunch with her family.

'None of them get me,' she said. 'Except Raymond, my older brother. My mum wants me to settle down.' She crooked her fingers, making quote marks in the air around 'settle down'. 'Find a husband, have babies, is what she means. You should come over. We could watch *Psycho* with Raymond although he doesn't like blood, and he gets annoyed when I explain how each film could be improved.' She didn't say when I was invited, and I wasn't sure if she meant it.

'I might take a blanket outside if it's sunny and sit on the grass,' I said. Sue was about to leave, and we were looking down into the garden from my window. We saw that it was a dank place, overgrown and gloomy, with a row of dustbins, and not somewhere anyone would want to sit. One of the tenants let his dog out there for a shit every morning – a little orange animal with a face like a squirrel. I didn't like gardens, conscious always of the small creatures in the undergrowth, the whine of insects, the crawling, inching things in the earth. Open University started at ten to seven on a Sunday; I would be spending the day in front of the telly.

At the front door, Sue shuffled her feet and shoved her hands deep into the pockets of her jeans. 'I hope you don't mind me mentioning it, but you left without paying last night. After all that stuff with Vince.'

I realized she was right. I'd been doing okay with money since I'd left Doughty House. Joy had helped me open a bank account and she was trying to teach me budgeting, making sure I saved enough for my rent and bills, having me write lists of purchases in a little notebook she'd given me.

'I made Vince pay for your dinner,' Sue said. 'And although he deserves it, he'll want to be paid back. He's such a tight-arse.'

'I've got some money in my room.' I turned and ran upstairs.

'It was nine pounds eighty-three pence,' she called. 'With the two steaks, the glass of wine and the tip.'

I had two five-pound notes in my purse. I took the money and ran downstairs.

'Here you are,' I said. 'He can keep the change.'

She looked at the notes and laughed, taking them from my fingers and stuffing them in her front pocket. I closed the door and went back upstairs, where I taped my poor drawing of Sue to the wall with the others. I sat on my bed looking at her drawing of me on my plaster cast, wondering if she was my friend now and whether that meant she would let me down.

5

On Monday I clocked in at seven, put my coat and bag in my locker, and worked alongside Terry logging the weekly equipment deliveries – bins of clay, printing inks, stationery for the main office, replacement easels and donkeys, all to be unwrapped and checked off. We also brought in the regular sacks of post from the Royal Mail van and handed over those for outgoing mail. When I'd first started, Terry, who was muscled and fit, had pulled one of the sacks off me, insisting women couldn't manage heavy loads, but Alan, resting on his elbows at his counter, said, 'Let her try,' and told me to use my thighs and stomach muscles to hoist the bag up and over my shoulder.

After the deliveries, Terry and I stood beside each other flicking envelopes like playing cards into departmental pigeonholes while he laughed about Friday night. He said he'd managed to get Vince home to his parents' house and up the stairs without them waking, and had left him on his bed on his side so he wouldn't choke if he was sick. Terry didn't mention Vince's obscene gestures and how he had howled like a wolf.

I walked through the main building with my morning deliveries, ending as always in Sculpture. Only one student was already working in the second-year studio, and I stood by the door, watching, poised to push my trolley onwards. He'd laid out a large piece of paper on the floor, the corners held down by stones. The sheet was as wide and as tall as he was, and he scuttled across it on all fours. Soft black lines flowed from his right hand, and in the other was a dirty rag that he used to smudge and blur and rub out. His whole body was drawing, performing a dance with arcs and shadows. I couldn't tell what it was supposed to be, perhaps it wasn't figurative. I'd taken O-level Art at school, but this had involved still-life drawings of jugs and dried flowers, or using primary-coloured poster paints splattered on sugar paper, or moulding lumps of clay into dinosaurs. I'd done well in the exam, but the art I'd made looked nothing like this. This student's work gave me a murky, excited feeling in my guts; that art could be created by making a mess and drawing could be a physical act using your whole body. I must have made a sound because the boy stopped, but before he could look up, my trolley and I were gone.

At morning tea break Sue and Vince were in the staff room, she in her office trouser suit and he with his hair in a bun. I looked at him differently now, knowing he'd been adopted, and gave him some leeway for his actions on Friday night, but I was also envious – what was it that had made him appealing to prospective parents when I had not been? Sue smiled at me, but we didn't talk.

Alan said, 'Drink up, lads,' and everyone except Sue and Vince put their cups on the table and filed out. Sue put her mug in my hands and said, 'Chop, chop,' like I was a fool to be washing up again. She nodded at Vince in a coded exchange and left.

One-handed, I collected the rest of the mugs and dumped them in the sink. I took off my jacket and put on the rubber glove. I shoved the hot water tap with my elbow, turned it on.

Vince cleared his throat. 'Apparently,' he said, 'I was

31

obnoxious on Friday. To be honest, I don't remember much about it.' He picked up the tea towel and sniffed it. 'Sue said I paid for your meal. Thanks for the money, by the way.'

'Yeah, you were obnoxious.' I yanked off the hot water, splashed in cold and squirted washing-up liquid into the bowl. Two cigarette butts floated to the surface. 'Go on, then,' I said.

'Go on then, what?'

'Apologize.' I sloshed a mug in the water and put it on the drainer upside down.

'I'm sorry.'

'Go on, then.'

'What?'

'Dry up.' I nodded at the mug, and he picked it up, stuffing the tea towel inside it, twisting it hard.

'Sue said you're looking for somewhere else to live.'

'Am I?'

'She said your place is a shithole.' He dried the outside of the mug.

'It is not.' I was defensive, although after Sue had left, the grottiness of the halfway house had become more evident: the smell of damp, the grimy windows, the understairs cupboard filled with old clothes and items previous tenants had left behind. Being placed with these men was not so different to being placed in the children's homes – all inhabitants strangers to me. I put the last mug on the drainer and plucked the glove from my fingers.

'She might not have used those words. She said you live in a tiny room in a filthy house with a load of flashers.'

'It's not as bad as that.'

He rubbed the tea towel around the mug's handle. It couldn't have got any drier. 'She says I have to tell you there's a room going in the house I'm moving into.' He put the mug in the cupboard and slammed the door. 'And that there's no rent.'

'Oh yeah? How come?' I put my jacket on and my arm back in its sling.

'No landlord.'

'Why isn't there any landlord?'

'I don't know, do I. The people who lived there before . . .' He paused. 'The wife went and the husband went too.'

'What's wrong with it?'

'Supposed to be haunted.'

'What?'

'Just a rumour. It's damp and falling down. Probably condemned.'

I didn't believe that places were haunted in real life, only in films. 'Why are you moving in?'

I put the mugs from the drainer into the cupboard, still wet.

'Had enough of my parents, and they've had enough of me, apparently.' He didn't expand. I knew he didn't want me to move into this house. I could tell he wanted this squat, if that's what it was, to himself.

'Where is it?'

He sighed. He'd lost. 'Barrow Road. The Underwood.'

These past thirty-six hours – is that all it's been? – I've managed a few hours of patchy sleep before I jerk upright, certain I heard a knock on my door, or the buzzer go, and I sit tense and silent, listening.

Six months ago, I was napping in the afternoon when the door buzzer woke me. I stumbled to the intercom and on the monitor I saw a woman, young, black hair in spirals, brown skin. A beauty, although beauty isn't something I've been interested in exploring, artistically. I knew who she was; still, I pressed the button to allow her to speak.

'Uschi?' the woman said. 'Is that Uschi? I'm Emma Zahini, I'm making the documentary? I sent you some emails? I just want to talk to you. Get your side of the story?'

I was surprised she'd come herself rather than sending a researcher, but maybe she thought her fame would open my door. It was true, she had sent me several more emails after the first, checking I'd received the previous one, almost begging for a reply.

I put my forehead to the monitor and closed my eyes. *It's not a story*, I might have said.

'Uschi,' Emma Zahini repeated, as though she were speaking in my ear. 'If you can hear me, I'd like to ask you some questions about what happened in the summer of 1987. It would be wonderful to speak to you.'

It occurred to me that it might be better to learn everything I could about the woman out there, and I opened my eyes. Maybe I should let her in. Emma Zahini took her mobile phone from her pocket and held it up to the row of buzzers and snapped a picture. *U. Major* it says beside mine, which I realized was a stupid mistake. She had found me, and my name confirmed my identity.

The man who lives in the ground-floor apartment came out of the front door while Emma Zahini was standing there. He seemed to recognize her too and held the door open for her with a smile, and she came inside. Sound carries oddly in this block, and from inside my apartment I can hear the lift: the ping of the call button, the metallic slide of the doors opening, the hollow clanging of the mechanism, the Judi Dench-type voice saying, *Doors closing, Going up, First floor, Second floor, Doors opening*. I don't mind. I like to think Dame

Judi is keeping an eye on things. That day I heard her voice, and the lift's mechanical clunk and whirr as it ascended, and then Emma Zahini was at my front door, rapping gently. I watched her through the peephole.

'Uschi?' she said again. 'Can we talk, off the record, whenever it's convenient? I left messages on your mobile phone.'

I'd listened to her messages; they were in the same style and tone as her emails: an overzealous saleswoman too convinced by her own product. I'd blocked her number. I'd disconnected my landline a long time ago and I rarely switch on my mobile, just taking it with me in case of emergencies. I could have counted on one hand the people I'd given the number to. Anger was replaced by a roiling fear as Emma Zahini knocked again.

'Uschi?' I could see a spiral of hair on the top of her head; she must have been pressing her ear against the door. I was never going to speak to this woman. 'Ursula?'

There it is, there it is, I thought. She knew who I used to be, which meant she knew everything. But how much was everything? If I let her in and told her what had happened, would she listen or did she have a preconceived idea of how her documentary would play out? No, I decided, I'd not been listened to before, and Emma Zahini had her own agenda. She isn't known for her subtlety and nuance. Her voice came through the letter box and I backed away. Since the events of 1987, I have never liked letter boxes. 'I should tell you that we've interviewed Suzie's aunt, and several other people have agreed to go on camera.' *Which other people?* I wanted to ask, but I knew if I started talking, she'd have got me. 'I'll leave my card.' She pushed it through and it dropped to the floor. 'Please give me a ring or drop me a line.'

Emma Zahini smiled at the peephole, her face rounded at the edges. I knew she knew I was there. She went towards the lift and I heard the doors opening. When I saw on the monitor that she had left, I put my shoe over her business card, opened my front door and slid it across the landing, then let it fall, scuffed and dirty, down the stairwell.

6

Before I left for the day, I went back to Sculpture and strode along the corridor like I was supposed to be there. I'd prepared an excuse that I was taking a shortcut if anyone questioned me. A student, a girl with straight brown hair and an unhappy mouth, was in the studio where the student had been drawing that morning. She was sitting on a piece of wood and frowning at the carving Ms Barker and I had discussed, and she glanced up when I came in, and seeing I was someone from the post room looked down again. She barely saw me. Although I was only four years younger, to her I was a different species, one that was almost invisible, blending into an underlayer of art school staff – the cleaners, cooks, maintenance men, technicians and porters – who were only acknowledged, called on or complained to when something went wrong. This student was wearing blue overalls and steel-toe-capped boots and was smoking a roll-up. She took it out of her mouth and looked at the end, which had gone out.

The male student's drawing was taped on the wall above one of the work tables. It looked even more dramatic here, face on. The smudged marks gave me a feeling of foreboding like the music at the start of a horror film, something glowering, moving too fast to see fully, as though a blackened body had swept parts of itself – an eyeball, a buttock, an elbow – up against the paper. I went towards it and saw, on the table, spilling out of a couple of boxes, the black sticks the student had used: WILLOW CHARCOAL, ASSORTED SIZES. I was aware without turning that the female student was watching me, curious about what I was doing, and I leaned across the table to examine the drawing more closely. At the same time, I wrapped my hand around three fat sticks of charcoal, angling them into my palm and up into the sleeve of my jacket.

'It's good, isn't it?' I said and looked over my shoulder. The girl stared at me, and as though in answer she flicked open her Zippo lighter and put the flame to the end of her roll-up, inhaling with a look of arrogance that said I had no right to be there and comment on a student's work. And it seemed to me that she could tell I had lived those years in temporary houses with no parents, without art or culture or knowledge, nobody to ask me who or what I could become.

A couple of evenings later I went to see the Underwood. Vince, who had yet to move in, said he'd get a key cut for me if I liked the look of the place, so this time I was only nosing around the outside.

The ugly bungalow hunkered at the lowest point on a strip of land formed where two roads diverged, an isosceles triangle with the building in the centre of the widest part. An open five-bar gate was being eaten by lichen at the top of a sloping drive, grass sprouting in the gravel. At the bottom, the detached garage was made of brown overlapping boards, and I didn't bother to look inside – I wasn't interested in the garage, not then. A concrete path led me towards the front door, between flower beds clotted with weeds and the occasional bright head of petals. There must have once been mown lawn up to the garden's vertex, but now the grass was thigh-high, and around its perimeter were overgrown hedges, nettles and bramble. At the point of the triangle, a tree with a trunk as wide as I was tall rose up far above the house, so that I had to tip my head to see its leaves, newly unfurled to a luminous green. I wasn't planning on getting any closer.

The bungalow was built in the 1950s – single-paned, metal-framed windows, poorly insulated and prone to condensation. It was made of brick with a concrete-tile roof, and as I approached the porch filled with last year's leaves, a soggy doormat and a milk bottle holder that was losing its plastic coating, I saw two cracks zigzagging down through the bricks and the mortar, both big enough to slip a finger into.

I pressed my face to the rippled glass in the top half of the front door but couldn't see inside, and I rang the bell to hear it chime. Down a short side alley, past an outhouse and around the corner, the blind at the next window was down, but I peered in, and where a corner was rucked I could make out a kitchen sink but not much else. I walked around the back and down the gap between house and garage, returning to the front, but the curtains were drawn at all the other windows and there was nothing to see. At the front door I bent to look through the letter box, where the interior was too shadowed to make much out. I put my fingers through and fumbled for a key on a piece of string but felt nothing. I had no idea what was inside, and I had some misgivings about living with Vince, but this undistinguished, down-at-heel bungalow seemed better than anything I'd been offered before.

In the halfway house, I took a fresh bin liner up to my room and started flinging in my belongings. The doorbell rang, and when I went downstairs it was, as I'd expected, Joy, come to check up on me as she did every other Wednesday.

She held something behind her back, and she was beaming.

'Would you like a cup of tea?' I said.

'Oh, Ursula, not yet, not yet.' She dropped her cigarette, ground it out with her shoe and pushed it over the edge of the step with her foot. 'You have to invite me in first.'

I held the door open and stood aside. I liked Joy. She was one of the better social workers of the long list I'd had over the years – patient, understanding, and she'd stuck around for a while.

'I'd love a cup of tea, thank you,' she said. 'Here, these are for you.' With a flourish she produced a bunch of flowers.

'What are these for?'

'Your one-month appraisal, of course. You passed! Mrs Rooney phoned me on Friday. I'm so pleased for you.' She gave me a hug, the smell of her cigarette lingering. We were about the same height, but Joy was thin, her face wrinkled from the smoking. 'It means your job is permanent.'

I thought of what Sue had asked me at the dinner – how I was planning on getting out of here – and now I wasn't sure being made permanent was a good thing. Joy followed me into the kitchen. Someone had done the washing-up and it was piled, mountainous and unsteady, on the drainer. I put the kettle on while Joy opened one cupboard after another, looking for a vase. 'Mrs R also said you were going out with your colleagues last weekend.' Joy was delighted, like a mother with a daughter who has finally made some friends after a long and lonely childhood. 'How did it go?'

'It was nice,' I said, not mentioning the knife and Vince's howling. 'I had steak. Two steaks.'

'Two?'

'And I ate some peas.'

'Oh, that is good.' She produced a pint of milk from her handbag and put it on the counter. Having given up on the search for a vase, she took an oversized mug from the drainer and caught a bowl before it hit the floor. She used one of the blunt knives from the drawer – the steak knife was still in my handbag – and hacked off the stalks from the flowers and crammed the heads into the mug. They looked nice.

'Are they chrysanthemums?' I asked.

'Asters.' Joy made the tea.

'Asters.' I fingered a petal. 'No one's ever bought me flowers before.'

We took the tea up to my room.

'Are you going somewhere?' she said when she saw the bin liner on the bed, my wardrobe emptied.

'I'm moving. To a place on the other side of town.' It hadn't occurred to me to let Joy know.

'What place?' she said.

'A bungalow. I'm tired of living here.' I took a sip of tea.

'I'm not sure about that. Who will you be living with?' She was beginning to sound shirty and it was pissing me off.

'Not with any more dirty old men, at least.'

'Now –'

'Men who open the door to my friends with only their boxers on.'

She clocked the word 'friends' at the same time as she winced. 'Maybe I should come and see it with you first, make sure it's suitable, safe.'

'I've seen it, and it's very suitable and completely safe.' I gathered the bin liner by its neck, dumped it on the floor and sat heavily on the bed.

'But don't you think a second opinion would be helpful?'

'I've made up my mind. And my friend Sue said she'd help

me move in.' Was she my friend? I wasn't sure, but she had offered to take me and my belongings to the house in her car.

'Who else will be living there? You know I have a duty of care for you. We've discussed this.' She sat beside me.

I didn't like her tone, all of a sudden talking to me as though I were a child. 'I can look after myself.'

'Are you sure you can afford it?'

'There isn't any rent, just 50p in the electricity meter now and again.'

'No rent?'

I gave the bin liner a nudge with a toe.

'Is it a squat? I don't know about that.'

'Vince at work is moving in.'

'Vince. Vince? Not Vincent Goldie? Oh, Ursula.'

'He's been very helpful.'

'It's just –' She paused. I knew she wasn't supposed to talk about other people she'd come into contact with professionally. 'He's a bit of a troubled soul. Too much alcohol a little too often, a difficult history.' Joy began to explain about squats and their dangers. Anyone could be hanging around, they were often unsecured, and with no landlord, the accommodation would be of poor quality, dismal, dangerous – she was going on as I spread my arms wide to include the room I was in, the halfway house, the whole world I'd inhabited so far.

Last night I dreamt I heard the lift in my apartment block: the whoosh as the doors slid open on the ground floor, Dame Judi's announcements and the noise like distant vacuuming as it rose. I heard it but I couldn't move from the sofa where I lay, my body filling with sand through an opening in the side of my head, too heavy and cumbersome to even turn over. And, as happens in dreams, a different perspective:

I was looking through the peephole in my front door at an eighteen-year-old Sue – the age she was when I first met her. Her pale eyes were wild as she beat on my door with her fists, begging me to let her in. We heard the lift clunk to a stop and the whoosh as the doors slid apart. Her hammering slowed but continued, steady as the beat of a clock, as she looked to her left at something out of view. My hand was on the first bolt, undecided whether to open the door or keep it locked, when I woke, my heart keeping time with Sue's fist. It's coming.

7

'Light me a fag!' Sue shouted over the wind that rushed through the open windows of the car and flapped the loose ends of the bin liners of clothes and bedding on the back seat. I lit two and put one in her mouth. 'Sorry about the crap. In the car.'

The passenger footwell was littered with crisp packets and sweet wrappers, and dust lay thick across the dashboard. 'I should tidy up. It pisses Raymond off, and it is his car. His dad gave it to him, he's rich, he's the one who keeps our family afloat even though he isn't anyone else's father, and Raymond can't drive.'

'Your brother has a car he can't drive?'

'He hasn't taken his test. He missed loads of school, and that meant exams, university, learning to drive, blah, blah, blah – got delayed. There's something wrong with his joints, or his muscles. He says they hurt all the time, but no one can work out what it is or what to do about it. Mum thinks he's making it up or it's growing pains.' She waved her hand, ending the conversation as we pulled up outside a semi on an estate of identical houses.

She didn't turn off the engine, just sat staring ahead, tapping the steering wheel as though trying to make up her mind about something. Eventually, I said: 'Is this where you live? It's nice.' I was excited and nervous about meeting her family, although I tried not to show it. She jiggled the gear stick and put the car into first gear, but as her foot pressed the clutch, from inside the house we heard someone shout, 'You flipping mongrel!' and we looked at each other and laughed.

'Some of my family have funny opinions,' she said. 'There's too many of them, and my mum's about to pop out another with a different man from my dad and from Raymond's dad, and from the twins' dad. It's gross. This one is already married, and he didn't want Mum to have the baby, so it won't have a dad at all. Anyway, we can stuff our faces with roast chicken and bugger off.'

Eating sounded like a good idea. We got out of the car and halfway up the drive she put her hand on my arm. 'Best not to mention Vince or anything about . . .'

'About what?'

'Let me do the talking.' She flapped her arm. 'They're my family.'

'We're all family here,' I said, parroting Alan.

'Family, my arse.' We were at the door, sniggering. 'One big happy family. Come on.'

The house inside was more full of sound than the car had been, and although noise was reassuringly familiar, I still had an urge to know the layout, who was in there and who was in charge. 'Mapping', as my current therapist calls it, allows my brain to anticipate threats, learn the escape routes, who's the top dog and where I might fit in the hierarchy.

We faced a narrow hallway, with an open door at the end and stairs on the left with a landing at the top. The noise swept us into a lounge on the right, where twin girls of five or six were lying upside down on the sofa, shouting and giggling, their legs over the back. A Labrador was woofing, and an old man was reading sections of newspaper aloud

45

as though someone were listening. I followed Sue through a dining area, squeezing past the table laid for lunch, to a kitchen where three women were dishing out a roast dinner. It smelled delicious.

'Suzie!' the oldest woman said. 'Where did you get to?' She clapped her oven-gloved hands over Sue's ears and kissed her forehead before bending to the oven. 'Which one is this?' She looked up at me. 'Not the one who came to lunch last month?'

'It's Ursula, Gran. Remember I told you she was coming?' Sue said, crossing her eyes and turning away so only I could see.

'Hello, love,' another woman said, pressing her permed hair out of her face, red from the heat in the kitchen, and I saw that her belly was enormous, pushing out through the fabric of her dress.

A whine started up and the third woman began to slice a chicken with an electric knife. Sue whispered, 'We could go, leave, right now. Out through the back door. They'd never notice.'

'You never said your name was Suzie,' I teased, quietly. 'Suzie, Suzie, Suzie.'

'Fuck off,' she whispered.

'Go and call your brother,' Sue's mother said, but stuck her head into the hall and yelled, 'Raymond, lunch is ready.'

The dining room was full of laughter and clamour, cutlery on crockery, the twins getting down and fetching beakers of milk, a bottle of lemonade being opened, everyone talking at once. No one else paid attention to Raymond coming into the room. Tall, with long arms and legs, he wore a suit and tie and polished shoes, and his eyes were large and protruding so that he looked younger than Sue. I tried to see whether he walked like he was in pain.

'Auntie Julie,' Sue said, pointing with her knife at the woman who'd carved the chicken. 'Mum's older sister.' She carried on around the table indicating each person in turn and naming them: 'Gramps; Twin One and Twin Two – Hannah and Jess; my mum – Anita; and the blob.' Sue pointed at her mother's stomach. 'Gran; and Raymond, my older, cleverer, better-looking sibling.' Raymond, sitting next to me, bobbed his head.

'You are the girl in need of a car,' he said, cutting a potato with the side of his fork.

'Ursula. I'm a friend of Sue's from the art school. And thanks for the car.'

'You can't keep it, you know.'

'It's for today,' I said. 'I'm moving house.'

Sue took a jug of gravy from Julie. 'That's Raymond's idea of a joke.'

'What are you studying?' Raymond asked.

And in my moment of hesitation, Sue said, 'She's studying Sculpture.' She didn't take her eyes from the gravy, which she was pouring carefully between each item of food, making islands of the slices of meat.

'What do you think of our Gainsboroughs?' Raymond picked up his plate and lifted it high, showing the place mat underneath. 'Jackpot!' he said. It was a painting of a woman in a large blue dress sitting on a bench in a field, with a man in a triangular hat leaning against a tree. '*Mr and Mrs Andrews*. All the others are muddy landscapes.'

I went to pick up my plate, out of politeness, still confused.

'Put it down, Raymond,' Sue said, and she caught a drip of gravy from the side of the jug.

Raymond put down his plate. 'What kind of sculpture do you do?' At that moment there was a break in the noise around the table, as though everyone was waiting for my answer.

Sue licked her finger. 'This and that,' she said.

'Can't Ursula speak for herself?' Raymond asked.

'Not to you lot.'

'Wood carving,' I said.

The table grew loud again, and a forgotten saucepan of cabbage was passed to Raymond. 'You should eat some vegetables,' he said and piled two spoonfuls on my plate. 'Vegetables are known for loosening the tongue.' But I suddenly found that I wasn't hungry, too full instead of family, inclusion, acceptance.

'You should always listen to Raymond,' said Gran, peering around him to speak to me. 'Raymond knows what he's talking about.'

'Have some cabbage, Gran.' He gave her a small amount. 'Gran's talkative enough.'

'Would you like me to cut your food up for you, dear?' she asked, looking at my arm.

'I'm fine, thanks.' I was touched that she had asked, that she had noticed I might need help, and offered it.

'Anyone who eats at our table is as good as family,' Gran said, and took a piece of meat from her own plate and held it under the table, where the dog brushed against my legs. She sucked on her fingers and said, 'Did you know my daughter is having a baby?'

'She can hardly miss it,' Julie said, cutting up food for one of the twins, who was shouting down the table that she was doing it wrong.

'Baby.' Anita drew out the word, caressed her belly and closed her eyes.

'Our mother likes babies best,' Sue said. 'Past the age of

48

three she loses interest in her children. She can't wait for me and Raymond to leave home.'

'That's not true.' Anita picked up her knife and fork.

'Remind me again how old you two are?' Sue asked the twins.

'Six,' they said, in unison.

'Oh dear,' Sue said.

'Don't be mean,' Julie said.

'Are you leaving home?' I asked Raymond.

He skewered a piece of chicken. 'I'm going to uni in September, finally. To study law.'

'You've got a good job,' Anita said to Sue. 'You need to settle down, save for a place of your own.'

'Find a nice young man,' Gran said.

'I don't need a nice young man, I've already got a bad one,' Sue said, but only Raymond and I heard. He turned down his mouth and shook his head in distaste as he mouthed Vince's name. Sue ignored him.

One of the twins asked whether she and her sister would still be the youngest when the baby arrived, and Gramps tried to explain how everyone would love them no matter what.

'Think of the things you could have done, if you hadn't had this rabble,' Sue said to her mother, cutting through the noise.

'Anita wanted to be a ballerina when she was little,' Gran said.

Sue licked her knife, one side and the other. 'So why didn't you?'

'Legs were too spindly,' Gramps said.

'That was just a childish dream,' Anita said.

'What about after that, when you were older? What did you want to be then?' Sue had turned aggressive.

'I can't remember.' Anita was defensive. 'I met Raymond's father.'

'And?'

'We rented a flat. I had a baby. It was 1966.'

'And he expected you to stay at home and look after it? Didn't you want to do something with your life?'

'I had a baby!' Anita said, finally risen to indignation. 'Babies need stability, continuity.'

I wasn't sure they did. When I was the twins' age, or a little younger, there had been an evening when Sadie left me alone in the driver's seat of her car, with a packet of crisps and a bottle of Coke. She must have been in the pub, playing guitar while the headlights from the road strobed me, my hands turning ghostly and then dark. I wasn't scared or sad or lonely; it was just difficult to hold the crisps upright and fit my mouth over the end of the bobbing straw.

'Babies need a home,' Gran said.

'Babies have no idea what they need,' Sue said.

Babies need their mothers, is what I thought.

'And how come these babies' fathers get to bugger off and do whatever they want?'

'Because that's the way it works,' Anita said, as though that was the end of it.

'But you could have done anything.'

'What, like make films? Go to Hollywood?' Julie snorted.

'Can't beat a good weepie in the afternoon,' Gramps said. 'Someone needs to make them.'

'Like anything!' Sue said, and I saw she was close to tears. 'Like travel, see places, learn things, make stuff. I don't know.'

'Anything except be a mother?' Julie's voice was hard. 'Is that not good enough for you?'

'I don't think that's what Sue meant,' Raymond said.

'What sort of example is this, though?' Sue had fought off the tears and now sounded angry again. 'To me, to Jess and Hannah?' The girls stared at her, their little mouths chewing. 'Raymond's off to university, but did you even consider that as an option for me?' she said to Anita.

'I thought you applied to do Film Studies at the art school,' Julie said. 'Didn't get in, as I recall.'

'I wouldn't study with those pricks if you paid me.'

'Language!' Gran said.

'When I said I was going to leave school at sixteen, did you try to stop me?'

'But it was your choice, you messed up your exams,' Anita said. 'I let you make your own decisions, and you have to live with them.'

'Choices, but not encouragement to try harder, aim higher. Apply to the NFTS.' She flung her cutlery on to her plate and her fork skidded on to the carpet, where I heard the dog licking.

'National Film and Television School,' Raymond said quietly to me.

'I didn't know there was another option! You didn't tell me!' Sue stood and squeezed past the backs of the chairs until she reached the kitchen. I looked over my shoulder as she went out the back door, slamming it behind her. Seconds later, we saw her through the French windows, lighting a cigarette and walking to the end of the garden.

'Well!' Gran said.

'She's always changing her mind, that girl,' Julie said. 'Itchy feet.'

I sat there awkwardly, wondering if I was supposed to go after her or stay.

'It's okay,' Raymond whispered. 'It's the chicken that does it.'

I hoped that was an invitation to stay, and so I sat with

the family while Julie collected the plates – mine still almost full – and sliced two Viennettas and they all bickered about whose turn it was to do the washing-up.

Sue came in as everyone was getting up. 'Ursula and I are leaving,' she said.

I stood too. 'Maybe I should help.' I looked at her family gathering plates and glasses, taking them to the kitchen.

'Let them do it,' Sue said. It didn't seem they needed me, but I hesitated, thinking again of the rota at Doughty House.

'I should help.' I picked up my plate. A painting of a shepherd with his sheep in a misty landscape was on my place mat. I would have liked to show Raymond.

'Suit yourself. I'm going for a walk.' Sue squeezed through the jam in the kitchen and went out the back door again, taking the dog and its lead with her, and I was sure I'd done the wrong thing.

Julie, her fingers covered in rings, lit a cigarette and stood next to the back door, blowing smoke over her shoulder and bossing Gran about. Raymond took off his jacket and tossed his tie over his shoulder. They talked about people I didn't know, Julie describing a neighbour whose rabbits had escaped into someone's vegetable patch, and Gran telling a long story about a friend of a friend who had escaped from her old people's home at night and was found frozen to death the next day. Julie said hypothermia was a good way to go. 'After the shaking stops, you fall into a coma and enter a state of bliss. Like dying in your sleep.'

'Crapola,' Raymond said, angled against the sink as though it were holding him up. 'How would you know?'

'Scientific studies,' Julie said, as she chucked her cigarette out of the back door and laughed.

Gran asked Raymond to sing something for her.

'What do you fancy?' he said. 'Elvis the Pelvis? Val Doonican? Andy Williams?'

'A bit of Andy.'

He sang 'Can't Take My Eyes Off You', and they were silent, watching and listening as he sang it to his grandmother. His voice was soft and deep. We clapped when he'd finished, and he bowed and returned to the washing-up. I watched this family as I dried the plates and cutlery, thinking I could easily fit into the bickering, the disagreements, the laughter, the singing. One more daughter would make no difference, surely.

Julie made tea and took a tray into the lounge. Anita, who'd been dozing on the sofa, woke up and poured. Sue hadn't returned, and I thought about her never coming back and no one noticing that I'd replaced her. The twins ran in from the garden, begged for biscuits, and were grabbed and hugged, or tickled, or spoken over the heads of until they gave up and ran out again. Beside me was a pile of papers with a spiral notebook and a pen on top. I picked them up, flipped to a blank page, and began to draw Anita: the way her hair had bunched up where her head had rested against the sofa, the dark mole on her top lip, and how her enormous breasts rested on her bump.

'Did you see *Crimewatch* last night?' Gran said. She sucked in air. 'A sixty-six-year-old woman beaten and left for dead in Crab Wood.'

'Not Crab Wood, Mum,' Julie said. 'Worlebury Woods, near Weston-super-Mare.'

'But her name *was* Helen, that's my name.'

'Helen *Fleet*.'

'So terrible.' Anita had tears in her eyes. I looked at her, looked at the paper, trying to capture her expression.

'Yet still you watch it,' Raymond said.

The twins had come in holding pink plastic watering cans. 'Watch what? Watch what?' they chanted.

'Nothing, darlings,' Julie said. 'Mind the teapot. Take the water outside.'

'So sad,' Anita said. I drew a tiny cairn for her belly button, turned inside out on top of the mountain of her stomach.

'We watch it to help find the killer,' Julie said.

'That's not why,' Raymond said. 'You watch it because you love being terrified. The same reason Sue and I watch horror films. But at least they're fiction. You watch because you want to know the worst that can happen, and if it happened to someone else then you're happy it didn't happen to you.'

'Raymond!' Anita said.

'The other one was worse,' said Gramps. 'She was a beauty. Blonde and only twenty-six.'

'The *other one*!' Julie said. 'Doesn't she have a name, Dad? Like it's worse to be murdered if you're young or beautiful.'

'She probably did have more life ahead of her at twenty-six,' Anita said.

'Her name was Shani Warren,' Raymond said.

I flipped the page and looked at him in three-quarter profile. I drew a line, another, and looked at him again. His sleeves were still rolled up, and he was bent forward on his seat, elbows on knees and hands clasped. I saw the hairs on his forearms, the muscles there moving as he talked to his family, his slender fingers. My pen traced his long nose, and I watched how his mouth moved when he laughed. Two wavy lines across his forehead in concentration, and his prominent eyes almost cartoonish. He turned his head and looked at me, surprise showing for a second, and then he smiled and I looked down quickly to my page.

'Someone must have seen something,' Gramps said. 'What kind of man would do that?'

'Who says it was a man?' Raymond asked.

'It's always a man,' Julie said.

'She'd been dumped in a lake,' Gran said. 'At sixty-six!' No one corrected her.

'You're all too ghoulish,' Anita said. 'Are you drawing Raymond? Can I see?'

I held the drawing up, but not for long. The pen wasn't good, the ink didn't flow evenly, and I wasn't happy with the result.

'Oh, that does look lovely.'

'Did Raymond say you're a sculpture?' Gran said.

'Sculptor.' And Sue was there, across the room, propped in the doorway, waiting.

'What did I say?' Gran asked.

'Sculpture.'

'Well, exactly.'

'What does your father do?' Gramps asked me.

I looked at them, knowing I was about to be found out, ejected from this ready-made family. A day – less than a day – was all I was going to get.

'He died in a tragic accident,' Sue said loudly, and they looked at her and away. Raymond made a murmur of sympathy, but none of them said anything until Sue spoke again, directing her question at no one in particular. 'Aren't you going to ask what her mother does?'

I loved her for making sure I didn't have to explain about the children's homes, my lack of parents, and quickly and roughly I drew her, standing in the doorway, getting her face down in a few lines. Julie sighed, as though she was tired of Sue.

'Suzie, take your wellies off in the house,' Anita said, in a despairing tone.

There was a fuss about making more tea. Julie and Gran wanted to look at my drawings, and they passed them to Raymond, who asked if he could have the one of Sue. I would have liked to keep it, but I shrugged and he tore it out and made me sign it.

To Raymond, I wrote. *A nice young man. From Ursula.*

Sue's arms came around me from behind, over my shoulders, wrapping me up. I could smell her floral shampoo.

'Don't you dare fall in love with my fucking family,' she whispered. Her breath tickled my neck.

'I'm not. I won't.'

'And don't make them love you back.'

'Okay.'

'It'll end in tears. I'm warning you.'

She let go and I turned to catch her expression to see if she was joking or serious, but she was announcing to the room that she had to take me away. 'Ursula's moving house today and I've got all her worldly belongings in the back of my car.' She stopped herself. 'Your car,' she said to Raymond.

The family made lots of noise and exclamations about how if they'd known they would have sent me off sooner. Anita heaved herself up and hugged me, her belly between us. 'It's been delightful meeting you. Please come back soon, love. I mean it.'

'I'll come with you,' Raymond said to Sue.

'Not sure what help you'll be,' she said.

'I can carry things in, one teaspoon at a time,' Raymond said. I was pleased.

8

Sue performed a three-point turn, and Raymond, who was sitting in the passenger seat, looked back to where I was squashed in with my stuff and said, 'I'm sorry about that nonsense at the table.'

'I think I'm going to kill her,' Sue said, pulling hard on the wheel. 'I might actually do it one of these days. You'll help me, won't you, Ursula?' She put her arm over the back of Raymond's seat as she looked out of the rear window to reverse. I watched her face, the stern concentration, and I wasn't sure she was joking.

'Oh, crapola,' Raymond said at something he could see out of the front window. Sue stopped the car, and we looked forward.

Julie was at the front door, waving her arms and shouting. 'The baby's coming.'

'Two minutes later and we would have got away,' Sue said. She parked the car and turned off the engine. Julie shouted for them to come in, but still we sat there. 'You know she can't have babies of her own?' Sue said. 'She had a litho . . . How do you say it? *Lithopedion.*'

'Sue, don't,' Raymond said.

'What?' She was indignant.

'What's a lithopedion?' I asked.

'It's a stone baby. A baby made of stone inside her womb.'

'That's sad,' I said.

'Not in her womb, in her abdomen,' Raymond said. 'It's calcification.'

'They had to take the whole lot out.' Sue made the noise of an ascending Swanee whistle. Raymond shook his head.

Back in the house, Julie, who I looked at with a new curiosity, was trying to organize everyone and getting nothing done. Anita sat on the wet sofa repeating that she wasn't ready, that she should have two weeks yet, while the twins shrieked about not being allowed watering cans in the lounge and everything being unfair.

Sue and I sat on the stairs while everyone ran around. 'I hate babies,' she said.

'I think they're sweet,' I said.

'Well, this one will be going spare.'

Raymond phoned the midwife while Sue helped Anita up to her bedroom, and it was agreed that Gramps would drive me to the bungalow in Raymond's car since it was out on the road and my belongings were on the back seat. Julie would look after the twins, and Gran would make tea. In the car, Gramps talked about how the world had too many people in it already. The only thing he asked me was for directions to the Underwood.

'Are you sure this is the place?' he asked as he pulled into the drive.

The bungalow looked desolate and empty after Anita's, and I would have liked for Gramps to take me back to the mess and noise of Sue's house, where the party was going on without me. But he and I carried my box of crockery, a bag of food and two bin liners of clothes and bedding into the porch. He looked in the car boot and seemed surprised this was all I had, and then he sped off to see the new addition to his family without a wave, and I unlocked the front door with the key Vince had got cut for me.

A short, dim hallway turned left out of sight, and a heap of letters lay scattered across loose parquet flooring. The place smelled of damp and cigarettes smoked long ago. A person stood to my left and my hand went to my throat, and I cried out, and the person's hand went to their throat and their mouth opened, and I huffed out a laugh at my reflection in the full-length mirror. It was part of one of those old-fashioned hall units with hooks and a couple of coats hanging there. A furled umbrella and a walking stick leaned together in a stand. Maybe Vince was wrong; perhaps someone did live here.

'Hello?' I called out. There was no answer. To my right was a doorway with a view of a cooker and before the hallway dog-legged to the left was another room with a bed in it. When I flicked the switch in the hall the lights didn't come on, but Vince had told me to expect that; the electricity meter was in the outhouse. I picked up the post and pushed the door to the kitchen wide, as though someone might be in there, sitting at the fold-down table, waiting. I saw a stainless-steel sink and drainer, high cupboards with sliding glass doors, and an electric cooker, the enamel scrubbed clean by a housewife. Light came in from the triangular gap in the window blind that I had peered through on the day I'd visited, and lined up along the sill were ceramic jars labelled SUGAR, TEA and FLOUR. I wiped a finger across the top of one of the jars and a layer of dust came off, and I saw that everything was dusty and no one could have been here for years.

Each cupboard and drawer I opened had its contents stacked neatly, knives and forks in order, tins and packets of ingredients in a pantry cupboard, a sour fridge with the remains of unidentifiable and desiccated food. I left the post on the table and went straight ahead along the hallway, pushing each door wide: on my right the first bedroom, a second bedroom, and at the end a narrow lounge, the width of the house, with a gas fire set into a brick surround and a mirror above. A clock sat on the mantelpiece beside two framed photographs of the same woman. I looked at them without touching. In the first the woman stood in the porch of the Underwood, smiling, a hand on her swollen belly although she seemed too old to be pregnant. I wondered how the birth had gone – did she have the baby at home with her family around her? In the second she looked down at the baby in her arms, its mouth open in full cry, eyes squeezed together, and I wondered why she hadn't chosen a more attractive image.

All the rooms in the Underwood were furnished with someone else's belongings, as though the woman in the picture, and presumably her husband – the photographer – had left moments before: lace doilies under china milkmaids, an armchair with a bag of knitting beside it, a record player with stacked LPs. Vince had said, 'The wife went and the husband went too.' Where had they gone in such a hurry? Or maybe he hadn't meant that they'd left.

It was eerie mapping a house that wasn't empty but had been vacated, although it was the bathroom that made me consider moving back to the halfway house.

It wasn't the lurid lime-green suite or the brown water stains that marked the basin and toilet, but the high and narrow window above the bath. The bathroom at the halfway house, although filthy, had been windowless. Nearly a decade had gone by since I'd been in a bathroom with a similar window, and I told myself that I would have to step into this one at some point, I would have to wash, I would have to use the toilet. For years I've worked with therapists trying to deal with my terrors: the dark holes insects might crawl out of, foul smells, chundering pipes, the gurgle of water. I stood outside the Underwood's bathroom for a minute more before I pulled the door closed.

In the corner bedroom, I opened the curtains, sat on the bed made up with a candlewick bedspread and bounced, like Goldilocks. A breath of warm air like the wind that blows from a vacuum cleaner rose up, but the room was a good size, and light, better than the smaller, gloomier bedroom next door, and I decided it would be mine.

I inspected the items on the dressing table – a small brush with a blue bunny on the back and soft bristles, various ceramic pots filled with hair grips and safety pins – careful to replace each back on to the dust-free shape I'd picked it up from. The presence of the woman, the baby and the unseen photographer was everywhere in the house, not only because their belongings lay on every surface and filled the cupboards, but in the concentrated atmosphere in each room, warm and soupy, like the air in a phone box after it has just been vacated. I wouldn't have been surprised if the couple had walked in and asked what I was doing in their house with all their things. I had lived in many houses in my sixteen years, some for a couple of nights, others for a year or more, and the children who'd come before me had left their mark: battered books and toys, names carved in woodwork, heights indicated on a door frame drawn by the child's own hand. I told myself that of course I could live at the Underwood, so what if it was full of stuff. The challenge of the bathroom could be overcome; I had navigated worse and survived.

The last of the afternoon sun glided into the bedroom. I thought about changing the bedding, but this was a double and the sheets and duvet I'd brought with me were for a single. I lay on the old bedspread thinking I must shake it out or wash it, my stomach rumbling, wishing I'd eaten more at lunch. I closed my eyes.

In *Dark Descent*, Julie, her smoker's face cut with hundreds of tiny lines, sits on a sofa with large white cushions that match her short white hair. I calculated that she must be approaching eighty. She wears small hooped earrings, many rings on her fingers and a V-neck top that rests slightly off-centre on her crêpe-paper chest. She will be annoyed about it when she sees it isn't straight, that Emma Zahini's assistant didn't adjust it. Behind Julie is a display cabinet crammed with majolica: a jug in the shape of a cucumber, cabbage plates and corn-on-the-cob mugs. Emma Zahini uses that device where the filming begins before the interviewee starts speaking, so as to make them appear more human as they clear their throat, pat their hair, wriggle in their seat to get comfortable. They are real people, the same as us, she's saying. Julie takes a last drag on a cigarette and moves forward to stub it out in an ashtray that is out of shot, carelessly waves her hand to clear the smoke and starts to speak. 'Suzie could be the very devil,' she says.

9

I woke on my bed in the Underwood to the sound of nails or knuckles or something else tapping. Three little beats. I stared up at the ceiling without seeing it, ready for fight or flight, body rigid, blending into the bedcover. The tapping came again. An old water pipe or the claws of a bird on the roof. I heard someone groaning and from the corner of my eye saw movement at the window, and I was up and off the bed, slamming my back against the dressing table with all the china pots ringing and the triple mirrors trembling. I clutched my pillow to my chest and my pulse thudded through the feathers as though the pillow had its own heart. At the window was a shape, contorted and unhuman, pressed against glass.

'Let me in, let me in,' it said in a low voice as it slid down the pane.

It was Sue, squashed up against the window so that the side of her face was pulpy, nose bent, splayed hands above her head, the fading light of the day behind her.

'Oh, bugger off,' I said, and chucked the pillow.

She peeled herself away. 'Your face!' she said, voice and laughter indistinct.

'Yeah, yeah. Very funny. I was trying to sleep.'

'Let me in, I've been knocking for ages.' She ran off around the side of the house and I put the pillow back on the bed and straightened my clothes.

At the front door she was doing it again, pressing her hands up to the frosted pane and moving her head forward, her face obscure until her puckered lips pushed hard against the glass and went white. I pressed my mouth against their shape and for a moment we were kissing before she opened her eyes and stepped back, and I was unsure whether it was from repulsion or a delighted shock.

'Come on, open the door,' she said. 'Stop messing about.'

'Has your mum had the baby?' I asked as I let her in.

'I am never having kids,' she said, giving an exaggerated shiver. 'Not in a million years. It's a boy. She's pleased. She likes boys better. It only took half an hour for it to pop out, flop out, slop out. Take your pick.' She went into the kitchen and flicked the light switch. 'Why doesn't this work?'

I closed the front door. 'Raymond not with you?'

She was opening cupboards, looking at the crockery and the stacked tins, labels facing out. She picked one up, new potatoes, and put it back. 'No, he stayed.' I was disappointed. When she moved on to another cupboard, I turned the potatoes face out again. 'He loves babies. My God, this house is so cool. It's the perfect horror film set.' She rotated, taking it in.

'What's he called?' I said.

'What's out here?' She opened the back door, went across the narrow alleyway into the outhouse, and I followed. 'What's who called?'

'The baby.'

'Oh, Andrew or something.'

The room was crammed with junk: a pile of old curtains, a dismantled cot and a twin tub for washing clothes. I found the electricity meter and pushed 50p into the slot, and as soon as I turned the handle the outhouse lit up and we could hear piano music coming from somewhere in the bungalow.

'What the fuck is that?' Sue said, and we clutched at each other, screaming and laughing.

All the house's lights had come on, and in the lounge, below the gas fire, a pile of plastic logs glimmered. The record player, the sort housed in a box, was playing piano music, slow and sad. I could hear the clunk as each key was pressed by the pianist, the hiss of the dust in the grooves of the vinyl.

'Who the hell would leave a house with the needle on the record?' Sue lifted it off, scanned through the other albums.

'Vince told me the wife went,' I said. 'And then the husband went too, and after that I don't know.'

'Went? What does *went* mean? They died. Can't you feel it?' She ran her hand along the top of a high-backed armchair and rubbed the dust between her fingers. 'Maybe he died in the house. Or she'd had enough and killed him.' Sue picked up the photographs, stared at them and put them back. She made no comment about the baby.

'I have to sleep here, you know.'

She opened the sideboard and handled the tiny coffee cups and matching saucers, the glasses of different shapes, examined the baize-lined drawer with the sections for cutlery.

I was filling the Underwood with a different family: one with two siblings, a father and a mother sitting at the kitchen table using the bone-handled knives and forks, parents who would look after me when I was ill, a sister who lent me her clothes.

Sue peered deeper into the sideboard. 'No alcohol, though. Probably a good thing.'

When she left the room, I adjusted the photo frames so that they stood where they always had, and followed her to the bathroom, hanging back beside the door.

'Jesus,' she said, bringing thumbs and forefingers up

to form a frame to look through. 'This must be where it happened, the murders. Red on green. Can you imagine? Maybe that could be the title.' She framed her own reflection in the mirrored cupboard over the sink, turned and put me in her frame. She dropped her hands and looked up at the oblong window where a fly buzzed, and then she stood on the edge of the bath and leaned across. I closed my eyes, sucked my cheeks to try to make my dry mouth moist. 'Gross,' she said. 'There's a mountain of dead flies up here.' She grunted as she tried to open the window. 'Nope. Won't budge. Sorry, Miss Fly, you'll have to die stupidly like your friends.' She hopped down.

'Come out, come out.' I launched myself forward, got hold of her jumper and pulled her from the bathroom, shutting the door.

'What?'

'It's a horrible room.'

In the hallway I put my back against the wall while she looked along a bookshelf. It was all DIY and car manuals, I'd already checked. 'What about if he sent his wife out to get motor oil?' I said. 'She was knocked over by a bus, lost her memory and forgot where she lived.'

'And he what? Dies of grief, leaving the lights and the record player on? I don't think so. What if she was bitten by a fly and went mad? Do flies bite?'

This was too close to the things I'd been trying for nine years not to think about.

'Bitten by a sweet little imp,' I suggested instead. 'A tiny devil.'

'An invisible devil with poisonous fangs.'

She went to the wardrobe in the corner bedroom and riffled through it. 'Mostly women's things in here, and baby stuff.' She pulled out a Moses basket and tossed in a bonnet and a roll of lining paper.

'Maybe they didn't do it any more, and she made him sleep in the spare room.'

Sue went into the other bedroom and I heard her in there, opening drawers while I looked at the things she'd taken out of the wardrobe, the skirts and dresses she'd disturbed. I didn't know how to put everything back so that it didn't look touched, so I left it. In the second bedroom, Sue held a pair of grey slacks up to her own legs, the waist near her chest. She put on a jacket, her hands covered by the sleeves, and after dumping that she put on a shirt that came down to her knees. I sat on the bed and watched while she went through the chest of drawers, worrying about the owner returning to this mess. She pulled on a pair of Y-fronts, stuck out her bum and wiggled her hips. In the bedside drawer she found a pair of glasses and put them on my face. They were round with thick black frames and thick lenses.

'Wow,' she said. 'What enormous eyes you have.'

'All the better to see you with,' I said in a low voice.

She tied another of the shirts around her waist like an apron and lay down on top of the bed.

'My husband is a heavy smoker and it's killing me.' She pointed upwards and I looked over the top of the glasses and saw that the ceiling was stained a dirty yellow, a denser shade above the bed. I leaned over her, pressing my fingers into the sides of her neck and below her jaw.

'The problem isn't my neck.' She gripped her stomach and groaned. 'I'm having a stone baby and it won't come out.'

'You're the mother and thou shalt not die,' I said in my deep voice. 'We're all family here.' We sniggered. 'And I have just the thing to help.'

I took a small brown bottle from the chest of drawers. Sue was panting and her legs were open, knees raised and her chin to her chest. Was this what she'd witnessed earlier that afternoon? I removed the cotton-wool wadding from the bottle's neck and tipped out four beige tablets, lozenge-shaped and talcy.

'Four tablets twice a day should get that stone baby out,' I said.

'Bloody babies,' she moaned, and then sat up, and I held out my palm, ready to close my fist and funnel the pills back into the bottle, but she bent over, lips to my skin, sucked the pills into her mouth and swallowed.

'No!' I yelled, stripping off the glasses. 'You didn't swallow them? Not really. Did you?'

She opened her mouth, made an *ahh* noise.

'You're such an idiot.' I stuffed the cotton wool back into the bottle, screwed on the lid. 'I can't believe you took them.' I read the label. 'Laprosyn. What's Laprosyn? What if it's poison?' And how – I didn't say – was I going to put them back?

'It won't be poison. It's in a prescription bottle.' She bounced.

I continued to read. 'Take one twice a day. Mr D. Bloodworth. Twenty-third February 1977.'

'Mr D. Bloodworth? That's who lived here?'

I could see him, tall and stooped with a cigarette cupped inward between thumb and forefinger, peering through his glasses.

'What a name,' Sue said.

'That's more than ten years ago,' I said.

'Medicine never goes out of date. It just gets less effective.'

'What do you think Laprosyn is for?' I asked.

'No idea.'

'It's from a chemist in Shanklin. I could call them. There's a phone number. Four three seven seven.'

'Where's Shanklin?'

'No idea.'

'There isn't a telephone in the house.'

'How do you feel, really?'

'Like we're all family here.' She bobbed her head and rolled her eyes.

'Idiot.' I flung the bottle at her, and it bounced off her head. 'Did you actually swallow them?' I was still worried, about her becoming ill and whether I'd get the blame. If she died I would be arrested and convicted, sent to prison or back to a children's home. Unthinkable.

As she opened her mouth to show me again that it was empty, we heard a key in the front door's lock. We clung to each other once more, laughing and making each other jump in turn, and I was sure that the owner of the house, the tall smoker, Mr D. Bloodworth with the pebble glasses, had come back.

'Hello?'

It was Vince.

As well as three boxes, suitcases, a television and video player, Vince arrived with fish and chips, and the smell made my stomach groan. I laid the kitchen table with place mats I found in the sideboard – with pictures of roses – and cutlery, and Sue laughed at me. While we ate, she told us about her brother's birth: the blue umbilical cord, slippery and coiled, coming out from between her mother's legs. Vince said she was putting him off his food, but her descriptions didn't stop me eating, and she said she'd have filmed it if her camera had been working. I was quiet while they talked, feeling like a third unnecessary part, and still unsure of Vince. He didn't scare me, no more than the men in the halfway house had, but I hadn't yet worked him out, whether he was the drunken bully from the Berni Inn dinner or a colleague who'd offered me a room. Maybe we all felt weird sitting in that house surrounded by the Bloodworths' stuff, like gatecrashers at a party that had finished decades ago.

Over the years and with several different therapists, I have tried to analyse my feelings towards Vince and Sue. These therapists have all come to the same conclusion, that what I felt wasn't sexual jealousy – I didn't want either of them in that way – but a fear of being left out, of Sue being closer to Vince than she was to me. All teenagers send out sexual and friendship signals: blasting out pheromones, looking for a fraction too long into every eye they meet, laughing at jokes too loudly. I had been launching messages into the dark for years and waiting to see whether I could spot the return flicker of a distant beacon. If I didn't see it, if I suspected rejection, I was always ready to withdraw or lash out. And these feelings were mixed with another emotion that I understood only subsequently: the shame that I might be unlovable.

Sue started her made-up story again of who had lived and died here, and I joined in, both of us coming up with scenarios from films we'd watched.

'The creepy neighbour came over,' I said. 'And put Laprosyn in the chocolate mousse and it made the wife go into labour.'

'The baby died and the father was persuaded by a priest to secretly adopt another,' Sue said.

'No,' I said. 'The baby didn't die.'

'Its ghost flies around the garden, climbing on the roof and knocking on the windows, crying to be let in.' She put her palms against an invisible window. 'Let me in, let me in,' she wailed.

'Never let it in,' I hissed.

'Never let it in,' she hissed back. We repeated the phrase with our eyes wide, our heads and hands stretching towards Vince.

He put his knife and fork side by side on his plate, and I did the same. Sue had picked at her fish and chips with her fingers. He interrupted with, 'Then the wife died, and the husband died, the end.' He had meant *died*. Sue was right.

'Vince,' she said. 'You always spoil everything.'

'It's not a joke,' he said.

'What isn't?' Sue asked.

'Death,' Vince said, sharply, and Sue rolled her eyes, but I could see that his response had quietened her for a moment.

I began to fold up the fish-and-chip paper. 'Are you going to direct your film as well as write it?' I asked her to fill the gap.

'Of course,' she said. 'It's going to be a horror film from a female perspective, and they'll have to let me in.' She stuck her tongue out at Vince.

'Let her in,' I said in a spooky voice.

When we'd all had a smoke and cleared the table, Sue said she had to go because her mother wanted her to put the twins to bed. Vince looked disappointed, and I wondered if he'd been hoping she'd stay the night now he had moved out from his parents' house. Washing his hands at the sink, he asked me for seventy-five pence towards the fish and chips. He didn't ask Sue, but I gave him the money. He said he was going to have an early night, and he and Sue started to snog, and I took the fish-and-chip paper out to the bin beside the gate and perched on the bonnet of Sue's car, sparking up my cigarette lighter, letting the flame go out, over and over.

When Sue came outside, I said, 'Give my congratulations to your mum.'

She pressed in close and I could feel her breath on my cheek.

'Your turn next,' she whispered.

'My turn next, what?' I pulled back, trying to read her face.

'I dared to take the pills. Your turn next.'

Vince was in the bathroom when I went back into the house, and I returned the things Sue and I had moved to their right places – there was of course nothing I could do about the missing tablets. I saw that Vince hadn't moved the items on his dressing table either, but had placed his own belongings amongst them. I bent in close to look at a framed photograph of a girl of six or seven. She smiled at the camera, her two front teeth missing. I searched on the floor for the bottle of Laprosyn, but I couldn't find it, and the dustless shape where it had stood had been wiped away.

1 0

In all the homes I'd lived in, we children had spent every moment we could in front of the telly. We argued about what to watch, but the strongest boy always won, which meant I watched a lot of football growing up when what I wanted was films. Television was our entertainment, education, babysitter and distraction from what we heard through bedroom walls and what sometimes went on in our own rooms. It had worked the same way in the halfway house. When I was home, I spent most spare hours watching telly and drawing, or if John was in the lounge watching one of his highbrow talkie programmes, I drew him. He was the only Black man I knew and the first I drew. He wore his hair clipped close to his head, which was easy to capture, but his face was more difficult – the line of his jaw, the single deep furrow in between his eyebrows, and his acne scars, which I wondered if I should leave out altogether.

In the Underwood, the telly was in Vince's room, and he had gone to bed. I was too pent-up to sleep, and so I spent some time taping up my old drawings in my room and sat on the bed to look at them. Sue might have said they were good, but as though I'd been given someone else's eyes, I saw them for what they were: tight, precise and boring. I ripped them off the wall. The violence of their destruction was exciting.

I remembered the roll of lining paper Sue had found,

but I hesitated before getting it out again – it belonged to someone else. But it was lining paper, no one was ever going to come back for lining paper. I unrolled it on the carpet, from my bedroom window to my closed door, pinning the corners with mugs from the kitchen. I found the pieces of charcoal I'd taken from the art school, got down on my hands and knees, and began to draw. An energy filled me, my right hand racing across the paper, drawing faces with eyes too big for their heads, and open mouths, grey teeth lining black holes, distorted heads and wild beards, ears and hands. Holding my broken arm, I used my sling to smudge in great sweeping arcs, blending faces and bodies into chaos. I drew until the three sticks of charcoal were dust. Artists have a word for this – 'flow' – but I didn't know any artists, unless I counted Ms Barker.

It was after midnight when I stopped, back aching and knees sore. I smoked a cigarette and stood in the doorway of the lit bathroom where the high window was a wide black mouth and a single fly threw itself at the central bulb. Where did they keep coming from? I pulled the door closed and went to the kitchen to wash the charcoal from my hands, and afterwards out into the garden where I peed in the moonlight. Gardens were marginally better than bathrooms.

The digital alarm clock Joy had given me when I started work showed that it was a few minutes after four. As my eyes grew accustomed to the dark, I looked at my drawings laid out on the carpet, and although they were hard to see, I felt they were good, great perhaps, and I fell asleep thinking that Sue was going to love them, and they would be my reply to her swallowing the pills, to her challenge that it was my turn next. But when my alarm sounded at six thirty, I looked again at what I'd drawn: heads being swallowed by open mouths, bodies within bodies, limbs that didn't seem to be quite human, and to be truthful I was frightened that I could have created such violence and malevolence. If I had analysed the source back then, if I had been in any way self-aware, I might have put it down to what I'd already lived through: Sadie's death, the short period with foster parents, my years in those seven children's homes. It is only hindsight that allows me to blame that murky creativity on whatever we set loose in the Underwood.

The piece of work that made me famous, in the art world at least, wasn't a drawing. I was thirty-five when my sculpture *The Lithopedion* won the Albrecht-Rosen Art Prize, but by then I'd changed my name to Uschi and refused to give interviews or have my photograph taken. As well as providing a life-changing amount of money, the prize arranged for the winner's work to be shown in various prestigious galleries, and I flew to New York to see the sculpture temporarily installed at MoMA.

Imagine a single visitor. It's ten minutes until the museum closes, and the place is emptying, and the visitor thinks, *One last room.* She pushes against the flow, hoping an attendant won't ask her to leave. Her feet ache from the walking and her brain is tired from the looking, but she comes upon a large room labelled *The Lithopedion* and goes in. The walls are white, the floor is white, the ceiling is white, although it's artfully lit by spotlights so that the room's corners are in shadow. A large object on a low plinth is spread out in the middle of the space. The visitor can't make out what it is, but the colour is a reddish brown and the object is long and she's approaching it from one end so that its shape is foreshortened.

As she walks forward, it becomes clear that it is an enormous animal lying on its back, perhaps rolling playfully, and she realizes it is an animal made from carved wood, gleaming where it has been oiled and polished, as though a thousand human hands have stroked its head and the point of its nose. She walks further into the space and understands that the animal is a bear, a massive supine grizzly. When she looks at its face the eyes seem to look back at her with pain and pleading, appealing to her only, directly, following her as she walks. And with a start she realizes these eyes are blue, when surely a bear's eyes are brown – and with turquoise irises, black pupils and white sclera – a human's eyes. One more step and she sees the bear's open mouth and teeth, and again something is wrong – the ursine incisors, top and bottom, are missing. These teeth are all a similar size, yellowish and wonky – English teeth, rather than American, with their tidy dental work – but human, yes, she's certain.

The visitor approaches closer now, and she sees how the head rears back, and the angle of the neck, and that the four giant limbs are splayed, and suddenly everything is shockingly on show: the belly, slit up the middle, the fur and epidermis peeled back, all rich brown polished wood. The underlayer, the dermis, is also open, revealing, in the cavity of the creature's pelvis, a woman carved from stone. She is snugly curled on her side, breasts pressed against thighs, head tucked, the glimpse of a vulva. An adult foetus.

I carved the bear from the trunk of a six-hundred-year-old yew tree that was cut down in Gloucestershire to make way for a housing estate. Yew is a beautiful wood to work, dense but flexible, and naturally a rich reddish brown. The woman I carved from limestone that I sourced from a Portland quarry in return for a bottle of whisky.

When the piece had done the rounds, I had it moved to the middle of a remote Welsh forest owned by someone Claudia, the gallerist who represents me, knew, and I have let it decay. Every year or so I visit to take photos of its re-integration into the earth. One day, long after I'm gone, if I'm ever gone, only the curled stone woman will remain.

Emma Zahini contacted Claudia to ask her to appear in *Dark Descent*. She declined, but the request made her enthusiastic about a retrospective of my work, believing that the documentary was sure to give me more exposure. Before it aired, she'd had the vaguest idea of what had happened when I was sixteen, and she'd never pried. Since the broadcast, Claudia has left me voice messages and rung the buzzer downstairs, although I didn't answer. She'll be even keener about the idea of a retrospective or a new exhibition now, whereas I'm not sure I'll ever be able to work again.

I I

Sue called the phone box up the road from the Underwood when she got home after work. I was already there, waiting for it to ring and smoking a cigarette, adding to the stink of piss and bad breath. She and I had seen each other at the art school during tea break, but our lunchtimes didn't overlap, and I wanted to ask her whether she'd taken the bottle of Laprosyn. I knew she had, I just needed her to own up to it, and maybe I'd tell her about the drawings I'd shoved under my bed.

'Listen to what I have to put up with!' Sue said after I'd answered, without checking it was me. A baby was crying and the twins were shouting over the noise of the telly. The Underwood in contrast was oppressively quiet. Vince was out at football practice, and I didn't think I could go into his room and put his telly on.

'It sounds brill,' I said.

'My life is full of shitting and wailing. That is not brill. I'm coming over to yours.' It wasn't a question. 'I don't know how Mum thinks I might want this to be my life.'

She started in on how little sleep she'd got last night, dirty nappies and milky vomit. I'd never known any babies and I was curious about Andrew; I wanted to see him. I had once asked Mrs Hulse, my first foster mother, who had a wrinkled face, grey hair and a round tummy, whether she was going to have a baby, and her eyes had filled with tears, and she'd put the telly on for me before going to her room for a lie-down. When Dr Hulse came home he hadn't even bothered to shout at me.

Sue was saying she had no idea how she was going to finish her film script with this racket, but that when it was finished the head of Film Studies at the art school, a man of course, would never live down what a talent he'd missed. She still hadn't told me what it was about.

'He shouldn't even be the head,' I said. 'He should be out on his ear.'

'He's an imbecile with no eye,' she said.

'He's not one of the family.'

'He should be thrown in poor-taste prison.'

'Thrown in prison and made to clean the shitty toilets in the student halls,' I said.

'Clean the shitty toilets and lick the students' dirty arses.'

We snorted, hysterical, until we were weak.

In the background Anita complained about how long Sue had been on the phone, and did she know how much calls cost these days, and who was she speaking to anyway, and when Sue said, 'Ursula,' Anita said, 'Didn't you see her at work today?'

Raymond chipped in with, 'Tell her to come to tea,' and my stomach rumbled.

He waved a serving spoon at me as a hello while he dished up spaghetti bolognese and the twins squabbled about what counted as an equal share of grated Cheddar. I still couldn't tell them apart.

Anita, sitting at the table feeding the baby, gathered me into a hug with her free arm. 'Hello, love,' she said, and I bent close to her breast, seeing a bubble of milk in the corner of Andrew's mouth and a blue vein snaking under her skin.

'God, Ursula doesn't want to see that.' Sue sucked in a strand of spaghetti.

I was given the same seat as before as though it were mine, and as they ate and I chopped my pasta into tiny pieces – no longer hungry – they argued and laughed. They swept me up into their family, a new arrival like Andrew, welcomed and accepted as if I too had just been born.

Anita said she wished Sue didn't smoke, that it was a filthy habit, and Sue said it was the only thing that kept her sane. Raymond agreed with his mother. We checked under our plates to see who had *Mr and Mrs Andrews*, and pretended to the twins that pineapple rings grew on trees. In a funny voice, Raymond sang them the children's song 'My Brother' to make it up to them. I gave myself a milk moustache to distract Anita from the amount of food I'd left on my plate, and everyone did the same. I was aware of Raymond's gaze on my mouth for a fraction of a second longer than was necessary, and I licked the milk away, making sure my eyes only skimmed his.

'How's life at the art school?' he asked.

'He knows, by the way,' Sue said to me. 'That you aren't studying Sculpture; that you're a menial worker like me.'

I blushed, wondering if he also knew Sue had lied about my parents.

'There's nothing menial about secretarial work,' Anita said. She made no comment about working in the post room.

I drew Anita, Andrew and Sue, but I didn't draw Raymond again; I knew it would be impossible to hide my feelings if I looked at him that intently. My drawings had gone back to a scratchy tightness, and although they felt safer than the charcoal creatures I'd produced the previous night, I didn't like their prissiness, how tentative and dull they were.

After we'd helped clear the table, we went upstairs. Sue shared a room with the twins, but she spent most of her time in Raymond's because he had a telly and a video player that his father had given him. I sat on his bed and saw he'd Blu-Tacked my drawing of Sue to his bedroom wall. The three of us watched *The Exorcist*, and when we reached the scene where the possessed Regan smacks Dr Klein in the face, Sue said, 'Serves him right. Bloody male doctors. Where's the female doctor? If a female director had made it, they'd have had a female doctor.'

'Female priests too, I suppose?' Raymond said.

She rolled her eyes and decided it was time to take me home – she didn't invite me to stay the night. We spent several evenings like this, with Sue and me talking on the phone and her collecting me for dinner, which I rarely ate, and Anita hugging me, and Raymond singing and cooking. Every night Sue drove me home and Vince would be out. I couldn't work out if they were girlfriend and boyfriend or not, since they hardly spent any time together. He and I sometimes saw each other in the mornings in the kitchen, when he seemed tired and hungover and never asked where I'd been.

I would have been happy for this to continue indefinitely: being at Sue's house full of noise, watching horror films, pretending not to watch Raymond. One evening he didn't appear downstairs, and when Anita said it was beans on toast for supper the twins complained and Sue snapped that they should show a little consideration for their brother, he was in pain. Anita muttered something and Sue shouted; the twins cried and Andrew wailed. I would have liked to go upstairs to see Raymond, to ask if there was anything I could do, but didn't think I knew him well enough. The next time Sue rang the phone box, she said she was coming to the Underwood – she'd had enough of her house, and she'd got me a present.

I sat on my bed and watched her picking through the stuff in my room again – a few items of mine amongst the previous owners' belongings still arranged on the chest of drawers and in the wardrobe, where I'd moved the clothes aside to fit mine in. Sue offered me a cigarette, and I hesitated and then shook my head, and she lit one for herself. She sprayed old perfume into the air and moved her head forward to sniff, and picked up one of those small softcover Bibles and thumbed through it. 'Well used,' she said, putting it back down. She opened the little boxes filled with buttons and safety pins, and pulled back the curtains to look out at the garden.

'I nearly forgot,' she said, reaching into her bag, which she'd dumped on the floor. 'Here's your present.' She tossed a heavy object on to the bed. It was a chisel with a wooden handle and a scooped and shining blade. If I'd admired the knife I'd taken from the Berni Inn, this was in another league. I ran a thumb against the edge. It was sharp.

'This is for me?' I asked.

She was pleased that I liked her gift. 'I thought you said you were a wood carver.'

Had I said that or had she? 'I haven't got anything to carve.'

'There's half a dead tree out there in the garden.'

I hadn't been into the Underwoods' garden except to pee.

'But I can't carve with only a chisel.'

'Use a hammer.'

'It's called a mallet.'

'Well, get a fucking mallet.'

'Where from?'

'From the same place I stole this. If you don't want it . . .'

'You stole it?'

'Of course. From the Sculpture studio.' She was offhand about the theft. 'When I was little, we had this cat,' she said, opening a drawer, shifting the contents around. 'A skinny little tabby. And sometimes she'd go mad, running into the middle of the room and twisting her head and licking her back like a maniac.' She closed the drawer, looked at me. 'She always did it in front of us, I never caught her doing it in a room on her own. I feel like that when I'm in the Underwood. Full of bad energy, like when it's windy outside and a storm is coming and you want to jump up and down and shout. But everyone has to be watching. Can you feel it too?'

I was about to show her the drawings under the bed when we heard from the kitchen, 'Fuck!' and the clatter of something falling. We laughed. Vince was cooking sausages and mashed potatoes, and I was starving.

'Vince wants me to do it with him,' Sue said.

'Do what?' I asked.

She rolled her eyes. 'Fuck.'

'Oh, sex,' I said with a nonchalance I didn't feel. I'd never had sex, had never had a boyfriend, but I'd watched a girl and boy doing it in the home I'd lived in before Doughty House. The laundry-room door had a window in it, and another boy was charging ten pence to stand on an upturned bucket and have a look. We formed a queue, and when it was my turn I stood on the bucket, wiping at the glass with my fist where it had been steamed up by the child who'd stood there before me. The couple inside had arranged themselves on a trolley loaded with towels, and although I couldn't see the boy's face, the girl's had such a look of boredom. Many of the films I watched had sex scenes, but I knew their satin sheets and saxophone scores were not real life.

'I need to focus, keep my eye on the goal, my film,' Sue said. 'Finish writing the script, get my camera back. Keep Vince at arm's length. You give away something when you have sex. There was a bloke last year who I was crazy about. Or I thought I was crazy about him. I followed him to Scotland.' She laughed, self-deprecating.

'What was it like?'

'It rained a lot.'

'No. What was the sex like?'

She eyed me. 'Oh, you haven't? Well, you know.' She blew out air. 'I don't like how it makes the man think he owns me for however long it takes him to finish. Have me. Possess me. It's weird too, that a part of someone's body is inside someone else's. You should be careful about who you give your body to.'

'Be in love, you mean?'

She laughed again. 'Just don't do it with a crazy person.' She tapped her temple. 'Like Vince. You know he was nearly selected by a pro football club, except he drinks too much and takes whatever drugs are on offer.' She picked up the chisel from the bed, held it over her head and made the slashing knife movements with her own version of the high-pitched violins from *Psycho*'s shower scene. Hers was better than mine. 'That's how the Underwood makes me feel. You must feel it too. Like I want to tear the place down and break my own rules.'

'We're all family here,' I said.

Growing up in care, there'd always been items we considered fair game for theft: sweets and small toys from Woolworths, cheap jewellery from Boots, sometimes cigarettes. But these were for ourselves, swiped in passing, unplanned, and never as a gift for someone else.

Sadie, though, would steal whenever she could get away with it. Cereals and milk from supermarkets, running away from ice-cream vans without paying, getting me to swipe my hand along the collection trays at the bottom of penny arcade machines. She would run along the street yelling 'Fuck capitalism!' and I would run with her, and she claimed our stealing was justified because we needed food and were homeless. She often took clothes from charity shops without paying. The winter before we left for Morocco, in a Save the Children shop she made me try on a duffel coat, blue and warm and with buttons like the horns of tiny animals. I paraded up and down while Sadie stuffed a child's woolly hat and a scarf into her oversized bag. Loudly, she told me the coat was too expensive and I should return it to the rack. After we'd left the shop, the manager came after us and Sadie shouted for me to run, but the woman caught us up and gave me the coat for free. I howled when Sadie told me Morocco would be hot and I had to leave it behind.

I'd only taken from shops where I believed, incorrectly, I wasn't doing people any harm. I'd taken the knife from the Berni Inn and the sticks of charcoal from the art school, but it had been three sticks from a whole box and I was sure their loss wouldn't be noticed, whereas the chisel, probably nabbed from the student who was doing the carving of the ribs and intestines, must have been expensive and would be missed. Sue's boldness thrilled me.

'Don't forget, you have to do something,' she said as we went into the kitchen. 'It's your turn next.'

12

After work, I stood outside the camera shop and looked at the window display. I'd been trying to think of what I could steal for Sue, and the only thing she was desperate for was a new video camera. Gramps, she told me, had given her his old Canon Super 8 and three cartridges of film, and after a lesson in how to use it she'd made two short films that came back blank from the developer, and she'd sent the Canon off to see if it could be repaired. She wasn't hopeful.

Through the window I could see the salesmen behind the counter and the male customers. I'd never thought before about who made the films I watched until Sue pointed out that it was nearly always a man shooting, directing, editing, making the choices about what was filmed, whose stories got to be told and how. I'd been inside the camera shop on a previous day, and after loitering, one of the salesmen had approached me and said they didn't develop snaps and it might be best if I tried Boots the Chemists. If I were to steal a camera, I'd have to steal some film too, and that seemed impossible.

Vince was out at football practice and Sue and I had invited Raymond to the Underwood for a film night. She came over after her workday finished, to cook before going to collect her brother, and since she was in the house, I made myself have a bath. It felt safer with someone else about.

I've always left bathroom doors open – something that got me into trouble in the children's homes and that Joy said I shouldn't do at the halfway house. The feeling I get in bathrooms disorientates me, and it was – still is – a kind of claustrophobia. The horror of the door becoming jammed and not being able to get out is worse when there is a window that I think is too small and too high for me to escape through. But that evening I was standing up in the water, having reached into the bathroom cabinet over the sink to look for a razor, when Sue pushed the door open, asking whether it was okay to cook sprouting onions. She stopped mid-sentence when she saw me. I'd given up shaving the downy tufts that sprouted from under my arms, and tweezering the hairs that circled my nipples was too painful. A thicket flourished between my legs and advanced down the inside of my thighs, and this I'd never tackled. All these areas were hidden by clothes, but not the hairs on my calves. These I shaved several times a week at the kitchen sink when Vince was out.

'Wow,' Sue said, a cigarette in her hand. I stood there, pinned by the intensity of her gaze. No one had seen me naked since before I'd been taken into care, not even myself.

I covered myself with my hands. 'That's some serious hair,' she said, taking a drag. It was a statement rather than a judgement, and I uncovered myself.

'It came with the body,' I said, and stuck out one hip, put my hands behind my head, stuck out my other hip, and then, becoming shy again, sat down in the bath, square knees hiding my breasts.

'Was your mother a bear?' she asked.

'A grizzly,' I said, looking at the razor. It wasn't mine. This was metal with a blade either side of the head.

'I've heard they're very protective of their young. Very loving.'

'I was found in the woods when I was a baby. In Canada.'

'That's cool. I've never been out of the country. Unless you count Scotland.'

'I can't speak Canadian, though.'

She almost laughed, and then she saw the razor. 'Are you shaving it off?'

'Only my calves.' I lifted a leg out of the water and rested my foot beside a tap.

'You should let it grow like the rest. Be a she-bear.'

'You can see it through my tights.' I soaped my leg. I was also thinking about Raymond coming over.

'Then don't wear tights.' She folded her arms in the doorway, watching, cigarette between her lips.

'I have to wear tights, with the skirt, for work.'

'Wear trousers. Why should you have to wear a skirt to work? Terry doesn't wear a skirt, Alan doesn't wear a skirt.'

'Yeah, right.'

'What would they do?' she said as she was turning to go back to the kitchen. 'Send you home?'

I looked more closely at the razor and saw against the blades a clutch of short dark hairs which weren't mine.

Alan was interviewed for *Dark Descent*. Thirty-six years on from when I wore skirts and tights to work and washed up his teacup, I watched him on the television, smooth-pated and hollow-cheeked, with a nailbrush moustache. He sits in a chair in what might be a room in an old people's home, shuffling the knot of his tie. Behind him is a chest of drawers with only a couple of framed photos of trees and dogs on it. He starts by saying it was like one big happy family at work until it wasn't. He says nice things about me but ends with his belief that I'd made poor choices in the company I kept. 'Naive,' he says. 'Easily led.'

'Hold still,' Sue said to me. 'Or I'll cut you.'

Raymond made a moan of distress. 'Is that blood? Is that red blood?' He wasn't even looking. He was tilting back on one of the chairs in the Underwood's kitchen with an unused sanitary towel laid over his eyes. Raymond was the first male – boy or man – I'd known who hadn't joked about or been sickened by the idea of menstruation, although he didn't like the gory scenes in the films we watched. He said there was nothing illogical about being pro-women and therefore pro-periods but to feel faint at the sight of blood. He said he didn't know how girls managed to carry on walking and talking, and bleeding at the same time.

'I could look in the outhouse for wire cutters,' I said. 'This is going to take forever.'

I was sitting on a chair with Sue bent low over my arm, nail scissors inching through my plaster cast, white powder and the fluffy stuff from the inside messing up the table. She'd wanted me to kneel with my forearm in warm bathwater for twenty minutes before she went at it with the scissors, but I'd said I'd soak it in the kitchen sink.

'There won't be any red blood if Ursula keeps still,' Sue said.

'It might not have mended,' Raymond said. 'The bone might be sticking out.'

'It's been weeks.' Actually, I couldn't remember how long I'd had the cast on for, and since I hadn't told the hospital that I'd moved, I hadn't had any letters reminding me about appointments.

'How did you do it again?' Raymond asked.

'Someone pushed me off a bunk bed.'

'Pushed?' Sue sat up. 'I thought you said jumped or fell.'

'It was a fight. An argument. It's what happened in that place. There was always fighting and arguing.'

'Fell, jumped.' Raymond took the sanitary towel from his eyes. 'I still think you should go to the hospital and let them cut the cast off.'

'I can't be bothered.'

'Well, be bothered.'

I looked at Sue and she crossed her eyes, and I started giggling and she began to laugh until she did nick me with the scissors, and I yelped. Raymond put his head in his hands. 'Please, God, make them stop,' he prayed, amping it up to make us laugh more. Blood mixed with water ran down my arm and dripped off my elbow. I smeared some on Sue's face and she smudged some on mine. Sue placed my arm back on the table, picked up the scissors and resumed her careful cutting, humming along with the strange, sad piano music that was playing in the lounge.

Raymond levered himself to his feet using the table. He never talked about it, but I could see he was often in pain.

'Oh God, oh God,' he said, looking at us. 'You're savages.'

He took Sue's shepherd's pie out of the oven with a pair of matching oven mitts. 'This house is incredible. It has everything you could ever want.' He put the pie on a trivet. 'Like a show home but from the 1950s. Oh, but I forgot, one thing you don't have.' He took a package from a bag he'd brought with him, flat and thin and wrapped in Christmas paper. I took it, but he took it back to open it for me. He handed it over and, when I turned it the right way up, I saw it was the place mat of *Mr and Mrs Andrews*.

'But I can't have this!' I said, although I was delighted. 'This belongs to you, to your mum.'

'It's not ours,' Raymond said. 'I found it in a charity shop. One little place mat all on its own.'

I clutched it to me. 'Well, thank you.'

'Done!' Sue said. 'Try that.'

I pulled at what was left of the cast and it slid off my arm. Underneath, my skin was covered in long brown hair, and Sue and I stared at it. The blood from the little cut had stopped flowing and my arm ponged like ditchwater. When I lifted it, it felt so light it might have been floating. I waited for Sue to tell Raymond how hairy I was elsewhere, to say, *Now you match the rest of your body!*, but she offered me a cigarette. I stroked the hairs, as soft as a cat's belly.

'I've given up,' I said, although I wanted one.

She regarded me, open-mouthed. 'Since when?'

'Good for you,' Raymond said.

I shrugged. Since Anita said she didn't like smoking.

We ate the shepherd's pie sitting on Vince's bed, watching *Rosemary's Baby*, Sue in the middle talking about men controlling women and how the only thing Rosemary does without the agreement of a man is have a haircut. When it was finished, Sue drove Raymond home.

I brushed my teeth at the kitchen sink, and when I was peeing in the garden, the lights of Vince's car came down the drive.

'Who's there?' he called when he was out of the car.

'It's only me,' I said, coming forward into the light of the open front door.

He had his hand on his heart. 'Jesus. What were you doing?'

'Peeing,' I said. He followed me into the house.

'In the garden?'

I shrugged. 'How was training?'

'Not good. Don't want to talk about it.' He got himself a glass of water. 'Want one?'

I nodded. Vince and I had been alone together in the house before, but we'd not spent any length of time in the same room, just the two of us.

'Been having fun at Sue's house again?' he asked in a sarcastic tone.

'We were here tonight. But I like it at her house, her family are nice.'

'If they're your kind of thing.'

'What's that mean?'

'Nothing.' He finished his water and started unpacking his kit bag. 'Forget it. Great, if you're having a nice time.'

I sat at the table with my glass. 'Sue told me you were adopted.'

'Did she now?' He flapped out a towel and hung it over the back of a chair. 'So it won't be a surprise that she told me you grew up in a children's home.'

'Several children's homes. Why did you move out of your parents' house?'

He took out a T-shirt. 'Because they were always on at me to do better. Always reminding me about my education and how much it cost. My dad's a barrister.' He sniffed the T-shirt under the arms. 'He wanted me to be a lawyer, or anything rather than work in the maintenance team at the art school. I'm sure they were pleased to see the back of me.'

'What about the football?'

'*Football is too common, Vincent,*' he said in a posh voice. 'Apparently, it's rugby I'm supposed to be good at. Being good at rugby runs in the family. But I don't run in the family, do I? If one of them sneezes someone will say that sneeze sounds like Auntie Anne, or if they don't like eggs, it's because neither did Great-Uncle Geoff; if they take a shit it smells like Granny's. I'm tired of it. The only person who gets me is my grandfather – my adoptive grandfather – and he hasn't got long left.' He folded up the T-shirt and put it back in the bag. 'Why were you peeing in the garden?'

'I don't like the bathroom. Sue reckons there's something weird about the Underwood.'

'Sue finds weirdness everywhere.'

'Then how do you explain the lights and the music coming on when we put money in the meter that first evening?'

He sat down and put his hands behind his head as though thinking. 'Who knows? A rozzer who wanted to play a joke?'

'A policeman?'

'Could have been anybody. It was easy enough to break in, and then I found a set of keys in the table drawer.' He tapped it.

'But it was you who told me it was haunted.'

'Did I?' He reached for my glass of water, fished out a speck with his little finger and passed it back. 'You never heard the rumours? I thought you and Sue must have known.' I leaned forward. 'That stuff you were saying the night we arrived, about the man who died and his wife.'

'No,' I said. 'I only knew what you told us – that they'd gone.'

'It was all everyone talked about in the pub when I first started going out drinking. This couple were found dead a few years ago. The woman had a baby when she was in her forties, and he was even older.'

'What, and they lived here?'

'Their bodies were found in the garden.'

'In this garden?' My voice was rising. 'Here?'

'The husband killed his wife and then he topped himself. Jumped from the roof apparently, although it's not very high.'

'Christ.' I put my hands on my cheeks. 'What happened to the baby?'

He looked at me, making an assessment. 'No idea.'

'Why didn't you tell me?'

He shrugged. 'Sue wanted you to move in, and what Sue wants, Sue gets.'

13

Sometime after Sue gave me the chisel, I went into the second-year Sculpture studio again, in the early morning when it was empty. I took more pieces of charcoal, slipping them up my sleeve like before. The wood-carving student had worked more on the ribs and intestines, but it hadn't improved. Three chisels lay on the floor beside it, together with the wooden mallet, which I picked up. It was heavier than I expected, and I slapped it into my opposite palm with a satisfying whump. I put it in my trolley under the post. Ms Barker had received another postcard from Samuel. It was a black-and-white photo of a herd of buffalo standing in front of a forest of pine trees; in the distance were mountains. BANFF, the inscription said again.

I don't know what the plan is any more, Samuel had written. *Stay by the phone at our usual time and I'll call you.*

On the following Saturday I stood at the kitchen window of the Underwood, eating a slice of toast and Marmite, looking towards the tree at the end of the garden. Sue had told me it was a horse chestnut – the tree that produces conkers in the autumn – and I remembered what she'd said about the chunk of wood in the garden. I wasn't sure I even wanted to live in the house any longer, and I'd thought a few times about phoning Joy and seeing if she would find me somewhere else.

But I finished the toast, took the mallet and the chisel Sue had given me, and went outside. I stood there a while in the long grass, everything about me green and blooming. I shaded my eyes and looked up to the roof. Vince was right, it wasn't very high, but I imagined a man with a beard and glasses that magnified his eyes, standing up from a crouch, arms out, balancing. I wondered where his wife's body had been discovered, and I looked around as though I could recognize the spot. The baby, though, I was sure had been fine – found, cared for, adopted, happy.

The garden was distressingly noisy: the buzzing of an insect inside a flower, flies that I could hear but couldn't see, birdsong above me. I found the branch Sue had told me about: thicker than a human torso where it had once joined the tree, and dividing into two further branches, the wider one arching away from the centre. When I nudged the bark with the tip of my shoe, it dropped away in large plates, and I fell back, landing in the grass as what seemed like hundreds of woodlice were revealed, antennae waving and their tiny insect legs working as they scurried from the light. I scuttled backwards on my bottom and closed my eyes until I thought they had gone.

Already I could feel the energy rising in me, the same murky flow I'd experienced when I was drawing, and with no idea of what I would create, I picked up the mallet and the chisel. I put the blade against the wood and hit the handle with the mallet. The chisel stuck, and I had to hit it sideways to get it loose. Slowly, I learned how to tap the end of the handle enough for the chisel to move forward and a curl of wood to form before the blade, but not so hard it got stuck again or veered off. The first knuckle on my left hand became enlarged and purple from my frequent misses, but eventually I lost awareness of my surroundings, didn't hear the *pock*,

pock, pock of the mallet on the chisel, and moved my body as I worked, straddling the branch to achieve the correct angle. Vince came out and asked if I wanted a cup of tea; he came out later to say he was making himself a sandwich and ask whether I wanted one, but I couldn't stop. He came out again and put his hand on my shoulder, and held out a glass of water and said I had to drink. He asked what I was making and I said I had no idea. Vince made no comment about the work and said he was off to football.

I drank the water and would have started work again, but a car was beeping on the drive – Sue had come to pick me up and drive us into town.

Outside the cubicle of the Woolworths photo booth I whispered, 'Sue,' into the closed curtain.

'I'm adjusting the seat,' she said.

I heard it turn and saw her feet planted on the floor. 'I did it today.'

'Did what?'

'Your dare. I did it.'

I heard her put the money in.

'You know – *your turn next.*'

A flash went off and she pulled back the curtain. 'It wasn't a dare.' She said 'dare' like it was a pathetic word.

'Okay, not a dare. But I did it.'

She stood up and came out.

'I stole a mallet from the art school.'

'A mallet. What am I going to do with a mallet?'

'Not for you, for me, and I've been carving. That bit of tree in the garden you told me about.'

'Sculpting.'

'Sculpting, yes,' I said.

'Right,' she said. And I knew I'd made a mistake and she'd meant something else.

Her strip of photos dropped out of the machine and she examined them.

'Maybe I should get my photos done while we're here,' I said. 'Apply for a passport?'

She blew on the strip. 'If you want,' she said, distractedly.

'Then I could get out of here.' I wondered if she remembered our conversation at the Berni Inn dinner.

'Get out of where?'

'Go to America too.'

She squinted at me but didn't answer.

I put coins in the machine and had my photo taken, knowing she'd forgotten about her invitation. This moment, though, was when the idea settled in my head: visions of the Columbia Pictures lady with the torch, and Paramount's star-ringed mountain, which grew into the certainty that she and I were going to America.

After I'd got my photos, we went into the cubicle together, and Sue was back to her old self, giggling as we balanced on half of the circular seat, deciding which colour curtain to have behind us and pulling a new face after each flash: with our tongues out, with our fingers made into circles for glasses, looking straight ahead, our lips thin and straight, foreheads furrowed. A double police mugshot as though we were Bonnie and Clyde, caught and documented. Partners in crime.

I was disappointed when she wasn't bothered about splitting the pictures and having two each but let me keep all four. I put them in my bedside drawer and occasionally I'd take them out to examine them, trying to work out what Sue was thinking.

*

Recently, I was sent a photo of Sadie and me in Marrakesh. It is the only picture I've seen of us together. It must have been taken by a street photographer soon after we arrived because our faces are pale and our matching djellabas look clean. In Sadie's lap is a snake, its head blurred with motion as it twists up her wrist. She is laughing, delighted at our escape, and I am smiling too because Sadie is smiling. It's the late 1970s, and I must be seven and she is twenty-three. I found a magnifying glass and through my tears I examined her skin, trying to find the mosquito bite that killed her.

'Who would you choose?' Sue asked. 'If you had to kill someone?'

We were in a café in the centre of town, above a bakery. The funk of warm cheese wafted greasily from the floor below. I'd had tea that tasted of the metal pot it came in and a Chelsea bun. Sue, who'd only had a coffee, dared me to eat the bun without licking my lips or wiping my mouth, and we'd laughed loudly as I did it, and now my cheeks were sticky and covered in sugar. She said I had to go downstairs and order more tea just as I was, and when I told her I wouldn't, she said, 'Okay, you have to tell me who in this room you would kill.'

I was facing the window, she was facing the room, and I looked to my left and my right. It was after we'd done the photos, a Saturday, and the place was full of shoppers, older women out together, families, couples. 'I wouldn't kill any of them.'

'You have to pick someone. Or they'll all die.' She lit a cigarette. I still wasn't smoking. I'd told her it was a filthy habit, and she'd laughed at me.

I swivelled in my seat, looked around: an elderly man

eating a sandwich, a child in a high chair, the waitress placing a bowl of soup in front of a woman paging through a magazine of hairstyles.

I stared back at Sue. 'This is a stupid game.'

'All right. Someone you know. Someone at work, Alan or Terry. If you don't choose, everyone in the whole world will die.'

I wiped my face with the back of my hand, feeling the scrape of sugar.

'No one. I'm not picking anyone.'

'My mum. Or the baby.' She never called Andrew by his name.

'What is this?'

'Raymond?'

'You're sick.'

'Or Vince?'

'No,' I said.

'All right.' She stood, picked up her bag.

'What?'

'Nice work.' She strode across the room to the stairs.

I swung around to watch her.

'You just killed everyone!' she shouted, and the shoppers and the couples and the waitress turned to look at her and then at me.

14

A journalist sits in his car in *Dark Descent*. The sign for Barrow Road can be seen over his right shoulder. He takes a sip of coffee from a reusable cup and places it back in the cup holder. His car looks as though a crime has been committed, it is so dust-free and clean. To the camera he talks about me and my work, like he knows me, and he talks about journalism and missing persons, and how *missing* can mean different things.

Joy came round the following weekend, the last day in May. Warm enough for Sue to take a blanket out to the long grass and sprawl across it next to Vince, beneath a blue sky. I was carving under the horse chestnut, which was in flower, a beacon, flaming white, and the hawthorns were draped in cream and green, and the scrubby edges of the garden were giving off an earthy scent, hinting at the beginning of summer.

Sue was talking about women filmmakers and how it wasn't right that male directors got the breaks and the rec-ognition. She said the five nominations for Best Director at the Oscars in February had all been men.

'And guess who won?' Neither Vince nor I answered. 'A man,' she said. 'Last year, five men were nominated, and the year before that, and the year before that, and the year before that. You have to go back eleven years. Back to nineteen fucking seventy-six, when Lina Wertmüller was nominated, to find the first. The actual first woman nominated after I don't know how long. How long have the Oscars been going?' I stopped carving and she raised herself on to her elbows to look at us, shaking her head at our ignorance.

'Don't know,' Vince said. He was rolling another joint on one of the DIY manuals from the bookshelf.

'Come and smoke this, you monomaniac,' Sue said to me and patted the blanket. I didn't want to put down my tools. I was still blocking out the sculpture, but I could see it now, in my head at least: two figures, one kneeling with her arms by her sides and her hands resting on her thighs. Her head was tilted all the way back and her mouth was stretched wider than it was possible for a human mouth to be. Falling into it was going to be the other figure, neither male nor female yet, head inside the other's mouth, body, legs and feet in the air.

'Stop,' Sue said, and I shook out my hands and drank from the bottle of milk I'd brought out with me. It was warm and thick, almost on the turn. Sue had run the cut quarters of a lemon along strands of her hair to lighten it – an activity she'd read about in a magazine – and the air smelled of lemon and weed. Vince had bought the weed from Terry, and we'd been smoking all afternoon; I told myself that the tobacco in a joint didn't count. Vince became quieter and more morose the more he smoked, Sue louder and more excitable. I only wanted to carve.

A car slowed on the road, and by the music coming from the open window, some rockabilly band, I knew it was Joy before she'd pulled into the drive.

'Who is it?' Sue lifted her head from the crook of her elbow.

'My social worker,' I said, sitting down on the blanket.

She knelt up and I could sense a buzzing excitement running through her, as though having a social worker was thrilling.

'Shit. On a Sunday?' Vince finished licking the cigarette papers and tucked the joint behind his ear, dropping his hair over it.

'Checking up on me, I suppose,' I said. 'You should light it. Joy won't mind. She'll probably smoke it with us.'

'I don't think so,' Vince said.

'She's cool.'

'She's not like any of the social workers I ever had, then.'

'Did you have a social worker too?' Sue asked.

'Duh, I was adopted.'

Sue didn't take offence, she just asked another question. 'But that was when you were three?'

'And they liked to stick their noses in when I was older.'

'Did she get you your job at the art school too?'

Joy seemed to have paused in the car, gathering strength.

'I got my job through skill, ingenuity and sheer good looks,' Vince said.

'Why is she here?' Sue was too enthusiastic, too keen to hear about atrocities rather than real stories about complicated childhoods.

'To make sure I'm not doing anything stupid like living with a druggie,' I said.

Vince laughed gruffly.

'What would happen if you were?' Sue asked.

'She'd send her back to where she came from, to a children's home,' Vince said. Was he being mean for the sake of it, or was it true?

'She can't do that.' I wasn't sure.

'She bloody could. How old are you? Seventeen?'

'I'm never going back there.'

'Just like that!' He clicked his fingers.

'Was it bad?' Sue asked, too curious.

I shrugged. I didn't want to go into the details with her; I was learning that she couldn't be trusted not to tell. Joy turned off the car's engine, the music stopped, and the sounds of the garden resumed: the buzz of flies, the birdsong echoing in the horse chestnut.

'Hello there,' she called as she came towards us. She must have come from a dance practice because she was wearing a rockabilly dress, big red roses on a full cream skirt over a full net petticoat, and low-heeled lace-ups. 'Hello, Ursula. And Vincent, how nice to see you again, how are you?'

'Shit,' he said under his breath, then, 'All right,' with a nod of his head.

'Your cast has gone,' Joy said to me. 'You got to your appointment okay?' She was a tall silhouette with the sharp outline of the house behind her.

'I made sure of it,' Sue said, giving Joy her biggest smile. 'I'm Sue.'

'Is this it?' Joy looked back at the Underwood.

'The famous squat,' I said, and Sue laughed too loudly. Vince nudged the ashtray of roaches under the blanket.

'Would you like a cup of tea?' I shaded my eyes to look up at her.

'If that's what you would like,' Joy said. I was embarrassed by her extravagant dress, her kindness.

'A guided tour!' Sue jumped up and pulled me up too. Vince stayed in the garden.

Sue led us into the house, Joy following and me trailing behind. Sue presented each room and its eccentricities with pride, as though it were her house: the dressing table in my room with the lace doilies trapped under glass, the baby's brush, the boxes and their contents.

'Are you sure the owners aren't coming back?' Joy frowned as she looked around, her hand at her throat, above the sweetheart neckline of her dress.

'Nah,' Sue said. 'They're long gone.' After she picked up each item, I moved it back into place.

We went into the kitchen and Sue chattered on, exhibiting the packets of food that had been left, the crockery and the pots and pans. Joy gave a tiny belch and coughed to cover it up.

We traipsed down the hallway to the lounge, and I could sense something in her, antipathy or revulsion, and I knew she wanted to get out of there. Little blisters of sweat were emerging along her hairline where she'd pulled her hair into a ponytail, a style I thought was too young for her. Her questions were short and practical: about the hot water tank, the meter, whether I'd been writing down my expenditures in my notebook. She didn't listen to our answers. When we got to the closed door of the bathroom, the colour had seeped from her face, her hand was over her stomach, and her throat was working up and down. Quiet bumps and angry buzzing came from behind the door, and I felt the cold rushing again, through my body – that something terrible would be in there, a sight worse than flies trying to escape, and I thought Joy could sense it too. Sue pushed the door and it swung open. Nothing else was in the bathroom, only the fat bluebottles battering themselves to death.

Joy made a noise, a kind of *oh* in the back of her throat, and clamped her hand to her mouth and ran around the corner and out through the front door, and we followed. She bent over and vomited into the flower bed.

'We could get rid of her,' Sue whispered. 'It would be

easy.' She drew a finger across her throat. I shook my head. 'No?' She smiled. 'Not yet, then.'

I smiled back, thinking, if I grinned enough, I could turn Sue's words into a joke. 'Go and get her a glass of water,' I whispered back.

Joy straightened and wiped her mouth with the back of her hand. Her eyes were red and watery.

Sue returned and held out a glass, and Joy looked at it as though it was horrific, as if Sue might be offering a severed finger or a turd, and Joy took a step away from the house, her hand back on her stomach.

'I have to go,' she said, and almost ran to her car. Sue and I went after her and stood side by side with our arms around each other.

'You don't need to worry about Ursula,' Sue said, although Joy was fumbling in her dress pocket for her car key and not listening. 'She's not going to be here much longer. We've applied for our passports.' I hugged her into me; we would be going to America together.

Joy found her key and tried to insert it into the lock, cursing under her breath. 'Passports,' she said, without looking at us. 'That's great.' She got the door open and clung to it like it was a defence, a barrier between her and us and the house. 'That's wonderful.'

'Do you want to see the sculpture I've been working on?' I pointed across the garden, beyond where Vince was sitting on the blanket. He had lit the joint and the smell of the weed was drifting across.

'Next time,' Joy said, weakly. She got in the car.

'Honestly,' I said. 'It's okay here.'

'Great. That's great.' She slammed the car door, and although a scrap of her dress, a red petal, was trapped and sticking out, she reversed quickly up the drive. Sue and I watched as she backed out on to the road and drove away.

'Well,' Sue said. 'That went fine, I think.'

'Like we're one happy family,' I said, and Sue drank the glass of water.

We returned to the blanket.

'She spewed up in the flower bed,' Sue said to Vince. 'I don't think she liked the Underwood. But at least Ursula isn't going to be sent back.' We sat down. 'I charmed her.'

Vince inhaled deeply on the joint. 'Don't you believe it. Those social workers can turn.'

'I'm not going back,' I said. 'I'm not officially on her list.'

'When are you eighteen?' He talked with his throat closed, the smoke held in his lungs.

'In a year and a bit.'

'You're not seventeen yet?' He let the smoke go and it rolled upwards, over his top lip where his insubstantial moustache grew and into the sky. 'Well, behave and you might be okay. She won't be able to touch you when you're eighteen. File closed.'

'Didn't your parents nearly send you back?' Sue asked him.

'No,' he said. 'Of course not.'

'That's what Terry told me. Something about your sister.'

'Terry likes to talk. And she wasn't my sister, she was the daughter of my adopted parents.'

'And?' Sue said. 'He told me you got drunk when you were babysitting.'

Vince took another drag, held the smoke in, let it go and passed the joint to Sue.

'Go on, what happened?' she said.

Whatever this story was, I didn't think he should tell it, not to Sue, not to anyone.

'It shouldn't have been my job to babysit, should it? Not when I was twelve.'

'Oh my God,' Sue said. 'You were drunk and in charge of a child.' I knew she was trying different tactics to draw the information out of him.

'Are you going to smoke that?' he asked.

Sue put the joint between her lips and took it straight out.

'My sister was being annoying,' he said. 'Swigging from the bottle of whisky I'd taken from the drinks cabinet, trying to get my attention, thinking she was clever. I locked her in her room and she hurt herself.'

My arms were goosey although it was warm.

'How old was she?' Sue asked.

'I don't know. Seven?' He liberated the joint from Sue's fingers. I tried to catch his eye to stop him from speaking, for his own good and because this wasn't what people like us did – talk about our histories.

'But they forgave you?' Sue said. 'They didn't send you back?'

'Nope.' He held the joint out to me and I snatched it from him, sucked in smoke.

'Nope they didn't forgive you or nope they didn't send you back?'

'Nope to both.' His brown eyes were liquid. He took the joint and pressed the lit end to the back of his hand, and I smelled the acrid odour of burning skin.

'Jesus Christ!' Sue shouted, and she and I jumped up. 'No!' She knocked the joint from his hand. It landed near me, and while she was yelling, dragging his body upwards by the wrist and towards the house, the kitchen tap, I ground it out under my shoe.

15

Me, Sue and Raymond spent a lot of evenings at the Underwood in those few weeks: laughing, eating together, watching a film in Vince's room if he was out training or drinking, sitting in the kitchen and talking if he was home. It was quieter than Sue's house, more orderly, but I liked spending time with the siblings.

One day, I showed them my sculpture in the garden. I'd been working on it every afternoon – racing home after work, changing my clothes and grabbing my tools. Already they were *my* tools, not borrowed, not stolen, and I no longer worried about the garden and its insects. The piece had come a long way, and the figure falling into the mouth of the other was clearer now. *Not falling*, I thought as I looked at it with them – *being swallowed*. Raymond stared, but Sue was excited. She paced around it, examining the two figures from each angle.

'You can really do this,' she said, as though she hadn't expected it. 'You're good.'

With that encouragement I took them inside, into my bedroom, pulled out the drawings from under my bed and unrolled them.

'Oh,' Raymond said. 'Dark.'

Sue was even more animated than usual. She made me tape them to the wall and asked unanswerable questions about what they were, what I was trying to express and why I hadn't shown them to her before.

'They're very Goya-like,' she said, standing back. 'That painting he did of the giant eating his son.'

I didn't know it; I didn't know who Goya was.

'Saturn,' Raymond said. He was lying on my bed – his joints seemed to be hurting him that day.

'He painted it on the wall of his dining room in his house in Spain,' Sue said. 'Can you imagine eating your dinner and looking at that? You should go to art school.'

Sitting on the edge of the bed, I cast a glance back at Raymond for confirmation or reassurance, but his eyes were closed. Sue told me how I should get a portfolio together, that it might not be too late to apply for September's intake – although we knew it was – and how I would easily get on to one of the Fine Art degree courses in London. I knew too that people like me didn't go to art school. 'Don't apply to *our* art school,' Sue said. 'It's all male heads of department who wouldn't be able to recognize if genius hit them between the eyes.'

'I can only do this stuff when I'm here,' I said. 'At the Underwood. The place makes me draw differently.'

'Exactly.' She took my arm and shook it. 'Exactly. I knew you'd be able to feel it too. There's something about the place that infects you. Like a virus. You touch a door handle or a cup or the kitchen tap, and it spreads. It'll always be in you even when you think it's gone. Raymond says it's nonsense.'

'What's nonsense?' He sounded sleepy.

'The feeling is strongest in the bathroom,' she said. 'Maybe that's why you don't like going in there.'

'It's rubbish. We should believe in science and proof.' Raymond, still lying down, folded his arms.

'You think scientists won't discover anything new?' Sue

said. She was pacing in front of my drawings. 'That we know everything there is to know?' They were sparring good-naturedly, like they often did. 'I don't like your materialistic philosophy.'

He laughed. 'I taught you that and now you throw it back in my face. I believe in the unexplained, not the paranormal.' He shifted on to his side, wincing.

But it was hard to stop Sue once she got an idea in her head – not even Raymond could slow her – and so after dinner we found ourselves in the kitchen, sitting around the table with a candle and a glass of water between us. She said the bathroom had better seance vibes, but I'd vetoed its use, and it was too small for three of us.

She lit the candle and the reflection of the flame trembled in the kitchen window, and I wondered how we appeared from the outside. If anyone was looking in, we wouldn't have known.

'Really?' Raymond said. 'We're going to do this?'

Sue held her index finger in front of her face and, bending it, she spoke in a high, croaky voice. 'Whatcha scared of, Raymond?'

'I'm not scared, it's just pointless.'

'What's the harm in it?' Sue's finger said. 'Maybe Ursula wants to speak to her dead mother.'

'Mother?' he said. 'I thought it was her father who was dead.'

'Don't try to catch me out with which of Ursula's parents is dead,' Sue said in her normal voice but feigning outrage. 'Maybe it's both.'

Raymond dropped his head and closed his eyes, raised it and looked at me – an apology. Sue was bluffing; I hadn't told her anything about Sadie.

'You want to do this?' he said to me.

'It's a bit of fun.' I still hadn't fulfilled Sue's dare, and I didn't want to be the one to put an end to her entertainment.

'We have to hold hands,' she said, taking hold of mine and Raymond's. He and I stretched our arms across the table and his long, warm fingers gripped mine.

She let a moment of silence fall, took a breath and said, 'Is anybody there? If anybody is there, move the glass.' Then, 'No, wait. What's your mum's name? I mean, what was her name?'

'Sadie,' I said. How long had it been since I'd said her name aloud? Raymond gave my hand a gentle squeeze. The candle lit our faces from beneath, making shadows of our cheekbones, and beyond the table the corners of the kitchen were dusky.

'Now we have to close our eyes.' Sue closed hers and I closed mine. 'Raymond,' she said, and I heard his puff of air.

Another pause. 'Sadie,' Sue said. 'Are you there?'

Raymond squeezed my hand a second time. Sue's fingers were cool and dry, neither gripping nor relaxed.

We waited. What did I think about seances and the super-natural then? When I was watching horror films, I liked the feeling of being scared while knowing I was safe; that I could move my eyes away from the screen and be in the real world. I didn't know whether this, in the Underwood's kitchen, was real or pretend.

'Sadie, if you're there, move the glass.'

I could hear the drip of the bathroom tap, the buzz of a fly at one of the windows and the tick of the clock on the mantelpiece in the lounge.

'Sadie, are you there? Just move the glass.'

Raymond sniffed. 'Can we stop?' he said, and I opened my

eyes. He pulled his hands away from us both. 'This is ridiculous. Nothing is going to happen.'

'No, we cannot stop,' Sue said. 'We've barely started.' She lunged for his hand and held on to mine more tightly. With resignation he stretched his arm out across the table once more and took my hand. 'I reckon Sadie is busy tonight,' Sue said. I thought about suggesting they pick one of their own dead relatives. 'We could try your dad,' she said to me. 'What was his name?' She was fishing.

'Sue,' Raymond said. 'Don't.'

'Okay, then,' she said huffily. 'We'll ask for whoever happens to be around.'

The knocking, Sue's tapping at the window, the tick of the clock seemed to start up inside me, a drip, drip, drip of the blood in my veins.

This time we kept our eyes open. Raymond managed to look both bored and irritated, while Sue gazed into the candle.

'Is anyone there?'

Again, we waited. A car went past on the road outside, the engine whining as the driver changed gear for the uphill climb.

'If anyone is there, move the glass.'

I heard a scraping and caught a shift from the corner of my eye. I couldn't say I saw the glass move, but Sue, bending forward so the candle flickered, said, 'There! Did you see it? Look.' A droplet of water on the table reflected the flame.

Raymond's face was serene, his skin clear and smooth, almost burnished. I looked at his eyes and then his mouth, the pinkish lips, the way they curved up at the ends. He made a guttural sound and his body twitched. His hand clamped on to mine and Sue's so that we both squawked and had to yank back from his grip.

His chin jerked upwards. 'Thirsty,' he said, although the voice wasn't his; it was similar to the one Sue had just used, an attempt at the imaginary Tony from *The Shining*, scratchy and from the back of his throat.

'That isn't funny,' I said, but Raymond didn't respond, he only looked around the kitchen, turning his head one way and then the other, eyes blank. I pulled my hand out from Sue's too.

'I don't want to do this,' I said.

'No, wait,' she said, studying Raymond's face.

'Thirsty,' he said again in his Tony voice.

Sweat broke out across my body, but my hands were freezing. I wrapped my arms around my torso, tucked my hands into my armpits.

'Who are you?' Sue said, and Raymond slowly turned his head towards her, and his expression was puzzlement, as though he didn't recognize his own sister.

'Let's stop this.' I rocked forward. 'This is stupid. Raymond, please stop joking around.' I didn't really think he was joking, he never joked like this; I just wanted him to say that he was.

'Water,' Raymond said.

'Who are you?' Sue repeated.

Raymond seemed to hear her now and looked straight at her.

'Raymond?' she asked.

'Guess again,' he said in that other voice, and loomed across the table towards her. She let go of my hand and reared back in her chair, tipping it on to two legs, and I knew the power in the room had passed from sister to brother.

Sue's eyes were wide, frightened, and I cried again, 'We should stop this!'

As I spoke, Raymond turned his head towards me. His gaze was intense, and I understood this person was no longer Raymond.

'I know what you did and I know what you're going to do,' he said to me. He was still speaking in that horrific raspy voice, but low now, his words hard to make out.

'What is Ursula going to do? What's she done?' Sue's voice was timid, and her brother's gaze shifted back towards her.

'Thirsty!' he roared, and the cords in his neck stuck out and his eyes bulged as though they might pop from his head.

I jumped up and rushed around the table and turned on the light. The strip bulb buzzed, and Raymond grunted and folded sideways, sliding on to the carpet tiles, knees bent. His body spasmed, saliva foaming thickly at the corners of his mouth, his eyes rolling backwards so only the whites were showing. I was stuck there, turned to stone, but Sue got down on her knees and cradled her brother's jerking head in her hands.

'Fetch a pillow,' she said. 'Now.'

16

I brought a pillow from my bedroom, and Sue put it under Raymond's head and stroked his cheek with the side of her finger, crooning about how sorry she was, how she didn't mean to hurt him and that she would never do it again. It seemed to me that she was saying those things to calm herself as much as him. When she was silent and sitting on the floor beside her sleeping brother, I said, 'Will he be okay?'

'He's had them before.' Her back was to me and she spoke quietly. 'Seizures, fits. He has epilepsy.'

I'd seen a child have a seizure in the last children's home; I knew that's what had been happening when Raymond fell to the floor.

'Was he having a fit earlier too?' I said. 'When he spoke in that voice?'

She turned and looked up at me and I saw that her face was white and drawn. I wanted the jokey, irreverent Sue, but this one shrugged. I got down on the floor and saw she was shaking. 'He'll be all right, won't he?'

'What is it that you've done?' she asked. 'And what are you going to do?'

'I have no idea what he was talking about.' This wasn't completely true: I knew of course what I'd already done. 'Maybe everything he said was because of his epilepsy.'

We were whispering, our sentences punctuated by Raymond's sonorous breathing.

'That wasn't Raymond speaking,' Sue said.

'Who was it, then?'

'I don't know.'

I didn't like this version of Sue.

'You mustn't tell him,' she said. 'About that voice, the way
he looked.'

'Won't he remember?'

'Probably not. He always forgets the last few minutes
before a fit starts, although he hasn't had one in years. He'll
be embarrassed or worried he wet himself.'

Raymond began to stir, and when he'd fully woken we
helped him to a chair and he sat with his knees up. I made him
a cup of sweet tea, and Sue promised she wouldn't tell Anita
about his fit. Their mother, they agreed, would make him go
to the doctor, and doctors never believed anything he said.

We heard a car on the drive and Vince came in. We were
sitting at the table, withdrawn, silent. When he asked what
had been going on, Raymond and I didn't look at him, and
eventually Sue said, 'We tried to have a little seance, that's all,
but Raymond was ill.'

'I told you not to mess with that shit,' Vince said.

'I need some air,' Raymond said, and he stood, holding
on to the table and the back of the chair. I helped him out,
hearing an argument start behind us.

'I'm sorry you had to see that,' Raymond said. We perched
on the bonnet of his car. The night was warm and the stars
were out. For a moment I thought he meant the things he'd
said at the table, and he was going to tell me what it was I
was going to do. I didn't want to hear it. 'I haven't had a fit
for years,' he said. 'I used to know when one was coming,

get an aura. I'd smell burnt rubber and have a weird taste in my mouth, but I didn't get those this time. The funny thing is, right before it started, I did feel something.' He glanced at me. 'It was as though my body had changed, like it wasn't my own.' I wished he would stop, worried he would say that he knew what I'd done. 'But now, sitting out here with you, I've just realized what was different this time. All my pain had gone.' He laughed. 'And it was amazing. I've forgotten what it's like, to have a body that works without even thinking about it. After that, I must have conked out, and when I came round, it was back. The pain.'

'I'm sorry,' I said.

'I'd give anything to be back in that state. Don't ever take it for granted.' He turned to me and I was aware of his body more than ever, its warmth, his smell, the sleeve of his jacket touching my jumper. I turned my face towards his. And Sue came out jangling her car keys, and Raymond and I pulled back.

'I'm sorry about your mum,' he whispered. 'And your dad, both of them.'

After that evening, Raymond stayed away from the Underwood for a while. I thought he must have been ashamed, as Sue suggested, or maybe he was unsettled by the house, as I was. When I couldn't sleep, I thought about the energy that Sue had talked about, and the virus, and I wondered if it had infected Raymond, if he had caught it from the Underwood during the seance and who he was going to pass it to next. They were dark, middle-of-the-night thoughts that made no sense in the morning.

I also began to daydream more about going to America with Sue, although these ideas weren't realistic either: Anita and Raymond were there with us, and baby Andrew too, living together in a fancy house with a pool. Sue would be a famous horror film director and I'd be a successful artist. All I had to do was finish the sculpture in the garden.

Sue arrived one evening as the light was fading. She'd stayed away for a couple of days, and by unspoken mutual agreement we hadn't had our evening phone calls. Neither had we talked much at work, both of us withdrawn, scared, I supposed, about what we'd witnessed, and unable to explain it. Still sitting in the car, she wound down the window and shouted across the garden: 'Ursula! Want to be in my film?'

I stood upright, shading my eyes. 'You've finished the script, then?'

She got out and came towards me. 'Not that one. I've had a new idea. A much better idea.'

She looked at the house, made the square frame with her hands and turned it on me. She was jumpy and excited and, without understanding why, I felt a leaden dread at whatever her idea was.

'Wow,' she said, looking at the sculpture. 'This gets more and more amazing.' She wasn't really interested, she only wanted to tell me her idea. 'You could fuck the system with this one,' she said. 'You could have your own exhibition, I bet loads of galleries would want to show this. You should take photos and –'

To stop her flow of words, I said, 'So, what's your new idea?'

'Wait, wait. Let's find Vince, and I'll tell him at the same time. You're both going to be in it. And Raymond.'

'Raymond? Really?' I said, doubtful. Vince and Raymond didn't mix.

She grabbed my hand and pulled me towards the house, shouting for Vince, but before we got to the door another car swung on to the drive.

'Terry,' she called. 'Terry's going to be in it too.'

Terry tucked his car behind Sue's and Vince's.

'Tell me your idea,' I said. 'Tell me now.'

'You're going to love it. Oh my God, it makes sense of everything.' I stood in the porch and watched as she bounced over to Terry. 'You'll see!' she shouted back to me. And then I heard her ask Terry, 'Did you bring some? Have you got it?'

'I've always got it for you, darling,' Terry said.

Terry had been to the house before, picking up Vince to go jogging or to deliver weed, and if Sue was around, he'd stay longer and they'd gossip about which tutors were having it off with each other, which were having it off with students and which ones he'd like to have it off with. Terry hadn't come out, although we knew he liked men. We'd seen the advert on the telly with the gravestone being carved and falling over, and we knew the chimes of the hammer on the chisel were from *The Shining*, and when the 'Don't Die of Ignorance' leaflet came through the letter box, Sue read all of it. Vince and I stayed out of their shared confidences and frank conversations about sex.

In the lounge, Sue put on the sad piano music and started dancing to it like the woman in the opening credits of *Tales of the Unexpected*, arms spiralling above her head, hands and wrists twisting. I wondered whether I could leave, say I felt sick and go to my room. Vince joined us and poured cider into four glasses.

'Apple juice,' he said to me with a wink. I sipped at it.

Terry parcelled some speed into cigarette papers and lined these up where our glasses had been. He swallowed his first, and then Vince, washing it down with a swig of cider. Sue made a fuss about hers, making sure we were watching as she put it in her mouth. I didn't want to take mine, but she said it would stop me being so uptight. 'Help you relax,' she said with a laugh. I took it.

After twenty minutes we were all dancing, then it was eleven and the four of us were in the garden doing the same. Sue and I were at the kitchen table and there was lots I needed to say about the dark feeling that made me want to carve. It seemed necessary to explain it over and over. It was after two when Terry stripped down to his underpants and ran around the outside of the house, ringing the doorbell, banging on the windows, and then he decided it would be a good idea to carry the sofa into the garden. I could tell that Vince was as uneasy as I was about moving a large piece of furniture from the house, but Terry managed to tip it on to one end, and he and Sue used a rug to slide it into the hallway, around the corner and out through the front door. They carried it into the garden, placing it so that it faced the horse chestnut, in front of the blanket, which had been left out since Joy came round. Someone decided we should go into the garage. It was three in the morning.

The double doors were made of the same wooden boards as the rest of it, and although they were unlocked, we had to tug on them to drag them over the grass growing in front.

The garage was empty, and it stank of underground places, cellars and caves, of damp crawl holes and rotten wood. Vince found the pull for the overhead light, which swung, unshaded, back and forth, chasing our shadows into the corners. Suddenly silent, we stood on the earth floor looking around while I thought about millipedes and beetles, and the insects that live in the dark.

At the far end a workbench had been built to fit the garage's width, and on the wall above was a perforated board hung with old tools. As the undulating shadows slowed to stillness I saw a large handsaw, a hacksaw, screwdrivers, spanners of different sizes, a spirit level. A rack to the side held gardening equipment: a fork and a shovel, trowels, two sorts of rake, a ladder and a pair of shears. Everything was rusty and dusty and strung with lengths of old spiderweb. Someone had drawn around each tool in red.

'Look at that,' Sue said, and walked forward. She reached across the bench and tapped an empty shape: the distinctive blocky head and flat nose, and the backward-pointing spikes like reversed horns. 'It's only the bloody claw hammer that's missing. Oh my God. There's a claw hammer in my new film. I can have a scene in here.' She spread out her arms. 'In the garage.' She turned, admiring it.

'This isn't a good place,' Terry said. 'Bad vibes.' He was still only wearing his underpants.

'What new film?' Vince asked.

'The one that you, you and you are going to be in.' She pointed at each of us in turn.

Vince gave a dismissive *pfff*, but Sue continued. 'It's about the Bloodworths.' She said the name breathily in a horror film way.

'Mr D. Bloodworth?' I said. 'From the bottle of pills?'

'About his wife, and a murder. Here, at the Underwood.' Vince must have also told Sue about what had happened.

'No,' Terry said, backing away. 'I'm not going to be in it, no way.'

'Don't worry, it won't happen,' Vince said. 'I've lost count of the number of films she's supposed to be making. How many screenplays have you written? How many times have you said you're going to America? Girls like you don't become horror directors. Get real.'

'Oh, fuck off,' Sue said.

'No, you fuck off. And you know what? I'm bored of all your crappy ideas that go nowhere. I'm bored of everything you have to say, in fact I'm bored of everything about you.'

'And I'm bored of you,' Sue said. 'Always asking me the same thing. *Please, Sue, please, Sue.*' She spoke in a begging tone that Vince never used. '*Please can we have sex? Just a little bit of sex. Please?*'

I was mesmerized by them, and something about the garage, the reek of it, the taste of it, wormed its way into me, down my throat, and kept me there, watching. A real-life horror.

'So, what happens in your film?' Vince said, moving closer. 'Does Mr Bloodworth whack his wife with the claw hammer because she's such a fucking tease?' With his index finger he tapped out the last four words on Sue's forehead.

Terry winced, and Sue swept Vince's hand away from her face. 'No, she kills him.'

This Vince scared me like the drunk one at the Berni Inn, and the night felt uncontainable, like something bad was coming, and Terry felt it too. Before Vince could answer, Terry cut through their argument with a high-pitched scream. He spun and crashed into me. I tried to grab him as he flailed, but he launched himself towards the open garage door, slipping on the packed soil of the floor, yelling and scrabbling like an enormous four-legged creature. He got up, was out the door, and we went after him.

In the kitchen, he wouldn't stop shouting that he wanted to go home, that this was a bad place. I took his car keys off him and Sue slapped his face. He stopped shouting and began to cry.

'He's having a bad comedown,' Sue said.

'He takes too many drugs too often,' Vince said.

★

We stayed up most of that night, Sue calming Terry and supplying us with pints of water. Somehow we made it into work. The look on Alan's face when he saw me and Terry was one of disgust, and I too was disgusted with myself, miserable and even more anxious about the house and now Sue's film. As Terry and I were sorting the post – no competitive firing into the pigeonholes that morning – he told me that disgust, anxiety and depression were usual symptoms after taking speed.

'And it makes your willy tiny.'

'I don't have a willy,' I said.

We weren't capable of laughter.

Of course, Terry was in *Dark Descent*. Still muscled inside a tight shirt, buttons straining, his hair thick, handsome in a beefy, big-jawed way. He sits relaxed, legs wide, on a large L-shaped sofa, tasteful prints behind him, a potted fern, the corner of a fireplace. Everything says he's done well for himself. Whatever his job is, it isn't working in the post room of an art school. *Friend of Sue and Vince*, the caption says, when his name comes up. The camera rolls, but he's unaware as he picks an invisible piece of lint or cat hair off his jeans and sweeps at the spot with the back of his hand. He still likes to talk. He speaks about the art school, the tea breaks and working with me. He fiddles with a strip of paper he has with him and calls Vince volatile. As I watched, I remembered what Raymond had once said about true crime programmes: we watch because we want to know the absolute worst, and if it happens to someone else we are happy it didn't happen to us. Even better, I thought, if we could nearly have been the victim, have once walked the same streets in the same town; then we can be horrified, empathetic and relieved.

17

Before *Dark Descent* streamed, but after her visit, I received another email from Emma Zahini. She explained that a short film Sue wrote and directed as well as acted in had come into her possession. Emma Zahini said it revealed the crucial dynamics between the major players in the events at the Underwood in 1987, and would I like to comment? I was more interested in who had given her the tape, but I didn't ask her that, I didn't reply at all. At that point I'd never seen Sue's film, but I knew what it was about because I'd been in it.

Early on an art school closure day, Sue, Vince, Raymond and I gathered at the Underwood to shoot Sue's film. She'd been unable to persuade Terry to be in it – he'd said nothing would induce him to go back to that house. The ancient video camera Gramps had given Sue had been returned as unrepairable, and she'd worked on Raymond until he asked his father if he could borrow his. It was a JVC GR-C1, the same make and model as the one used in *Back to the Future*, a film too cute and funny for our tastes. According to Raymond, the camera cost thousands and he'd told his father he needed it for a pre-university project, and his father had made him promise that no one else would use it. In the kitchen, Sue argued with Raymond, cajoling and joking and then shouting that she needed to be behind the camera as well as in front of it, but Raymond wouldn't budge. I felt his reasoning was more to do with Vince being there than anything about cameras.

Vince left them to it and went into the garden, and I trailed after him, not wanting to be drawn by Sue or Raymond on to one side or the other. In the garden he sat on the damp sofa, took a can of cider from a plastic bag and cracked it open. He held it out to me and I shook my head, trying not to look appalled. I hadn't yet had breakfast.

Raymond won the argument, and it was agreed that he would do the camerawork under her direction. She would play Mrs Bloodworth, Vince would be her husband and I was the manifestation of their baby's cry. 'Manifestation' – that was the title of the role in the script. Vince, I supposed, agreed to be in the film as an apology for the things he'd said in the garage, but I could still feel a simmering antagonism between him and Sue, as well as the tension between him and Raymond, who'd never liked each other. Even before Vince started drinking, I had bad feelings about how the day was going to go. Sue's script was hardly legible, and even as we gathered for the first scene she was rewriting the pages, crossing out and muttering to herself as she spoke the dialogue under her breath.

Emma Zahini's *Dark Descent* showed half-a-dozen clips from Sue's film, as well as stills of the house and garden, and she replayed certain scenes over and over. The colours are washed out and the dialogue is muffled as though we're speaking underwater, requiring subtitles in certain sections, and in the outdoor scenes you can sometimes hear a car going past. I watched the full version later, and unedited there is no music as it opens, no title or credits. It starts instead with a handheld shot from the top of the drive, panning across the garage and the house to the front door. Off camera, Sue says, 'The Underwood Possession, scene one, take one.'

Sue, dressed as Mrs Bloodworth in a frilly apron over a blouse with a ruff, is pruning the scraggly roses in the front garden, a younger Carol Van Sant from The Stepford Wives – but as she stands upright, we see she's heavily pregnant.

In the kitchen she argues with Vince, dressed as Mr D. Bloodworth in an oversized suit and the pebble glasses. They argue in the bathroom and in the lounge. He arrives home from work wanting to know why his dinner isn't on the table, why the house isn't tidier, why she doesn't want sex.

'I don't have to do what you tell me to do,' Sue as Mrs Bloodworth says.

'You're mine,' Vince as Mr Bloodworth replies.

On Vince's bed, in a long white nightie, Sue as Mrs Bloodworth gives birth, knees up, head to chest, grunting, while Vince as Mr Bloodworth paces the hallway, sometimes staggering. An umbilical cord made from a length of melted tubing snakes from under Sue, and one of the twins' dolls supplies a first glimpse of a baby, bloody and smeared with petroleum jelly. A recording of Andrew crying plays on a portable tape recorder hidden under the bed and doesn't stop. The crying continues for almost all of the rest of the film, a soundscape for every shot, until even the couple's rowing voices are drowned out.

As the crying goes on, there are glimpses of my face and open mouth as I hide under a bed, or in a wardrobe, or in a corner of the outhouse, in the long grass, and under the kitchen table, my tongue painted black with Marmite or red with tomato ketchup.

Raymond takes shots of flies on the bathroom windowsill,

rooks rising noisily from the horse chestnut, a worm inching its way across the drive. In the shadows of the garage, we see Sue as Mrs Bloodworth digging a hole the length and width of a body. The earth flies from the shovel and a mound of soil grows beside the grave. Sue as Mrs Bloodworth rests, leaning on the shaft and panting, and the camera slides from her sweaty face as her eyes move to a shape on the wall, outlined in red: the missing claw hammer. The camera is behind her now while she walks into the bright garden: a silhouette of a woman holding a hammer, narrowing to a charcoal line of darkness. There is one shot of the hammer held high against the sun, and another of the back of Vince's head.

The final scene is Sue and Vince, Mrs and Mr Bloodworth, lying beside each other in the grass, faces to the sky, the bottle of Laprosyn in the wife's hand. They could be dead; they might be sleeping. Inside the house, the sound of a baby crying starts up again and the woman's eyes flash open. This is supposed to be the final image, but the original continues past that final frame and shows us Vince refusing to play dead. He coughs and twitches, complains the grass is tickling him, his nose itching.

'For fuck's sake, Vince,' Sue says. 'Keep still. Two seconds.' He lets out an enormous belch and laughs. 'Please,' she says.

'You know it didn't happen like this, right?' Vince says. '*He* killed her, and then he topped himself.'

'I don't care,' Sue says. 'Lie still.'

Now, Vince sits up, legs out straight and wide like a doll's. He takes a flat bottle from the inside pocket of his jacket and drinks. 'Shoot your stupid little film in your own fucking garden,' he says. The viewer hears an audible breath from out of shot: mine. 'What?' he says, looking beyond the lens. 'Aren't you enjoying seeing us play dead in the grass?'

'This is Sue's film and you've been drinking all day,' Raymond says from behind the camera.

'It doesn't matter,' Sue says wearily, getting up. 'It's over.' She waves her hand towards the camera. 'You can stop filming. Cut. Cut!' But the camera swings from Sue to Vince.

'What are you going to do?' Vince says. 'Video me to death? Ouch, ouch, Raymond. You're hurting me.' He tips the bottle again, missing his mouth and spilling whisky on his shirt. He wipes at his chest and tries to get up, his legs sliding out from under him. We hear Sue gathering together her papers and props, talking about getting on with the editing, but Raymond keeps the camera focused on Vince, collecting evidence. And now I am just in the edge of the shot, coming into view.

Vince sways, speaks: 'What about you, hairy bear-cunt?'

I am frozen, as though my section of the screen has stopped working.

'Yep, that's right,' he continues, putting on his bad American accent. 'Sue told me you're as hairy as a bay-er, down there.' He indicated his own crotch with the neck of the bottle. 'All the way down to your knees.' The camera jumps, zooms into some grass and goes to black.

Vince continued speaking: 'I bet you, little lover-boy,' he pointed the bottle at Raymond, 'didn't know hairy bear-cunt was brought up in children's homes, did you? Did you? I bet you don't fancy her so much now.'

Heat rose from my chest, and Sue, crouching, looked up at me, her shock mirroring mine and guilt flashing across her face. Our eyes moved away from each other, and Raymond looked stunned.

'You're a nasty piece of work,' Sue said to Vince, as though she had no blame in disclosing these private things.

'*Ooh, you're a nasty piece of work,*' Vince repeated in a high voice, his drunkenness making him capable only of insults and repetition.

'Stop it,' Sue said. I knew she was looking at me, but I couldn't look back. 'Come into the house, let me explain.'

'I'm not going anywhere with you,' I said, surprising myself. I strode off and Raymond reached for my hand, and our fingers touched before I pulled mine away. I could hear him asking questions and Vince whistling after me.

In my bedroom, I closed the door and lowered my back down it until I was sitting on the floor. I wept silently with my mouth wide. I didn't want to give any of them the satisfaction of hearing me.

After ten minutes, when I had crawled into bed and was lying in a ball on my side, I heard a tap on my door.

'Ursula?' Sue's voice. 'I'm going to take Raymond home and then I'll come back. Okay? We can talk.' I didn't answer. 'Vince is in his room. I'm sure he won't be any trouble.' I heard a whispered conversation between her and Raymond, with Sue persuading him not to come in to check whether I was okay, that she would give me time and talk to me later. Finally, I heard the car leave.

I was awake for hours, waiting for Sue to come back so I could have it out with her. I thought about the things I'd say, my reasoning perfect and justified, and in every scenario she apologized, weeping and begging me to forgive her. But the car didn't return in the time it would have taken her to drive home, drop Raymond and come back.

I became angry with Vince in the next room, sleeping off his drinking. Making him say sorry wouldn't be so easy; he would never apologize or grovel. I thought about putting a pillow over his face and pressing down, but he would thrash and kick and fight back. As I fell asleep, I imagined getting the Berni Inn steak knife from the cutlery drawer but wasn't sure I'd be able to use it.

18

The next morning, Vince's door was closed. I had hardly slept, alternately burning with shame or fuming with anger, turning over in my bed, making plans that seemed ludicrous in daylight. As I dressed, I thought instead about the things I'd say to Sue when I saw her at the art school, or how I'd cut her dead.

It was one of those cool summer mornings where you know the cloud will burn off and the day will be roasting, but I was chilly as I walked through the town, the chisel and mallet in my bag, knocking against my hip. I had decided to return them; they weren't mine, but really I was doing it through some warped idea of getting back at Sue. She thought my sculpture was good, therefore I would stop being able to sculpt. When I got to work I transferred them to my post trolley, tucking them under the letters and parcels, and I did my usual rounds. In Sculpture I didn't see Ms Barker or any other tutors, and the studios were empty of students, but an official-looking poster was pinned to the noticeboard:

Watch out, watch out,
There are thieves about.
Take your valuables home or lock them away.
The art school does not take responsibility for any
personal materials, tools or belongings.

In the second-year studio only work in progress remained – all the tools and equipment had gone. The sculpture of the ribs and intestines had been worked on but still hadn't improved. I took the mallet out from under the post. The handle fitted so well into my fist, a perfect extension of my arm. A twitch of desire ran through me with the thought of getting back to the Underwood and continuing the work, something physical, sensual, low down in my belly, an addiction.

I have often felt that way when a piece of work is going well, or the ideas are coming. I once had an exhibition of wood carvings of small mammals, inspired by my drawings of roadkill – muntjac deer, badger, fox – each destroyed in some way. For the private view I placed the sculptures on the gallery floor with red lines around them. Some days I removed the 'bodies' and on others I left them in place. From the outset, I knew that exhibition would be a success.

I pushed my trolley out of the studio with the chisel and mallet still inside. They were mine.

Sue wasn't in her usual place in the main office; instead, her colleague stood behind the high reception desk, poring over the ledger and running a finger along the rows. She was an older woman whom Sue said kept a tin of Winter Mixtures in her desk drawer and unwrapped them without offering any.

'Where's Sue?' I said. The office was stuffy and stank of warm cinnamon breath.

The woman looked up and pursed her lips. 'We haven't heard from Sue.' She tutted, picked up an eraser and rubbed out a number, blowing flecks off the page. I turned to go. 'Aren't you forgetting something?' The woman had one hand out and it took me a moment to remember I hadn't given her the post. Ignoring her outstretched hand, I put the bundle on the edge of the desk where she would have to reach for it.

'Make sure you deal with those quickly.' I tapped the pile of post. 'You wouldn't want anyone to steal them.'

As I made my way to the post room, I had a horrible thought that Sue's passport had arrived and she'd gone to America without me. She couldn't do that. She wouldn't.

She wasn't at tea break and Vince didn't show up either, but that wasn't unusual, his maintenance jobs occasionally took longer than expected. I made the tea and slumped in my usual chair, imagining Sue and Vince kissing goodbye at the airport, laughing about me. I could have wept; I could have thrown my mug at the wall.

One of the maintenance team stood and held his cup out in my direction, and this time, I didn't take it. 'Do your own fucking washing-up,' I said. The room fell silent. Someone whistled. 'What?' I said to Alan. 'I'm not doing it any more.' If Sue had been there, we would have high-fived, except I was supposed to hate her. I wished I was wearing trousers.

On my way home I went into the phone box and called Sue's house. Raymond answered. It was warm in there, and I put my palm on one of the window panels and when I lifted it off a sweaty imprint remained. Raymond sounded pleased I'd called and I felt a flutter at hearing his voice. He was worried about me, he said. He'd been concerned all day about how I was feeling after what had happened the day before. He thought Vince was unpredictable, the atmosphere at the Underwood unstable. 'Why don't you start looking for some-where else to live?'

'I'm going to America with Sue, didn't she say?'

He made a non-committal noise.

'As soon as our passports arrive, as soon as she's edited the film.' As I said it, I knew the statements contradicted each other.

'That's what you want to do, is it? Follow Sue?'

I shrugged, although he couldn't see me.

'She changes her mind a lot, Ursula, and she's done this before, you know. Had other friends she's let down.' Did he mean the man she'd gone to Scotland with? 'She's my sister and I love her, but you need to work out what you want to do with your own life. Don't do what Sue is doing.'

'I know,' I said quietly. I exhaled on the glass, drew a heart, rubbed it out.

'You've got your carving.'

'Sculpting,' I corrected.

'Sculpting.'

'Is she there, at your house?' I asked.

Raymond paused, perhaps taking in that I hadn't called to speak to him. 'Sue?' he said. 'Wasn't she at work?' And I knew she'd be at the Underwood, lying on the blanket with Vince, getting stoned, looking up into the leaves of the horse chestnut. It was the perfect day for skiving. The pips sounded and Raymond shouted over them, 'If I could drive, I'd come and –' The call ended.

I jogged down the hill through air smelling of rotten vege-tation, as though with one hot day, summer was over. Just before I reached the gate, I heard Sue's voice, the tone of it – the light, jokey way she liked to tease Vince – although not what she was saying, and I couldn't believe I'd doubted her; of course she wouldn't go to America without me. I heard Vince's voice too, needled, angry.

The blanket and the other things Sue had taken outside over the weeks were strewn about the lawn: kitchen chairs, glasses, mugs and plates, ashtrays, a paper parasol with Chinese dragons flying across it. She and Vince were on the sofa – its back still to the house – kissing, their faces grinding, mouths open. As I watched, Vince pressed forward, pushing Sue backwards, her head resting on the sofa's arm, out of sight. She laughed and said something, a question, but I didn't hear Vince's reply because I ran inside, knowing they were unaware that I'd arrived home. I paced the lounge – the room furthest from the garden – and then went into my bedroom, but I'd left the window open and it was Vince I could hear now – the whole world could hear him grunting. I went into the kitchen, thinking I'd bang on the window to make them jump, make them stop, like cats or foxes in the night, but I saw that they'd moved to the blanket, Vince on top of Sue, trousers and pants around his thighs, bum pumping. I couldn't see her; I only heard her give a single cry. I returned to the lounge where I put on the sad piano music at full volume and lay on the dusty carpet where the sofa had been.

When Sue came into the kitchen, I was sitting at the table drawing shapes on the back of an envelope. I had made egg bread and had eaten three slices to make myself feel better. Sue's hair was rucked up at the back and her lips were reddened, puffy from kissing, I supposed. I pierced the final corner of egg bread with my fork and dipped it in a puddle of tomato ketchup. Vince had gone into the bathroom – I heard the squeak of the tap over the sink as he turned it on, and the water running. I thought he must be washing.

Sue stood in the kitchen looking out of the window, not speaking, and I knew something was off, but I didn't know what, too consumed by my own anger.

I put my plate and cutlery in the sink, making a noise

about it, wanting her to react, trying to force her to turn on me because that would scratch the itch under my skin. It would be scratched and scratched until it bled. Making it happen was better than the anticipation.

'So, you decided to do it?' I asked. She continued to stare as though she hadn't heard me, her arms hanging by her sides.

Her cigarettes were on the table, and I wanted one. I rattled the packet and she finally turned to look at me. Her face looked empty, devoid of emotion. I took a cigarette and lit it, inhaling once, and passed it to her. It made me feel sick. We heard Vince leave the bathroom, go into his bedroom and close the door. 'Why did you do it if you didn't want to?' I asked sharply. 'I thought you said he was crazy.'

She dragged hard on the cigarette. 'Did I?' Her voice wobbled but she rested her elbow in the cup of her other hand, so that the hand holding the cigarette was raised, accentuated, like she was acting in a film, trying to look in control but failing. 'It doesn't matter.'

'What doesn't matter?'

'Nothing.' She shook her head, trying to convince herself. 'Nothing, nothing, nothing!' Her throat was splotched with red and the rims of her eyes were pink.

'Are you going to apologize?'

She looked up at me quickly.

'For telling Vince about me. About my body.'

'Oh,' she said. 'That. Yes. I'm sorry.' She didn't sound it, and I might have stepped forward and slapped her except that we heard Vince call her name, short, like a bark. She turned to the sink and stabbed her cigarette out in the remains of the tomato ketchup on my plate. 'I am sorry,' she said kindly. 'Truly. We can talk tomorrow. We'll make a plan, yes?'

I watched her leave the kitchen, her fingertips on the doorpost for stability, or because she needed to touch something solid and real. She opened Vince's door and went into his room.

There's a retired detective in *Dark Descent*, with tufty hair and a face like a knot in a tree. It isn't a face I remember or a name I recognize. He sits in a wicker chair in a conservatory with orchids in pots lined up behind him, and I think caring for them must be his hobby. He clears his throat for a long time, shifting phlegm and swallowing before he says a cliché about this being the case that has haunted him for his entire career.

19

Small animals wove nests in the grass, ants made tracks in the flinty soil, worms went deeper to where the earth was damp. I'd lain in bed that morning – it was a Saturday – trying to puzzle out the previous night's conversation with Sue, and listening to the phantom *plock, plock, plock* of the mallet on the chisel echoing below the horse chestnut like a drum, as though another Ursula was carving.

Someone got up and went out, closing the front door, but I didn't know if it was Sue or Vince. I dressed, took my tools and a cigarette out to the garden, hunkering down to look at my sculpture, the cigarette unlit in my mouth. After a while a shadow fell across the carving, and I looked up, shading my eyes against the sun.

'All right?' Sue was a small shape against the sky.

I took the cigarette out of my mouth but didn't speak. She sat down on the blanket a little way from me and started unlacing her pumps. She was wearing a dressing gown that I knew had been left by the previous owners, silky with a paisley pattern, and underneath, a pair of Vince's shorts and a vest top.

'Phew,' she said. 'Hot already. I've been up the road to the phone box to talk to Terry.' She was chatty and normal, or she was acting that way, and I was amazed she could be so casual after everything that had happened. I waited to hear about the plan she'd mentioned yesterday. Would it be about when we were going to America, or finishing her film? Or maybe she'd announce that I should kill Vince. Wouldn't that be the dare to end all dares?

'I know I'm a bad person,' she said. 'I'm rubbish at keeping secrets.' She worked at a knot. 'No one should ever tell me anything.' The knot came loose, and she heeled off the pumps. 'I should never have told Vince about your body. I don't know why I did. It's this place. It makes me do things I shouldn't. It's making everyone behave weirdly, don't you think? Vince too.' She picked at a hole in the blanket, forcing her finger in and making it bigger. 'Please don't be cross with me,' she said. 'I can't stand it when you're cross with me.'

I said nothing.

'Are you going to smoke that?' She pointed at my cigarette, and I came over with it, still holding my chisel and mallet, and handed it down. She lit it and blew the smoke in a slow stream into the leaves above our head. I wanted to start carving again, to have the physicality of it remove me from my thoughts. Sue took something from the back pocket of her shorts.

'My passport arrived a few days ago.' She held it up to me – black with the golden lion and unicorn on the front – as though she wanted me to take it. When I didn't reach out, she flicked to the photo page. 'I look like a criminal.' She wanted me to look, to engage, to laugh with her, although I'd been there when the strip of pictures had popped out of the photo booth, and I knew what she looked like. I sat on the blanket so I wouldn't have to take it. 'I put "Film Director" in the occupation box.' She tried out a laugh, but it arrived stilted. 'You should put "Sculptor" in yours. Because you are. A sculptor. Look at the amazing work you're doing. You're going to be famous one day.'

I knew this pep talk was leading somewhere, but before I could work out where, Vince came out of the house with his holdall, a small suitcase and a duffel bag. Sue watched him and I watched Sue.

'Hey,' Vince called, and like an obedient dog she stood, and then threw the cigarette aside and went to his car, crossing the gravel gingerly in her bare feet and watching while he arranged things in the boot. She opened the suitcase to check something and closed it again. He took her by the shoulders and kissed her, and her arms were loose, and her head was loose, and it might have been that when he let go she would flop to the ground. He got in the driver's seat and raised his hand at me.

I started to raise my mallet in reply and then lowered it. Vince drove away and Sue came back to the blanket.

'He's going to see his grandfather in Manchester for a couple of days,' she said. 'He's not well.' I didn't respond; I didn't care what Vince was doing. She sighed and tried another subject. 'Raymond's car failed its bloody MOT yesterday. They wouldn't even let me drive it home, something about the tyres and a crack in the windscreen. Do you think he's going to be mad? I know he'll be mad.'

I didn't respond to this either. Instead I said, 'I don't want to be famous. I don't want anyone to know anything about me. I only want to carve.'

'No, okay,' she said, leaning forward, keenly. 'But you could rent a studio so you can work in the winter. Get out of that post room. Do something with your life.'

'I am doing something with my life – we're going to America.'

She hesitated. 'But that's *my* thing. You need to do *your* thing.'

'My thing?' There was a buzzing in my head, a pain in my side like a stitch and a taste like soap in my mouth.

'Vince wants to come.'

'Vince is coming with us?'

'He thinks he's coming, but I'm going to meet him on Monday at Manchester Piccadilly and I'll tell him then, at the station, that he isn't, that he can't.'

'Tell him that he isn't coming with us?'

'He thinks he's coming with me to the airport to buy tickets for the next flight.'

'But what about my ticket?'

She gave a slight shake of her head. 'He and I talked last night, about his drinking, his anger. You know that thing he did with the joint? He's done it before, he showed me. On the inside of his legs. He says it makes him feel better, calmer or something. He told me what happened with his sister. He didn't lock –'

I held my hand up to stop her talking.

'No,' she said. 'Okay.'

'And I need to wait for my passport.'

'It doesn't matter. That's what I'm trying to tell you. I'm going on my own, after I've told Vince that he's not coming.'

'What?'

'I need to go alone.'

'No,' I said, sitting upright, facing her. 'We agreed. You said I needed to get out of this place.' A familiar feeling of devastation washed through me. Not again. This couldn't happen again. The terror of starting over, of being alone, of being nowhere with no one.

'I'm going on my own. And didn't you say the other night that you didn't want to go anywhere with me?'

'But I didn't mean America.'

'Well, this is how it has to be.'

'No,' I repeated. 'This is not how it will be.' My heart was dark but on fire, the flames licking up into my head, and I brought the mallet up and out, and swung it sideways. Swung it without thinking so that it tapped her on the side of the head as I said the word 'not'. There wasn't much of a sound, a dull thud at most, no crack.

'Ow!' She brought her hand to her temple, her eyes wide with shock. 'What did you do that for?'

'Oh God,' I said. 'I'm sorry. I didn't mean to. Let me see.' I was appalled by my own actions, like a toddler who sweeps her bowl to the floor in a fit of temper and afterwards stares at the chaos of broken crockery and spilled food, amazed by her own power. Sue checked her fingertips, but there was no blood, and on her temple there wasn't a bump, not even a red mark.

'It's all right,' I said. 'It'll be okay. I'm sorry.'

'I want to see,' she said and went inside to the bathroom, and I followed. I stood in the doorway and watched her examine the side of her head in the mirror, pushing back her hair and twisting.

'There's nothing there,' I said.

She opened the bathroom cabinet and rattled through the old medicines, plasters and a plastic bottle of Johnson's Baby Powder, saying, 'Why haven't you cleared out this crap?'

I didn't like her touching it, messing it up. I wasn't sure what went where and whether I'd be able to put everything back in the right place.

'Do you have a headache? Vince might have headache tablets in his room.'

She didn't answer but sat on the side of the bath and let me press a wet flannel that I had folded in half and half again to the side of her head. 'Would you like a cup of tea? Toast?

Tea and toast always makes things better. It must be the after-noon, and we haven't even had breakfast or lunch.' I was suddenly famished. She didn't move, and so I took her by the elbow and led her into the kitchen and sat her at the table while I put the kettle on and took the last four slices of bread from a packet. I kept an eye on her, lifted the flannel from the side of her head where I had her pressing it to her temple. Still no mark. She watched me as I moved about the kitchen. I was sick with the thought that she'd been planning to go without me.

We went outside and sat on the sofa, facing the horse chestnut, drinking the tea and eating the toast. I let her have the last of the blackcurrant jam.

'As well as telling Vince you're hairy, I said you were found in Canada with a bear when you were a baby.' She spoke flatly and didn't look at me, and I felt terrible for hitting her.

'That's okay.'

'He didn't believe me even though I swore it was true. It's not true, is it?'

I stared at her. I knew she knew it wasn't true. What baby is raised by a bear? Everyone knows the bear would eat the baby.

'No, it's not true.'

'Tell me.' She faced me and put her feet up on the cushion as though she was waiting for a story. Her calves were smooth, shaved.

'About my mother?' I put my trainers on the sofa, so that we were face to face.

'Yes,' she said.

I'd never told anyone how I came to be placed with foster parents and put in children's homes, and the idea of saying it aloud made my fingertips sweat and my insides jitter, the same sensations as when I'd gone on a trip to the coast, and on a clifftop with a long drop to rocks and the thrashing sea, I'd had an unnerving desire to see what would happen if I jumped.

'I didn't know my dad,' I started. 'It was always just me and my mum. She made me call her Sadie, although I'd have liked to call her Mum. She was brilliant. She played the guitar, and we travelled around busking and sleeping in her car in the summer. But the car broke down and it cost too much to get it repaired and she said she was tired of England and the people in it, so we went to Morocco. I remember the heat and the dust and the noise – shouting and music and the clucking of chickens and, oh, the smell of roasting meat. I was seven, nearly eight.' Sue rested her head against the sofa, listening. 'No one got Sadie's music in Morocco, it wasn't like theirs, and they thought she was wicked because she didn't wear a veil in public, and we were about to come home when she got ill. She said it might have been the water, though we always boiled it, and she said maybe she had the flu. She wouldn't go to the hospital because she said we couldn't afford it. We were staying in the cheapest place she could find – the third floor of a small block, with thick walls and tiny windows and a bed and a stove. There was a toilet off a narrow hallway, which was just a stinking hole in the floor, but she was pleased because we didn't have to share it. The "crapper trapper", she called it, or the "highway to hell". I must have been naughty, but I can't remember why, I only remember locking myself in the toilet and Sadie banging on the door for me to let her in because she needed to use the loo.'

I remember waking to the sound of a fly buzzing at the oblong window high up in the wall above the sink and the smell of the musty hand towel under my head.

It's getting dark and, aside from the fly, it's quiet in the toilet. Sadie has stopped banging. *Has she had dinner without me?* I wonder. *Is she better? Is she sleeping in our lumpy-bumpy double bed with the sausage-shaped pillows and the blankets as heavy as rugs?*

I get up and pull the light cord and unlock the door but the stupid thing swings outwards and it will move only a finger's width because something is blocking it. 'Sadie!' I call through the gap. 'Sadie!' I shout, as loud as I can. I push the door with all my strength, feet braced against the tiled floor, but it won't budge. I shout again and again, and I get a finger and thumb in the gap and manage to pinch something, and it's a bit of the silky fabric Sadie wears over her head to try and blend in with the Moroccan women, she says, and I understand that what's blocking the door is Sadie herself, lying on the floor, wedged in the hallway. Now I'm the one banging on the door, pushing it, bumping it against her and calling and sobbing. She doesn't move, she doesn't make a sound. I cry myself to exhaustion. There's water in the bathroom – a warm trickle from the tap over the sink – but I know we're supposed to boil it before we drink it. My mouth is dry, and my throat is dry, but I don't drink. I put on the light and lie again with my head on the smelly towel watching the fly circling the bulb, round and round until it goes out through the gap in the door. There's a sweet smell out there but it's better than the stink from the highway to hell. I sleep, and when I wake I watch the bright rectangle that the window casts travel across the floor. I am so thirsty. I call for Sadie again, and when she doesn't answer, I stand and shout at the window: 'Hello!' and 'I'm stuck in here,' and 'Help!' The shouting makes me thirstier. I sit and watch the tap for what feels like hours and I get up and I drink from the tap and I lie down and wait to be sick, to have the squits, to die. I can hear the flies on the other side of the door. I don't die.

The window is closed, and I work out that on the other side, three floors down, is the alleyway Sadie and I sometimes run along with our hands out, brushing the sides until our fingertips are yellowy-orange from the dusty plaster. I climb on the sink, and I find that if I stand on my tiptoes, I can reach the window, and by stretching an arm and balancing on one foot I can push the window open. A slice of yellowy-orange wall. I shout again, up at the open window, but my little voice sails out over the flat roofs with their spiky aerials. I will never be able to climb up there and get out, I would never fit through such a tiny frame. More flies come, circling the bulb and going through the gap in the door, finding their way to Sadie. I hear them buzzing. I close the door. I open the door because I don't want to be alone. I think about the crawling things coming out of the cracks in the walls and up the plughole and down from the ceiling. And I cry and I sleep, and I use the revolting crapper trapper, and I drink from the tap and I stand on the sink and I call up to the window, 'Help! Help!' Night comes again and I'm very hungry. There's nothing to eat and I try the soap, the eroded oval of Imperial Leather that Sadie loves, which is all that's left of the block she brought with us from England. I bite into it, but it tastes of bitter fat and I scrape at my teeth and rub my mouth on my sleeve and spit. My child-sized tooth marks are in the soap.

I drink water to take away the taste and I pee into the highway to hell. I sleep on the floor while the flies buzz. When it gets light, I crouch for hours with my hands cupped, waiting for a fly to land, and when one does I snap my hands together like a Venus flytrap. Twice, three times, a fly lands and I miss it, but on the fourth, when I snap the cup closed, I've got it. It buzzes and bumps against my palms. I am so hungry. I put my mouth to my bent thumbs and make the tiniest of holes, and I suck. The fly comes into my mouth and I swallow it down, gagging and choking, but I keep it down. I am still hungry.

I carve *Help Me* into the soap with my fingernail and stand again on the sink. I throw the soap at the open window. It hits the glass and bounces back into the room. I have to climb off the sink each time to retrieve it and climb back up to throw it at the open window. I sit on the floor and sob, and I climb on to the sink and I throw the soap again and again, until it goes through. And then, a miracle! Someone calls up, and I remember I should have been shouting in French, I should have carved the words in French, not English. French is the language Sadie has been speaking in Morocco and teaching me when she remembers. 'Aide-moi! Aide-moi!' I shout. Finally I hear footsteps thumping up the stairs of the building, voices in the hallway. And somehow, I am taken back to England. Sadie's body comes too, and then I find myself with Dr and Mrs Hulse.

'Oh, Ursula,' Sue said. I'd almost forgotten she was there. 'This is what Raymond meant, wasn't it? When he said he knew what you'd done. But you didn't do anything.'

We sat for a while longer and I brought out more tea and fish fingers with tomato ketchup, which we ate while the light in the garden faded. I got the blanket from the grass, and Sue and I spooned on the sofa with it over us, me behind her, both of us facing out, our knees locked together, her hair in my face, and I was sure she wouldn't leave me now. In the morning when I woke, she was dead.

20

Whether the act of killing is murder or manslaughter is said to come down to intention: did the perpetrator intend to kill the victim or cause grievous bodily harm, or was it accidental? This is what the law says, as if intentionality is clearcut and recognizable, and in the millisecond when I swung the mallet towards Sue's temple, I might have had time to consider what I was hoping the outcome would be, or as though even in retrospect I might have been able to access and analyse my motive. What was I feeling? Frustration, disappointment, jealousy. I might have wished her dead or grievously harmed for a fraction of a second. That, then, is murder.

Time is a trickster. Days spent wondering what to do, minutes performing a job that took hours. It magics events into the wrong sequence, people in the wrong places, hats out of rabbits and rabbits out of scarves.

My ear against Sue's chest as she lay on the sofa. How she was colder than any living person. How I heard nothing in the ear pressed against her body, but a cacophony of sparrows in the other. How the morning sun was turning her skin the colour of lining paper, pale and matte, casting shadows from her eyelashes. How her hair had fallen away from her face to show me her ear where the cartilage furled, sculptural and waxen. How she had been sick in the night and how I wiped it away with the edge of the blanket, and her eyes stared, and her mouth remained open.

I sat beside her while the shade of the tree crept across the grass and the sun ran away down the drive. I can't say what I was thinking; my mind had been hollowed out. Something tiny landed beside me and I gazed at it, uncomprehending, as it rubbed its front legs eagerly together and up and over its dish-shaped eyes again and again until, swearing, I swiped at the fly and it took off with a buzz.

Down the telephone line I heard ringing as I turned my back on a white splatter of bird shit on a glass pane, until a twin was reciting their phone number like a poem, and I shoved in coins from my pocket. I asked for Raymond, and without asking who was calling, they said, 'I'll see if he's available. Hold the line, please, caller.' But Jess or Hannah replaced the handset, and the continuous call-ended tone was in my ear. What would I have said to Raymond? *I've murdered your sister?*

In the credit card compartment of my purse, I found the slip of paper with Joy's phone number and dialled the first two digits and then put the handset down. The phone box door was heavy against my shoulder. It closed me in again and I dialled 999.

'Emergency – which service do you require?'

I didn't know. I couldn't speak. Sue had dared me to choose someone to kill, and I had chosen her. I had done it, actually done it, and it made me want to throw up.

Back at the Underwood nothing had changed. It was dusk and the sofa was still on the lawn, the drive empty. I clung to the rotten gate and opened my mouth, wailing without a sound, tears falling down my cheeks and neck, legs weak.

And when the crying jag was over I went into the garage and looked at the hole in the earth floor that had been dug for Sue's film.

Was I thinking about my years in care, in someone else's home, in institutions? Was I thinking I didn't want to go back to being watched and supervised and judged, and once again rejected? One thing I'd learned in my sixteen years of being a looked-after child was how to avoid notice, how to blend in, keep to the back of the crowd, how to disappear. Let someone else take the punishment. I thought of Sadie and the freedom she had relished, and I knew that no matter what I'd done, I would not return to confinement.

By moonlight I tried to lift Sue using my thigh and stomach muscles and hoisting her body over my shoulder, but a dead body is heavier than you could ever imagine and so I rolled her on to the blanket and dragged it across the lawn, the flower beds, the path, to the garage. I didn't think about what I was doing, not while she travelled, not as I pushed her into the shallow grave. I could hardly see, but I made sure the blanket lay over her body and head, and then I took down the shovel that had been put back on the wall after Sue's film and blindly began to backfill. In the end I got on my hands and knees and pushed the soil over her with my hands. There seemed to be far more than had been taken out, and I knew that if anyone were to look in the garage they would see the disturbed earth, a mound. Averting my face, I pushed the garage doors shut from the outside.

I considered washing myself under the outside tap, but that wasn't going to work in the dark. I put the boiler on, and in the hall I undressed, leaving my muddy trainers, jeans, shirt and underwear in a heap in my bedroom. When the water was hot, I pushed open the bathroom door and stood looking into the room. There was no noise of Sue laughing, or Raymond in the kitchen making dinner, no sound of Vince's telly; I was alone in the house, but I took a step forward. In the mirror I was wild-haired, mud-streaked, my lips retracted in a grimace. I turned on the taps and didn't look at the high window.

Earth ran off me in streams, leaving a layer of grit between my backside and the enamel. I scrubbed at my hands and saw that the long hair that had been under my plaster cast had gone. I topped up the hot water, catching myself again and again with a jolt at this new reality, that Sue was dead and I had buried her in the garage. I knelt up and dry-vomited into the water.

The first sound was two slight taps against the window. I pulled myself into a crouch, water sloshing, to listen: the familiar gurgling in the pipes, the boiler puffing. I listened harder, but the taps didn't come again. It was rain, I told myself.

In the kitchen I fried an egg and sat at the table in my pyjamas to eat it, together with a cold sausage I'd found in the fridge. I was empty, but I pushed the plate away and put my head between my knees and then sat up and ate the sausage and the egg. What are you supposed to do when your best friend is under the earth in the garage, and you put her there? None of the horror films I'd watched had a template for this; none of the fake fright had prepared me for the true feeling.

Random memories dredged themselves up: Dr Hulse making me wash my hands with the Imperial Leather that was kept in the downstairs loo. He said Mrs Hulse wasn't feeling well, and then I was back in the social worker's car with my shiny new shoes resting on my suitcase. A man coming to Doughty House to select girls for a trip to the cinema. Lining up in the car park and not being chosen.

Later learning he'd been caught 'kiddie fiddling'. A school PE teacher catching a glimpse of the hair on my chest and not hiding the shock on her face.

I drew mindlessly on an envelope as I tried to remember what Sue had said about work. If she didn't turn up on Monday – how was it possible that she would never turn up again? – would they assume she was ill again? Surely you were supposed to call in every day you were sick. On the envelope, I'd drawn Sue's face over and over: her silky hair and her eyes, which sloped down at the ends. I screwed it up and threw it in the bin under the sink.

Silver trails crossed the kitchen floor, and I scuffed them out with my toes. I ran from the back door across the alley to the outhouse, hopping from one bare foot to the other on the cold concrete as I pushed three pounds in fifty-pence pieces into the meter to make sure the lights stayed on. It was when I went to go back inside, crossing the little alleyway again, that I saw that the ground was dry and there hadn't been any rain. I looked out at the night garden to make sure and then hurried inside, putting on all the lights. I climbed into bed, muscles aching, hands sore.

21

I didn't sleep, not properly, overwhelmed by images real and hypnogogic: me in Sue's bed in the twins' room, Sue tipping back tablets from a bottle, Raymond shaking me, asking, *What have you done?* With a start I woke to darkness and music, painfully loud, inside the house. It was the sad piano music that had made us laugh and scream when it'd come on that first day. *Sue!* I thought, followed again by a surge of unreality that she was dead. With another punch of alarm, I thought that someone must have come in and put the record on. Vince? I pulled the covers over my head and wailed, a high keening that sounded like it was coming from someone else. When I stopped, the music was still playing, the roar of it so loud it throbbed through the roots of my teeth, the bones of my face. What if the noise made the neighbours come round or call the police?

I got out of bed. My alarm clock showed 1.15 a.m. My bedroom light didn't work, and the whole house was dark although I'd left the lights on. The loudness of the music made it difficult to think, to work out how the record player could be playing if the electricity was off. I had put loads of money in the meter. How long did it last if you left all the lights on? I covered my ears, ducking. Perhaps the lights had fused, but I had no idea where the fuse box was. In the hall I flicked the switch: no light. I spread my arms wide as though to scoop and contain the distorted blast of music, and my fingertips touched either side of the hallway: open bathroom door on my left, Vince's closed door on my right. Had it been closed when I went to bed?

In the lounge, in the dark, I found the arm of the record player and lifted it from the record. Instantly the silence massed into a thick flow, filling the gap the sound had left, seeping around the standard lamp with the fringed shade, the two hulking armchairs, the sideboard with its twisted legs. There was a faint smell, unidentifiable but nasty, something in the garden or a bird rotting behind the gas fire.

Outside Vince's room I put my ear to his door. 'Vince?' I knocked. How was I going to tell him what I'd done? 'Vince, are you back?' No reply. I put my hand to the doorknob, paused, then opened the door with enough force for it to hit the wall behind. The lights were off in his room too, but I saw a shape in the bed, a head on the pillow, knees curled into chest. 'Vince?' I said again, louder. 'Something's happened.' My blood beat a rhythm in my throat and my eyes bulged into the blackness. 'Please don't play games.' My voice was thin, pleading. His light switch was beside my hand, and I flicked it, not expecting it to work, but his bedroom glared into view. The shape on the bed reassembled itself into old bedding, and I saw that he'd stripped his mattress and the items he kept on his chest of drawers, including the photo of the girl with the missing front teeth, were gone, and when I went forward and opened his wardrobe it was empty.

I sat on the edge of his bed with my head in my hands. He was still expecting to meet Sue tomorrow evening and catch a night flight to America. How long would he wait, and when he gave up would he drive straight to Sue's house? For the first time I thought properly about the twins and Anita, and Raymond, and I covered my open mouth and rocked.

I could never tell them. I began to sob, for Sue and her family, for Vince, and for myself.

I didn't think I'd fall asleep, but I woke on Vince's bed where I'd crawled, with the light on, to the same soft tapping I'd heard in the bathroom. If not rain, then water pipes, or twigs on the roof. I pulled the old cover over me and tried to do the alphabet game to get myself back to sleep, the one I would use in each children's home. I would visualize an animal beginning with each letter of the alphabet. No insects allowed. A for antelope, B for bear. If I was lucky, I would be asleep at F or G, but this time by M the tapping was impossible to ignore. It came every few minutes, irregular and insistent, from a location I couldn't identify, and finally I got up. I stood in the doorway of Vince's bedroom – the sound wasn't coming from his room, or the bathroom, but from my room. Something was tapping on the window that overlooked the back hedge. All my curtains were closed, but they were flimsy, and it was possible that anyone out there would be able to see shapes within my room even with the lights off. Was someone out there? As I thought this, the tapping seemed to get harder, and I retreated until my bedroom wall was at my back, squeezing myself between the open door and the dressing table. *Tap tap tap, tap tap.*

'Who is it?' I called, as though it was normal for a person to tap on the window of a house at night. There was no reply, but I was sure the person had heard me because the noise moved around the corner of the house to the next window – the one that overlooked the horse chestnut and the sofa. The sound wasn't the deeper rap of knuckles on glass but the hollower clink of fingernails. I needed to blink, but I was afraid in the second when my eyes closed something would happen and I would miss it; I needed to swallow but had no saliva.

The tapping stopped for a moment and came again, now from the kitchen, where there weren't any curtains. Someone was out there. It had to be Vince, Vince playing a stupid joke, but I stayed where I was, hemmed in and pushing backwards as though I might be able to dissolve into the wall and disappear into the fabric of the house. The sound became louder, changing to slapping, a palm against glass, demanding I come. Who would hit on the glass like that and not call out? Not even Vince would last this long before he said something or laughed. I put my hands over my ears and hummed. When I removed them, the noise had stopped. I waited, let myself breathe again, stepped out from my corner, and a rotten stench hit me, a decay worse than the smell in the lounge. I gagged, bending, hands on knees, and a splash of my stomach contents came up and I spat it on to the floor. I might have vomited everything except that the doorbell rang its two-tone chime. I stayed where I was, bent forward, and the doorbell rang again. Not Vince, no, he had a key. The doorbell rang a third time, and then, as though the person was keeping their finger on the button, it chimed over and over – the sweet ding-dong made malevolent by the repetition. I stood upright, and across the hallway I saw the shape of a person through the frosted glass.

'Go away,' I whispered, a prayer. 'Please go away.' The figure wasn't close enough to the glass to make out features, but it was about Sue's height, her build. The doorbell continued to ring. This wasn't real. I was still asleep. It was a dream.

I backed into my corner again, sinking to a crouch with my arms wrapped around my head, groaning to drown out the noise, tucking my nose into my knees to keep out the smell. I stayed there until I had pins and needles and my feet were numb. The doorbell continued to chime. It might have been an hour or more, but finally, with a long, low moan that rose to a shriek, I stood, ran into the hall, launched myself at the door and yanked it open. The sun was rising, and no one was there – only the chilly garden, the driveway, birdsong.

I ran back to my bedroom and put on my work uniform: shirt, jacket, skirt and tights, shoving my feet into my shoes, grabbing my coat and bag. Without looking at the garage, I ran out of the drive and up the road. Halfway to the art school, I stopped and rested on a lamp post, panting, feeling faint. A car pulled up beside me and a woman leaned out of the passenger window.

'Are you all right, dear?' she said. Perhaps it was her genuine concern or the delayed shock that made me bend over and throw up on the pavement. She made a grunt of disgust, the window rolled up and the car drove away. I sat on a bench next to the cathedral, nodding off while I waited for work to start.

At the post-room lockers I was light-headed, and I rested my forehead against the cold metal and took some long breaths. Terry shook his head at me and started to speak, but the post van arrived and he went outside to check the docket. Alan came in whistling, stopping when he saw me, and I stood straight, tugging on the bottom of my jacket.

'Worse for wear again?' he said, irritated.

'I'm all right.' I worked my face into a smile.

'You look peaky. Go home. We'll manage here.' He'd had enough of me.

'I'm all right.' There was no way I was going home.

'Another heavy night, was it?'

'Alan,' I started, ready to tell him everything.

Terry brought in the big packages by himself and didn't complain when I didn't help. I went into the toilets and lowered my face into palmfuls of cold water. In the mirror over the sink I looked dead.

I sorted the envelopes into the pigeonholes by myself while a voice in my head repeated, *I have killed Sue and buried her, I have killed Sue and buried her*. The voice questioned again how the record player could have come on, and what about the tapping and the slapping on the windows, the doorbell? And suddenly I realized and laughed out loud.

'Sorry I didn't answer the door last night,' I said to Terry, who was sorting boxes. 'I was really tired.'

'What?'

'When you came to the Underwood.'

'Wild horses couldn't drag me back to that place. But I did speak to Sue on Saturday morning.'

'You didn't ring the doorbell, knock on the windows?'

'She phoned me from the box up the road.'

'You didn't come round?'

'I'm a bit worried about her, actually.'

I opened my mouth to tell him and closed it again.

I delivered the post, and when I got to Sculpture my teeth were chattering and my frozen hands twitched on the handle of the trolley. I didn't notice whether any students were in the studios, I didn't look at what was new on the noticeboard, but I thought I could speak to Ms Barker. *I will tell Ms Barker,* I said to myself, otherwise I'd never be able to go home. It didn't occur to me that telling her that Sue from the main office was in the earth in the Underwood's garage would mean I'd never go home again. I knocked on the door of the Sculpture office but got no answer.

By the time tea break came I was sure I'd made it up. I bought a sausage roll from the canteen, and when I went into the staff room I was certain Sue would be there, grinding her teeth at every sexist word that came out of those men's mouths, and when she wasn't, I was equally certain that what I'd done was written on my face, but no one looked up as I boiled the kettles. I followed the list and made the teas and coffees and sat holding mine, feeling sick with tiredness and wide awake with dread. My stomach was empty but I couldn't eat. The sausage roll was fleshy, its pastry sweaty and its meat pink. I washed up. No one mentioned Vince or Sue.

22

My post-room shift finished at four thirty as usual, and I took my raincoat and my bag from my locker. In the daylight I was able to persuade myself that the knocking on the windows and the person at the door was a random lunatic. People escaped from mental institutions all the time, didn't they? Anyway, it happened in films. But as the afternoon had gone on, I realized there was no way I could go back to the Underwood sober. I loitered in town and huddled under the arches of the cathedral in the rain until the pubs opened.

At the bar of the Market Inn, I pointed at a pretty bottle, the barman poured my drink without asking my age and I took a corner seat. The vermouth was sweet, and I hoped I could drink enough of it to become invincible or pissed enough to get home and pass out until morning. Each time I lifted the glass to my lips, the ice rang, and I felt sicker. The pub filled with an after-work crowd, smokers in damp suits and a few women with big hair and wide shoulders. I gulped my drink and watched them until a man in a grubby shirt and stained jacket blocked my view. I looked up. It was John from the halfway house.

'Well, hello, Ursula!' he said over the noise. His upper-class voice had never matched his dishevelled clothes. I'd heard he'd been an accountant with a wife and child but was arrested for embezzlement and was put inside for four years. 'Long time no see,' he said. 'What are you doing here? On a date?' When I didn't answer, he said, 'Not been stood up, have you? Oh dear. What are you drinking?' He indicated my empty glass. I'd finished the drink, but it hadn't had any effect.

'Vermouth. Thanks.'

He pushed his way to the bar, the only Black man in the place, maybe in the whole town, and came back with a pint of bitter and a whisky, another vermouth for me and a packet of peanuts. We clinked glasses and drank.

'We've missed you in the house.' He tore open the peanuts, shook some into my hand and put his head back to tip a stream into his open mouth. 'Even more of a shithole than before,' he said, nuts churning.

'Is my room empty?' I had a sudden shot of hope that I could move back in, maybe that evening.

'That was filled. A fellow on the dole, I believe, like the rest of us. Good old Maggie, keeping us all in the drink.' He held up his pint – he'd finished the whisky. I gave his glass another clink. 'How's it working out at the post office?' I didn't correct him but answered blandly about sore feet and grumpy customers.

'I've always liked the look of it.' He took a drink of his bitter. 'Not the job, the uniform. Not a woman in a uniform, although that can be pleasant, just the actual uniform. Drink up.' He stood. 'Another?'

I hadn't finished my second. The vermouth was thick like the cough medicine Uncle Jimmy in Doughty House would spoon down us when we were ill, or sometimes when he wanted us to sleep. 'In a minute,' I said.

We continued in this way – John talking more as he drank and me becoming increasingly taciturn and drinking less as the hours passed – until the landlord rang last orders and time at ten thirty and the place emptied and my panic began to rise that I had to go home. The rain had stopped, and on the corner outside John patted me on the shoulder and started to say goodbye.

'Do you want to come back to mine?' I said. He hadn't asked me where I was living, and I hadn't volunteered the information, but I couldn't face that bungalow alone.

'Back to yours?' he said, surprised. 'Bit of an age gap. How old are you anyway?' He'd had at least five pints and several whiskies, but I wouldn't have been able to tell he was drunk.

'Sixteen,' I said.

'Christ,' he hissed, taking my arm. 'I'm thirty-nine and you let me buy you alcohol?' He looked around as though someone might have heard.

'You can have a nightcap and I'll have a coffee.' I wasn't sure we had any alcohol in the house, but John could have a cup of tea or a coffee with me, and I would persuade him to stay the night in Vince's bed.

It took a good half an hour to walk to the house with him rambling and getting mouthy about Margaret Thatcher and sounding off about other subjects. I barely listened to him. When we were near the Underwood and the dread had grown to a lump that sat solidly under my ribcage, I suddenly thought of an alternative.

'Why don't we go back to yours?' I said.

'Mine?'

'I'd like to see it –'

'But you already know it.'

'– again.'

'It's the same old shithole, I told you.'

'Please?'

'We must nearly be at your place.'

'Yes, but –'

'I'm afraid that my bladder isn't what it used to be, and I find I must urinate, and I'm not a man to urinate in a hedge.' He put an arm around my shoulders and pulled me onwards.

An oblong of yellow light shone from the Underwood's bathroom window, but the rest of the house was dark, and although Vince's car wasn't on the drive, I was sure he'd returned, and I was washed with relief that someone, anyone, would be there. I could invite John in, let him have a piss and send him on his way.

I unlocked the door and John followed me in. 'Vince?' I called out and flicked the hall light switch and it came on. 'My housemate,' I explained. There was no reply, and I knew the rooms were empty, too silent for Vince to be home, even sleeping. 'Fancy a cup of tea?' My voice was loud, too jolly. John stayed in the hall not moving, quiet after his previous garrulousness. Under the ceiling bulb the sockets of his eyes had become circular shadows and his cheeks looked clammy. Beads of sweat were breaking out on his forehead and a smell was coming off him, sweaty and rancid, although it might have been coming from somewhere inside the house. 'Are you okay?' I said. 'The loo's around the corner.' John didn't move. 'I must have left the light on when I went to work.'

He took a step backwards, into the coat rack, his hand to the side of his face. 'No,' he said, and his voice was quiet but clear, sober.

'What?' I raised my hand to my forehead to keep the light's glare from my eyes, to see him better.

'I have to leave.'

'Leave?' I stepped towards him.

'Sorry.' He spoke slowly, taking things in, formulating his words. 'Got to go.'

'But you needed to use the loo.'

'Things to do tomorrow.' He tipped his head up and I saw that his pupils were enlarged and staring, like a cat's when it stares at a spot in a room where you can see nothing. John was looking over my shoulder into the unlit kitchen, or further perhaps, out through the window to the garden, and it took all my willpower to resist looking behind me.

'Please stay. I'll put the kettle on.'

'No.' He stepped sideways towards the door.

'Vince might have something to drink in his room. I could check.' I scooted between John and the door, blocking his exit. 'Cider.'

He put his hands on the tops of my arms. 'I can't stay in this house.'

I stretched upwards – he was a foot taller than me – and pressed my lips against his, which were cold and soft and seemed to curl back against his teeth as though he was revolted. He pushed me away, almost lifting me sideways. 'Let me go.' His voice sounded strangled as he struggled with the door.

'Please, John, please stay.' I tried to close it and he tried to open it. The edge knocked against my forehead, and he had a foot in the gap.

'Let me out!' he shouted, and then he had the door open and was gone, blundering up the drive. I heard him on the road, panting and whimpering, his hard-soled shoes clacking and skidding as he disappeared into the night.

I closed the door, thinking that whatever was out there was worse than anything that might be inside, and without stopping I crossed the hallway and pulled the door to my bedroom closed without going in. I looked into Vince's room and was relieved that his curtains were drawn together as I'd remembered. The kitchen took more nerve, but keeping the light off, I reached over the sink and lowered the roller-blind without looking into the garden. The blind was water-marked and grubby, and it hung crookedly, creating a small gap where the night showed through, and I blocked this with old rags from under the sink.

My belly was an empty hole under my ribs. I'd barely eaten all day, just a bite of the sausage roll I'd bought from the canteen before my stomach refused it, and a few of John's peanuts. I heated a tin of beans, spooning some into my mouth before they were warm. I opened the fridge looking for cheese to grate on top. The interior was dark and warm, and it stank, but when I fiddled with the plug in the socket, it came back to life with a hum and a blink. Ham in an open packet had grown green and shiny, and a pepper had collapsed in on itself like the mouth of an old man with his teeth out – gone off too quickly for the length of time the power might have been out. There was no cheese. I swept the rotten food into a plastic bag and put it in the bin, and ate the beans straight from the saucepan, greedily.

I washed up the pan and then I washed the sink, sprinkling it with Ajax and scrubbing the water stains in each runnel of the drainer until they sparkled. I emptied the teapot, tipping out tea from what seemed like a week ago but had only been Saturday afternoon – two days previously – and washed that too, then moved on to the counter, sorting and tidying and wiping everything down, rinsing my cloth. The activity kept my mind occupied.

The food cupboard was next and as I reached in, I saw, on a box of Ritz Crackers, a slug. The cardboard was knobbled, the image gone where the slug had been eating, and it was working now on the edge of a hole. The creature had a wavy orange skirt, and when I looked closer, I saw tiny mites, white specks, moving across its ridged body. I slammed the cupboard closed, skin crawling, and leaving all the lights on went into Vince's room and on to his bed, getting under the old cover without undressing or brushing my teeth. He'd left his digital clock behind, one he'd brought with him when he moved in. I saw that the green boxy numbers were showing 1.30 as I fell asleep.

It was 2.17 a.m. This time I didn't wake to loud music or tapping, but a hiss and a scratchy click. I lay on my back gazing at the nicotine-stained ceiling and the peach-coloured lampshade. The bulb left a flash of light on the inside of my eyelids with every blink. I strained to hear the sound, which came again: the hiss and scratchy click repeated. This noise was coming from inside the bungalow, and it filled my head as insidiously as the tapping had the night before, a physical sensation as though my body contained only blood, which rocked and heaved against my skin. I made myself turn my head towards the door because not knowing was worse than knowing, and I saw that I'd left the door open and the hall light on. The strips of green that made up the digits on Vince's clock began to stutter, a couple going off, and then all of them winking out. The noise was calling me as the tapping had, and I sat up, swinging my legs to the floor. There was a stiffness in my shoulders from shovelling earth, a burn in my thigh muscles. In the L-shaped hallway all was the same. The sound was coming from the lounge, and I knew what it was but nevertheless I had to go and see.

The standard lamp was lit, and the turntable turned. The needle on the record had reached the end and it hissed across the dead space, clicked, and went back to the beginning of the end.

I couldn't remember if I had taken the record off the

turntable yesterday and put it away, or whether I'd just switched it off. I lifted the needle and put it back in its cradle and turned off the record player. I took off the record, held it over my head and brought it down hard on to the edge of the case. The vinyl broke into four or five large pieces that fell to the floor. I tensed, waiting for something to happen, and when nothing did I went to leave, and caught my reflection in the mirror over the gas fire and saw a wound in the middle of my forehead from where the edge of the door had cuffed me when John had left. It seemed superficial, but it must have opened again without me noticing because a trickle of blood had run down between my eyes and off the side of my nose, stopping in a crusted drip above my lip. I licked my finger and rubbed at it, smearing it across my face and rubbing at it with the sleeve of my post-room jacket.

Back in the hallway, I thought I'd have a go at trying to sleep again, but as I reached Vince's room, I heard another sound I recognized: the metallic rattle of the letter box as it was lifted from the outside. And that putrid stink came again, like something rotting. Around the corner from the front door, I was sure I could hear singing, no words, just a wavering and melancholic *la*-ing. It took a moment to place the tune and then I had it: the music from the record, the first few bars of the sad piano music, repeated. Incredulity wheeled into fear, and I sagged, guts plummeting and falling away like a split bag of salt, and I hunched over, clutching at myself, trembling. Perhaps I'd made a bleat, a noise, because the humming stopped and I heard a voice: 'Please. It's me. Let me in. I'm so thirsty.' It was Sue, softly pleading.

Sue! It was Sue. Urine flowed through my knickers and tights, warm at first, down the inside of my legs and pooling around my feet. And it occurred to me that I had buried

Sue alive. Perhaps she had clawed her way out of the earth, spitting soil and stones. *Should I let her in?* But Sue had been dead, absolutely dead, without doubt. *Yes, but what if I was wrong? Then why did she come at night? How was the record on? What had John seen?* I was scared that there were no answers.

'You're not real,' I said from around the corner.

'Ursula?' Sue said. 'Are you there?'

'Go away!'

'Ursula, please.' Her voice was urgent now she had heard me.

'Fuck off, fuck off, fuck off,' I said quietly, sliding down the wall until I was squatting.

'Please! I want to come in. I'm really thirsty. Just a glass of water.'

The letter box snapped shut, and I waited, two minutes, three, forever.

Too loud and too bright, the doorbell chimed. 'Let me in!' I heard again.

Whimpering, I lowered myself on to all fours and inched my way across the dusty parquet. I made myself raise my head and look up. The glass was dark, and I went past it, still on hands and knees, into the kitchen, where I reared up to open the cutlery drawer and scrabble amongst the contents until my hand closed around something. I heard the metal flap of the letter box being opened and, like a reluctant dog called by its master, I went back into the hall. Something was pushing through the gap, fingers searching blindly, earth under split nails. Sue's fingers. The stink was of old meat, fetid and ruined. With a screech, I flung myself forward and stabbed at the fingers with the steak knife from the Berni Inn. I stabbed until the fingers retreated. There was no blood. Before the letter box closed, I heard Sue's voice: 'Your turn next.'

23

Eventually the light through the glass of the door stirred me. I'd spent the night huddled in the corner under the coat rack, the knife clutched in my hand. My clothes were dirty and smelled of urine, and I stripped them off, dropping them on the hall floor, and went into my room and dressed in my spare work uniform. I put on my shoes, collected my bag and left the house, once more giving the garage the widest berth.

In the phone box I took out my purse and again found Joy's phone number. Her line rang for a long time before she answered in a sleepy voice and her throaty familiarity caught me off guard and I started to cry, sobbing into the handset and gasping, choking, trying to get out words that made sense.

'Who is this?' she said. 'Is that Ursula?' She let me cry some more and, when I slowed, she said, 'What is it? Where are you?'

'In a phone box, near the bungalow.' I gulped my breath. 'I can't live here any more.'

There was a pause. It was two weeks since Joy had been sick in the flower bed.

'What's happened?' she asked cautiously.

'I don't know,' I wailed. 'I don't know what it is.'

'You need to calm down.'

'I did something. Now there's someone, something, outside the house.'

'Who's outside the house? Is Vince there?' She was more urgent, pressing me for an answer.

'No, no, he isn't here.'

'Tell me what happened.'

'I can't live here any more,' I repeated, my voice wavering, high-pitched. I wanted to tell her about Sue in the earth and Sue at the door but didn't know how.

Joy was silent and then she said, 'I did tell you. What did I say about squats? You might like not paying rent, but they aren't nice places. The Underwood isn't a nice place.'

'No,' I said, composing myself, seeing a way in. 'You're right. I'm sorry.' I wiped my hand under my nose, sniffed. 'I should have listened. Can you find me somewhere else?'

'You need to stop being so impetuous. Try and think things through more.'

'I know. I will.'

She paused again and I waited. I heard her light a cigarette, inhale, exhale. 'I'll see what I can do.'

I would be able to leave. Joy would help me. 'Tonight? Can you get me a place for tonight?'

She snorted. 'Tonight? Unless you're in some sort of immediate danger, it'll take at least a couple of weeks, more like a month. Getting you into the halfway house so quickly was a fluke.'

'I am in danger!'

'What danger are you in, Ursula?' She sounded sarcastic but nervous too.

'It's Vince,' I said. 'He scares me.'

She made a noise of disbelief. 'I thought you said he wasn't there.'

'He's just come back.' And as if I'd conjured him, his car went past, heading towards the Underwood. I laughed and hammered on a windowpane as though he might hear.

'Right,' Joy said, and I knew she didn't believe me, but it didn't matter, all I cared about was that I was no longer going to be alone. I didn't think about Vince's drinking or what he'd called me.

'I've got to go! I'll phone you back.'

'Ursula!' I heard as I replaced the handset.

I jogged down the hill and on to the drive. I'd never expected to be pleased to see Vince, but what I felt was almost happiness, that there was someone else to take control, decide what should happen, get rid of that thing that came in the night.

'Vince?' I called as I stepped into the hall. He'd raised the kitchen blind and opened the curtains in his room, and he came out of the bathroom zipping up his trousers.

'What the hell happened?' he said. He meant the broken record, the puddle of pee, my scattered clothes, the knife. 'What have you done to your face?' He took hold of my chin and angled my head to the light.

'It's not as bad as it looks.' I pulled away.

'Did you and Sue have a fight? Is that why she didn't meet me?'

'How's your grandfather?' I needed to be nice to him, make him stay.

'Dying. Nearly dead. Where is she?' he said. 'What have you done with her?' He stepped across the hall and pushed my bedroom door open and looked inside.

'Who?' I said innocently, and practised a sentence in my head without saying it out loud.

'Don't be weird. Sue!' He came towards me and put his face close to mine so that I backed off. I could smell alcohol

172

on his breath although he seemed sober. 'I waited for her at Manchester Piccadilly all fucking night. I suppose you persuaded her not to come. Well, that's okay with me. I've had enough.'

I wanted to shout but I made myself be calm – being calm would work out better for me – and I picked up my knickers and my work skirt and folded them over my arm, trying to be as small as possible in my movements. In my head, I said the sentence again.

'My cousin was going to buy my car,' Vince ranted. 'And I've had to go back on that. So mortifying. And I was going to buy Sue's bloody plane ticket as well as my own. Do you know how much they were going to cost me? A week's wages, and instead I sat all night in the station car park like a pillock.' He quietened, visibly sagging, and walked into the kitchen and opened the fridge. 'Is there any food in the house? I'm ravenous.' He crouched. I knew the fridge was empty, and he let the door swing closed. I was ravenous too.

I picked up my shirt, jacket and tights from the hallway while Vince went out to his car. I folded these clothes over my arm too. I stood in the porch watching him and whispering the words. They didn't sound real, more like a melodramatic voice-over from a film trailer, American and deeply male. Vince slung his duffel bag over his shoulder and took out his holdall and came back into the house and I followed him to his room, watching him from this doorway instead. He let the duffel slip from his shoulder, dropped his other bag with exhaustion, and I wished he was Raymond, but Raymond couldn't drive, didn't live here, didn't know his sister was dead and that I'd killed her. I whispered the sentence and Vince looked up, saying, 'What?' and when I didn't answer he set about taking linen from the top shelf of his wardrobe and making his bed. He stripped down to his underwear and I waited for the words to come. He got into bed.

'I need to sleep,' he said. 'When I wake up I'm going to the supermarket to buy food, and afterwards we – you – can phone Sue's house and see where she's bloody got to.' He was almost asleep.

'Why me?' I said. I didn't want to speak to Anita or Raymond. I couldn't speak to Raymond. 'Why can't you phone?'

'Go away, Ursula. Go to work. Why aren't you at work? You should put a plaster on that cut or it'll get infected.'

I dumped my dirty clothes on top of the muddy ones in my room and stood at the kitchen window, staring out without seeing. What if Sue *was* at Anita's? Perhaps I was mistaken and on Saturday she'd caught a bus home and was now sitting at Anita's kitchen table with the twins. In the hall mirror my eyes were rimmed with red and my face was pale. I was famished and bone tired but knew I wouldn't be able to eat or sleep, not yet.

Outside, my mallet was still beside the sofa. I picked it up. It was unbelievable that I had used this to kill Sue. I saw it swinging, saw it touch her temple. How could she be dead, someone who had been so very alive? I picked up my chisel and with a grunt hit the end of it against my sculpture, and the movement, the act of carving, emptied my head. I defined the fingers of the man who was being swallowed, showing how they dug into the woman's shoulders. I gave her a waist, an indication of breasts, her hair hanging back-wards as she tilted her head to open her mouth. I took my jacket off and rolled up my sleeves. I carved for a long time, only pausing to roll the sculpture over and work at it from each side. Later I put my jacket back on, went inside with my tools and lay on my bed, my head again filled with thoughts of what was in the garage next door and what I had done.

Vince didn't wake until after one and said he was going to the greasy spoon café he liked to have one of their all-day break-fasts. I said I'd go with him, not wanting to be alone in the house although it was daytime. Maybe because he wanted to have someone to complain to about Sue, he let me.

Both our plates were piled with fried eggs, bacon, sausage, black pudding, grilled tomato and mushrooms. I ate mine without looking up, shovelling forkfuls into my mouth before I'd even swallowed. I sat back, belly distended, disgusted with myself. Vince repeated his complaints about the money and how his cousin was going to buy his car before he and Sue went to the airport, and how much two tickets to America cost. He said there was no way anyone was going to hire her as a film director, a fickle little girl from England trying to make a horror film. They weren't going to let her in. It was a closed circle, he said. You had to know people and he had contacts out there, and she should be grateful he'd offered to go with her. He told me more about his grandfather and how he'd sat beside his bed for two days and talked to him, a fellow Manchester United fan, about whether Alex Ferguson was going to come right for the team. Vince pinched the bridge of his nose and didn't look at me.

'I had to leave him to go and meet Sue, who never fucking turned up.' He told me he'd only agreed to lend her the money for the ticket to America so she'd let him fuck her. My own words were butting up against the inside layers of my skin, as though they would rush out in a bloody gush if I could make a new wound or open the existing one further, if I had the bravery for the pain and the consequences.

Vince asked the waitress for a slice of bread and wiped his eggy plate with it. I burped greasily, my fist over my mouth. When the bill came, he left it until I paid. I sat in his car feeling queasy and we drove to the new out-of-town supermarket. He got a trolley and filled it with tins and meat and bread, while I trailed behind and wondered what it would take for me to tell him, someone, anyone. I imagined shouting the words in the supermarket or grabbing the tannoy where staff made announcements about spillages, pressing the button and saying the words into the mouthpiece, and the customers with their shopping baskets and the staff standing behind the delicatessen and butcher counters swivelling to look at the loudspeakers.

We stood in line at the checkout, and Vince asked if I had any cash, and I handed over what I had in my purse without noticing how much it was, and as he paid he asked the checkout woman for some coins in the change.

Before we reached the Underwood, he parked beside the phone box, and when he got out and I didn't move he said, 'Come on, Ursula.' We squeezed into the box, Vince backed up against one of the side panels, me front on to the phone. My stomach muscles were jumping and I thought if I spoke I might be sick. 'Go on,' he said. 'I know you know the number.'

I dialled. One of the twins answered. I pressed in the money. 'Is Sue there?' My voice squeaked, and I coughed.

'She's not here,' the little voice replied.

'She's not there,' I said to Vince, my hand over the mouthpiece. Tears on the rims of my eyes were ready to fall.

'Ask for Raymond,' he said.

'Why can't you speak to them?' The handset began to shake in the way that the knife in Wendy Torrance's hand shook as she ran through the corridors of the Overlook Hotel.

'They won't speak to me.'

'Why not?'

'None of those fuckers will speak to me. They only speak to you because Sue lied for you.'

I didn't know what he meant.

'Raymond will!' I held the wobbling phone out to him.

'What the hell is wrong with you?' He shoved the handset back against my ear.

'Is Raymond there?' I said to whichever twin it was.

'Hold the line, please, caller. I'll just get him.' And I heard a long tone – Jess or Hannah had hung up again. I pressed the phone tight to my ear and didn't look at Vince.

'Hello. It's Ursula,' I said to the tone.

Vince nudged me. 'Ask if he knows where Sue is.'

'Oh, really?' I said. 'She didn't say that? What else was it she said?'

Vince said again more forcefully, 'Does he know where Sue is?'

'Do you know where Sue is?' I said in my brightest voice. It sounded like this was a hold-up and Vince had a gun in my ribs. I waited a couple of seconds. 'Oh, that's wonderful. Marvellous. Of course. At work, of course.'

The words slipped out even though I hadn't given one thought about work. It hadn't occurred to me to call in to say I was sick or worry that I might have been seen in the café or the supermarket wearing my uniform. When I'd skived off school, I'd stuff my school jumper in my bag and put on a hat and a jacket in the hope I wouldn't be spotted.

My ear was hot from the pressure of the phone. 'It's just

that I haven't seen her for a while.' I wanted to get out of there, I wanted to put the phone down and go home, to a good mother, surrogate or not, one who would make me a hot chocolate and wash my face with a flannel and tell me I was a brave kid.

'Thanks. Yes, thanks. I'll do that.' My tears overflowed.

I went to put down the handset. I put it back to my ear. 'Bye,' I said and replaced it.

'What did he say?' Vince asked.

'That maybe she's at work.'

He hit out at one of the panes of glass with the meat of his palm. 'Work! You think she'd go to work when she was supposed to be meeting me? Why not? I should phone the art school.' He was talking to himself, and as he squeezed around me to get at the phone book, I pushed the door open and stepped out. I went around the back of the phone box where there were no windows and tried to throw up, but my stomach seemed to want to hang on to that awful breakfast.

We got in the car and Vince said, 'I spoke to that woman in the office and she said Sue hadn't called in sick. Not today and not yesterday.' He turned towards me. 'When did she leave the Underwood to get the train?'

I opened my mouth and closed it again.

'She did tell you she was coming to meet me in Manchester?'

'She said you were going to America.'

He started the ignition and began driving. 'What if something happened to her on the way?' He took a hand off the wheel and rubbed his forehead. 'What if she's had an accident?' He glanced at me, his face creased with worry.

The words arrived. 'I murdered her,' I said, looking straight ahead.

'What?' The car swept up on to the kerb and back to the road, and I leaned forward to press my fingertips against the dashboard. 'You what?' Vince said.

'I murdered her.'

He began to laugh.

24

Vince parked the car on the drive and switched off the engine. We were facing the garage. A blackbird's alarm call sounded, a high-pitched motor turning over without starting, and I knew Vince was looking at me but I didn't look back. I sensed him shaking his head.

'God, you really do need help,' he said, irritated. He got out, went to the boot and carried the shopping inside.

A folded piece of paper with my name on it lay on the parquet floor, scuffed by Vince's shoes. It was a scrawled note from Joy saying she'd come round and I should phone again if I needed her. I knew it must have taken courage to return to the house, and I told myself to find that courage too.

Vince had put the oven on and was using a can opener aggressively to take the lid off a Fray Bentos steak-and-kidney pie. 'I suppose you'll want half of this?' He whacked it on a baking tray and doled out almost a whole bag of oven chips. I would have liked to have all of it. Joy would have asked where the green vegetable was, but I said nothing. 'Have you had any liquids?' Vince asked. 'Maybe that's why you've gone loopy. Or loopier than usual.' He shoved the tray in the oven, slamming the door closed with a foot, filled a pint glass with water and put it on the table. 'You have to drink this.' He dragged out a chair; it wasn't an invitation, it was a directive. 'Last year my Nanna Melanie didn't drink enough water, and she went crazy. She thought birds were getting into the house. So sit down and drink up.'

I sipped the water and watched him unpack the shopping, wondering whether the slug was still in the cupboard. Vince went to the outhouse and put some of my fifty-pence pieces in the meter. It would be dark in a few hours.

Vince laid out knives and forks and served the meal. He had sliced the pie in half with the Berni Inn steak knife, which I had washed and put back in the cutlery drawer. I bent my head over the plate and inhaled, and when I looked up Vince was watching but he didn't comment. We talked while we ate – about football and carving – easy, simple things. We didn't mention Sue. I cleared my plate – the chips and half of the pie cooked in a tin – in less than ten minutes. We stood at the kitchen window, me washing up and Vince drying and putting away.

'If she doesn't turn up tomorrow,' he said, 'I'm going to make an anonymous call to the rozzers and report her missing,' and heat rushed in to melt the ice that I'd let grow inside me like frost across a window.

'No!' I said. 'Not the police.'

'Oh, Ursula.' He sounded exhausted. 'You didn't murder her.' He took me by my shoulders, gripping me hard. 'You did not murder her. You argued with her, and she went off. Maybe she did catch the train to Manchester and something happened to her. Maybe I should go to the phone box and call the rozzers now, or we should phone Raymond again, see if she's turned up.'

I pushed his hands off my shoulders. 'I killed her. I'm not imagining it. I'm not loopy. I hit her on the side of the head with my mallet. I don't know if I meant to or not. We went to sleep and when I woke up, she was dead. I buried her, in the garage.'

He laughed and pretended to wipe under his eyes with his tea towel while I gripped the edge of the sink. It was dusk, and when I let my eyes lose focus, I could see a faint reflection of us in the window.

'You need some sleep. That grave was for Sue's silly film.'

'I'm not saying it wasn't.'

'I dug it.' He rubbed his palms together as though remembering the pain of it in his hands. 'She just pretended to dig it.'

'But that's where I buried her.' I began to cry.

'Show me, then,' he said, hard and fierce, flinging down the tea towel. 'If you buried her in that hole, show me.' He took hold of my wrist and led me out of the kitchen, not roughly but making sure I went with him. He opened the front door and we stepped outside. I didn't want to go to the garage and see that mound of earth again, to be presented with the bold facts of Sue's death and burial. But I went with him because I needed to make him see. We walked, almost hand in hand, along the path beside the bathroom where I'd first heard the tapping, beside the lounge window with its listless curtains, past the narrow gap between house and garage, and outside the double doors he let go of my wrist to use two hands to pull open the right-hand door.

It was dark in there, and it took a few moments for my eyes to adjust. It was not how I remembered leaving it.

'What's this?' he said.

The earth was no longer in a neat mound but scattered about in clumps either side of the hole, and the muddy blanket was flung open as though someone – Sue – had risen from her bed. Except this was a grave, and it was empty. I took a deep breath and put a hand over my mouth.

'Why did you bring a blanket in here? What's all this mess?' He went further into the garage and pulled at a corner of the blanket, partially lifting it, disturbing more soil and dropping it in revulsion.

When I took my hand away from my mouth, an involuntary moan came out. 'Oh God,' I said. 'She's gone. Her body's gone. But she was at the door, she wanted to come in.'

'What are you talking about?' Vince came to the doorway and took hold of me by my upper arms this time and shook me. 'Why didn't you let her in if she was at the door?'

'Because she's dead! I killed her, and she wants to come in.' I moved my head back and forth. I wouldn't look at him or the hole in the ground.

He released me, making a noise of frustration.

'No, you don't understand. There was a smell, and she was ringing on the doorbell for hours.'

'Okay, look.' He became efficient, practical, shoving me away, out on to the drive, pushing the door shut behind us. 'You didn't kill her. We dug that grave for Sue's stupid film. Don't you remember? There's no body. There isn't a body, yes?' It was hard to focus on what he was saying. It was too dark to remain outside; we needed to be inside with the doors locked. 'You went a bit batty, and for some reason I can't fathom you dragged a blanket in there and flung some earth around. That's all. That's all!'

'No, Vince. No,' I said. 'We need to go indoors. It'll be coming. Sue will be coming.'

'So she's not dead?'

'Yes! She's dead. She's dead! I killed her, but she keeps coming back.'

'You've been watching too many zombie movies.'

I took hold of his hand to pull him back to the house. We

stumbled along the path to the front door, and I tried again to explain. 'Sue wants to get in. She said she was thirsty. She said it was my turn next.'

'This is a story. It's Sue's fucking home movie. It's given you nightmares.'

'It's real. She wanted me to let her in. I think we started something with the seance, with Sue and me and Raymond –'

He yanked on my hand, making me stop. 'Look, Ursula. Look.' We were side by side in the porch. 'She's not coming, no one's coming.' He pulled me inside the house and released my hand. He locked the door and put on the chain, which we'd never done before. 'See,' he said. 'As safe as houses.'

'It won't come until the middle of the night.'

'Okay, all right. I want you to sit at the table, and I'm going up the road to phone a doctor, okay?' He spoke slowly, patiently.

'No!' I was shouting but I couldn't stop. 'You mustn't leave. You mustn't go. It's getting dark, it'll be dark soon! I don't want to be alone.' I was crashing about the kitchen, pulling down the blind, stacking whatever I could find in the gap, and I knew how he must view me, a deranged girl.

'All right,' he said again, palms out. 'Calm down. Deep breaths.' He took a deep breath himself, and I took one with him. We held it and he blew his out slowly and I blew out mine. In and out. I knew I needed to be calm to persuade him I was right, so we could come up with a plan. 'Let's sit,' he said. 'How about we stay at the Underwood tonight, and I promise you nothing will come.' I inhaled sharply. 'Nothing will come, we can sleep in my bedroom, and in the morning will you let me phone a doctor? Would it be okay if I did that?'

I nodded. A gesture of resignation. He could do what he

wanted in the morning. Although there was some comfort knowing we would sleep in the same room, the question was how we were going to get through the night.

We sat on Vince's bed, up against his pillows with his telly on and the curtains closed. The photograph of the girl with the missing teeth was on his bedside table. He had gone into every room in the house and closed the curtains at my insistence. The only window in the house that didn't have any was the one above the bath. He'd made us both a cup of tea – I'd been relieved that he hadn't bought any alcohol at the supermarket – but it was difficult to sit beside him, where I'd sat with Sue and Raymond. We watched a sitcom but we kept falling asleep, and then I would jump awake, hyperaware of my surroundings and listening for sounds under the canned laughter of the telly. I'd thought I would feel relief from telling Vince what I'd done, but I felt none, only more anxiety that it was night-time and he didn't believe me. Each time I woke beside a sleeping Vince I would shift or cough to wake him, and although I would have liked to discuss what we were going to do when the thing came knocking, as I was sure it would, I also knew he wouldn't let me.

'How did you know about all that stuff to calm me down?' I said, to keep him awake.

'What?' He picked up his cup from the bedside table and swallowed the rest of his tea.

'That deep breathing.'

'My mum. My birth mum. She wasn't well.'

'I thought you were adopted when you were three?'

'That's what I tell people, so I don't have to explain.' On the telly an awards ceremony had started and people were whooping. 'I was eight when I was fostered and adopted. By then I'd learned what to do when Mum had an episode. How to bring her down.'

'What do you mean, *an episode*?'

He glanced at me. 'Like hearing voices, imagining things.'

'Oh,' I said. 'Did she know when she was having an episode?'

'No. She was convinced it was real.'

We sat there, looking at the telly as an actress with shiny teeth held her statue over her head.

'What happened to her? In the end?'

He waited, considering. 'She was sectioned.'

Even at sixteen I knew what that meant. Uncle Jimmy liked to threaten it when we misbehaved, and other children would use it as a taunt. 'And after that?'

He paused again. 'She died a couple of years later. I didn't go to see her in hospital. They wouldn't let me, or I didn't ask. I didn't want to go to her funeral. I don't like funerals.'

'Do you think that's what I've been having, an episode?' I asked.

'I do. But it'll be okay. You can go to the doctor tomorrow and he'll be able to help.'

'All right,' I said. It wasn't possible to immediately believe that everything that had happened over the past few days wasn't real, that it'd been in my head, because my muscles reminded me that I'd backfilled a grave, and I had the cut on my forehead from when John had shut the door on me. John, who'd seen something through the kitchen window, or maybe I'd spooked him. And *where was Sue*? Or rather, where was her *body*? Perhaps it was possible to make it all up. But then, there definitely had been a thing at the door, a smell, fingers coming through the letter box. These things were too real to not be true.

'I'm so tired.' Vince got up and turned off the telly. 'I have to sleep. We can sort this out tomorrow.' He tied his hair into a bun with an elastic band. 'Off you go, then.'

My heart began to thump. 'Aren't I sleeping here?' I didn't want to be alone.

'What?' he said. 'No. Nothing will happen. Go to bed.'

I peed with the bathroom door open, and didn't bother brushing my teeth, and I didn't look up at the window. I lingered in the hallway, touching my forehead and checking my fingers for blood, until Vince came and closed his door further and switched off his light. Shivering, I put on my pyjamas and got into my own bed. It was quarter past eleven.

25

Claudia knew I'd been brought up in the care system, and she would sometimes ask if I was going to request to see my files. Social care assessments, daily record sheets, meeting notes: all the things social workers, head teachers and doctors wrote about me. I knew what I'd receive if I completed the request form: other people's opinions about my behaviour, which had followed me from foster home to children's home and back again. Read the file, why don't you? It's much quicker than getting to know the child and forming your own impression. This is what the record says, therefore it must be correct: disruptive yet withdrawn, difficulty making friends, prone to bouts of temper.

My care files were sent to me through the post, a fat folder with many sections redacted, and no offer of support to help me understand and process what I was reading. There was no specific reason to ask for them now, it was simply time. Included was the photo of me and Sadie in Morocco.

I learned that she died of dengue fever from a mosquito bite, which is easily treated if you get to a hospital in time. I learned about her parents. She'd never spoken about them, and at seven I hadn't thought to ask. It seemed they were alive or had been when I was a child. When Sadie was sixteen, my files said, she'd been raped, and I was the outcome. She'd carried that with her each day in the seven years we were together. Did she see him whenever she looked at me? If she did, she didn't show it, because I know she loved me fiercely – she demonstrated this to me every day. I sobbed over the paperwork, tear stains joining the rings from long-ago coffees, pen smudges and typos. Had I killed my mother by not opening that Moroccan bathroom door when she knocked? Could I have persuaded her to go to the hospital if I'd let her in? The first of at least two people whose deaths I take responsibility for. During the seance, Ray, or the thing that was Ray, said he knew what I'd done – killed my own mother – and somehow he'd known that I would also kill Sue.

Perhaps, I thought, Sadie's parents had wanted her to have an abortion, and she'd refused and left home, or they had made her leave. This information is not in my files.

After I travelled, by a means I have no recollection of, from Morocco to England, I didn't go immediately to a children's home; instead I was fostered by Dr and Mrs Hulse for three months. Three months before they said *No thank you* and had me packed off. What I learned from my files was that this couple were Sadie's parents, my grandparents.

I replayed my memories of them: the Chinese takeaway, a scratchy tablecloth, my bedroom, which they continued to call the spare room even while I slept in it; and I tried to slot child-Sadie into their house. Grandparents who hadn't told me that I was their grandchild and my mother was their daughter. I couldn't imagine the sort of people who would take a child in and then send her away. Sometimes, when I'm furious with them, I think they did it because they also saw my father when they looked at me, and other times, when I'm feeling more generous, I wonder if it was too painful for Mrs Hulse to see Sadie every day, echoed in her granddaughter's face.

My birth certificate says I was born in Reading. My surname is Major, but Sadie's was Hulse. I discovered recently that when a mother registers a birth, she can give her baby whatever surname she fancies. These days I like Sadie's little joke.

The clock beside my bed said it was ten past two when I woke to the sound of people talking in the house: an American woman giving measured views about female sexuality after sixty, followed by a strident English woman cutting in and declaiming that she wouldn't have come if she'd known all they were going to talk about was sex, she was here to talk about marriage and what that meant to women. I lay rigid in my bed, my hands on my belly over my pyjamas, my elbows by my side and my feet touching as though I needed all of my body to be in contact with the rest, no risk of an extremity being loosened from the other parts of me. I tried to work out where in the house these people were or whether they were in my head. An *episode* must be different in some way from real life, but I didn't know how. I breathed, in through the nose and out through the mouth, and pressed my hands to my ears for a count of sixty, but when I took them off the voices were still going: the American talking about how women are at a turning point and there's a choice to be made, how according to the women in her study they are still fighting. A few men began speaking over each other, but it continued as a quiet and reasonable conversation. Lying there listening was like the second when you know you're going to be sick but you have the unrealistic hope that if you stay motionless, only swallowing and sweating, the feeling might go away. It never goes away; you have to get up and vomit.

The more normal the voices, the more nightmarish and

sinister they seemed. I was desperate to check Vince was in his bed, and eventually I swung my legs out of mine and stood, sweat gathering under my arms and between my breasts, hands and feet freezing. I listened to the voices, and as if they were calling for me, like the tapping and the record, my feet took me into the hall and there I saw, in Vince's room, the telly casting its blue light over his bedspread, and Vince himself, in bed, asleep. On the television, a group of people were seated around a low table, talking together, drinking and smoking, and now I knew what the voices were, I found I liked their chat, the feeling of company, and I decided to leave the programme on. But as soon as I had this thought, the screen fizzed, lines of colour zigzagging, voices distorting. The image sucked itself into a central hole and with a pop the telly went off, and the house was pitch-black and silent.

Two taps. Not on Vince's window but from behind me at the high bathroom window, and my heart began to dance, a frightful bunny hop, telling me to run except I couldn't leave the house and go outside.

'It's not real. It's not real,' I muttered, lips barely moving. The tapping continued, and I could not turn to face that uncurtained window to see what was there. It stopped as I stood still, and stealthily the smell came, a sickening miasma of sweet shit. I went forward into Vince's room, shuffling in the dark and groping for his legs, feeling the shape of his ankle through the covers. I grasped it and shook it, and he groaned himself awake.

'Vince,' I hissed. 'Vince.'

'What? I'm sleeping.'

'I think I'm having an episode,' I sobbed. 'The telly was on, there were people talking and –'

'What time is it?'

His digital clock showed vertical bars and the two dots in the middle. I saw the lines and dots rise and realized he'd picked it up. He thumped it on the bedside table, and the bars disappeared and only the dots remained.

'It's two in the morning,' I said.

'Oh God, Ursula.' Another groan.

'It's all so real. I know it's real.'

'Oh my God.' He pulled his ankle out from under my hand. 'What is that smell?'

'You can smell it too?'

'Of course I can fucking smell it. The drains must be backing up.' I heard him gag.

'This is how it starts.' I backed away from his window and his door, into the corner of the room, clipping his bedside table, rattling a cup.

'Be quiet!' he said. 'I can hear something.'

I clamped my hand over my mouth, squeezed my eyes shut. I could hear it too, a sibilant sound, one word with two syllables, repeated, coming from outside. Vince slipped out of bed, and I heard the click of the switch on his bedside lamp, heard him say, 'Shit.'

I opened my eyes, but it was still dark.

'I put three pounds in the meter,' he whispered.

'It doesn't make any difference.'

'Who the hell is it?' He wasn't speaking to me. 'What's that fucking stink?'

He'd got up and was putting on his dressing gown. The voice, if that's what it was, was at Vince's window, as though someone was there behind his closed curtains, hands cupped around a mouth. I came out from the corner, knowing he'd go towards the voice. I reached for his arm, grabbed it.

'If that's Sue . . .' he said.

'No, don't.'

He yanked himself away, and I went to his room's light switch and tried it and then groped for the one in the hall, and with a hum it came on. Maybe water had got into the fitting because it lit up and went off in buzzing pulses, and I saw Vince move towards his window. In flashes of dark and light he yanked open his curtains with both hands.

'Sue!' he shouted at the glass, although there was no one there. 'About fucking time!'

His face and the things in the room were reflected back at us, and when the light went out, there was blackness. He paused, hands gripping the curtains, and I was motionless too, and we both heard the voice, louder now, coming from outside my bedroom window.

'Jesus Christ,' he said, and went past me, and I followed him into my bedroom and the hall light buzzed on again. 'Who's there!' he called with more trepidation. 'I'm going to phone the police!' A bluff, of course. He strode to my window and took hold of my curtains, pulling them so smartly that they ripped from the rail. Again, blackness outside and then our hazy reflections in the glass.

I didn't speak but he said, 'Wait,' as if I had. His hand was out towards me, his head cocked, listening. 'Wait.' I couldn't hear anything.

Then suddenly a bang on the window as though something bigger, stronger than two human hands, had slapped it, and Vince leapt away.

'What the fuck is that?' he said. 'What the fuck *is* that?'

This was somehow worse than anything that had gone before; a frightened Vince undid the flimsy armour that secured my terror, cutting it loose in a single snip. The slapping started on the kitchen window and neither of us moved. The stink had become stronger, gamey and nauseating. He put his hand over his nose. 'Go away!' he called out, weakly. We stayed in my bedroom, listening. But gaining strength from the sound of his voice, the beating on the kitchen window became frenzied.

'Thirsty,' I heard a constricted voice say. The throat was dry, full of earth.

'Is that Sue's voice?' Vince said.

'Don't let her in.'

The slapping moved to the back door, the one that led out to the alley and the outhouse, and Vince, beside me in the bedroom, jumped.

'It's Sue!' he shouted. 'Oh fuck, it's Sue.'

'It's not her. She's dead! She's dead!'

'Water,' the voice called. 'I'm so thirsty. Let me in! I just need a glass of water.'

'It's Sue!'

He ran the few short steps from my bedroom into the hall and to the kitchen, towards the back door, and I followed, grabbing the dressing gown's sleeve, and as I pulled him backwards a chair fell over and his arm or mine snagged the stack of saucepans we kept on top of the cooker, and they clattered to the floor. He tripped and I crashed into the rear of him, and I think he was calling to the thing outside and it was calling back, and I was shouting and shoving the table against the door, but it was dark in the kitchen and the two of us were grabbing at anything and falling over each other, and when I thought I had the table between him and the door, he went the other way, into the hall. The overhead light sent strobing images of him reaching for the chain, my hands pulling his hair, his face towards mine with all the fear and confusion showing.

'Let her in!' he yelled.

'Don't do it.' I had my hands on the catch. 'You promised.'

In one of those flashes of light I saw the face, or what had once been a face, come close to the frosted glass. Like a ghastly puppet, Sue's corpse with sunken eyes and a mouth of earth. Vince shoved out his elbow, catching me in the throat, and I fell backwards across the hallway, skidding over the parquet, hitting my head on the skirting board. The front door was open.

26

A cool breeze and daylight from the open front door brought me round. I didn't know how long I'd been out, but I sat up, neck stiff and head sore. From my position against the wall, I could see some of the mess in the kitchen – chairs overturned, pans and lids across the floor; and in the hall, the unit had been shifted out, coats strewn and the mirror smashed – a scattering of diamonds that the early-morning sunshine dappled across the ceiling. It might have been beautiful if my mind wasn't trying to make sense of the previous night. The same thing – Sue but not Sue – had been at the door. There had been that terrible smell, the face on the other side of the glass. I wondered again if I was wrong and she hadn't been dead when I buried her – but I could think of no reason for her to knock on the windows like that and scare us. I scrabbled for a rational explanation, trying to imagine what Raymond would say. But I couldn't go there, I couldn't think about Raymond when I'd killed his sister, buried her, seen her dead body at the door.

I got myself up. My throat was tender where Vince's elbow had whacked me, and I prodded at a lump on the back of my head where I'd hit the skirting board. The house was silent. I tiptoed around the pieces of shattered mirror and stood in the porch in my bare feet, feeling the freshness of the morning, hearing the birds in the trees and a faraway aeroplane overhead, going to America maybe.

Vince's car was on the drive, which meant if he'd left, he'd left on foot, or he'd stepped over me and had gone to bed. I peed in the garden and returned inside. There was no noise from his room, but I pushed his door open with my fingertips and it swung all the way to the wall with a clunk. His room didn't get the morning sun, but in its gloom, I could see his wardrobe, the chest of drawers, bedside tables, the few things he'd unpacked when he returned from Manchester and the empty bed unmade for the first time.

I got dressed in my work uniform although I hadn't decided whether I was going to work. I hadn't gone in yesterday and hadn't phoned in sick; Alan and Joy would be disappointed in me. Whatever I was going to do, I wouldn't be staying another night at the Underwood. It would be hard to leave my sculpture in the garden, but I could come back and get it another day. I was leaving, and if I had to sleep in a bus shelter I would. In a suitcase left by the previous owners, I shoved clothes, clean and dirty, the mallet and chisel, and tried to remember whether it was Wednesday or Thursday. Wednesday. I hesitated over the drawings on the wall, the ones Sue had said looked like Goya's paintings. I still didn't know who he was, what his work was like. Perhaps today I'd go to the library and find a book with them in. It struck me again like a physical blow that Sue was dead. She wouldn't ever again look at art, she would never make another film or edit the one she'd shot. I'd destroyed everything.

It was as I was reaching for a drawing that I became aware of a low hum, not an animal or human sound, but something made by humans, electrical. I stood listening, trying to work out what it was and where it was coming from, less frightening than last night, more curious. It wavered and a higher frequency joined it, oscillating over the top. I went to the door of my room and listened again. The front door was still open and the noise was coming from outside, so I crunched over the glass and stood in the porch. The sound was loud out here: a continuous bass note and the higher pitch. It switched to a blast of music, followed by the starts of words, back to the music, and once again the continuous hum. It was coming from Vince's empty car. It was the radio, moving along the dial as though someone was turning the button in and out of stations. But no one was in the car, no one that I could see, unless Vince or someone else was hiding in the passenger footwell.

Why does a character in a horror film go to investigate the unidentified noise? Why does she descend the cellar stairs when the electricity has tripped? Why does she climb to the attic with only a guttering candle? The sound pulled me towards the car, one foot after another, along the path to the drive. The noise continuing. When I reached the car, I looked through the driver's window, but there was no one there. No one was hiding in the front or the back. I tried the door, and it opened, the sound blasting out as I reached in. The interior smelled of cigarettes and sweaty football kit. I switched off the radio. I laughed and recognized my laugh as hysterical.

I went back to the house to finish packing, and in the hallway before I'd reached my bedroom, I smelled the stink, the same repugnant whiff. Maybe it was the fridge again. I looked towards the kitchen, but I knew it was coming from the bathroom. I stood at the closed door. A fly buzzed on the other side. I pushed the door open: the oblong window, the lurid bath, the sink. And Vince. He was standing on the bath mat, naked except for baggy grey Y-fronts like the ones Sue had once taken from the drawer and put on. Vince's shoulders were hunched and his hands, clasped at his chest, were

198

twitching, fingers wrapping around themselves. The noxious stink was in the room, and it might have been coming from him because he was smeared with dirt, and his hair was flattened to his head, soaked with sweat. A fly came at me, and I ducked, batting it away.

Vince angled his head this way and that, looking wildly at something I couldn't see, and then he noticed me in the doorway, taking him in.

'Thirsty,' he said, and I backed away without taking my eyes off him, about to turn and run when he began pleading, 'Water . . .' and I saw that his arms and legs were covered in red circles of pierced skin, painful-looking and bleeding.

'Vince.' I put my sleeve to my nose to block out the stench.

'I can feel her,' he said. 'In here.' And I knew exactly who he meant. He thumped his chest with his fist, and his eyes darkened, and he bent forward, his shoulders lowered. He raised his head towards me, opened his mouth and began to gag, a dry retching, his hands on his knees as his chest worked to rid itself of whatever was in there, as though he might vomit Sue out from the pit of his stomach. I watched until finally he stopped. His eyes were wide and streaming, and he stuck out his tongue, grey and flaccid, and a fly came out from inside his throat. It settled for a moment on his tongue and then took off in a lazy circle, around the room and to the window.

'Your turn next,' Vince said, looking straight at me, body still bent, head angled up.

I turned and ran. I left that place and my suitcase and everything I owned, and I ran out through the front door and away.

27

I'd gone a couple of hundred yards past the phone box when I turned back. I hadn't been sure where I was going, I was just running, but I stopped, panting, and went to the box and looked through the glass, the silver push-button numbers, the scratched Perspex over the notices, remembering the times I'd stood here waiting for the phone to ring, for Sue to call, wishing she'd invite me to her house. I pulled the door open and stepped into that familiar smell of old cigarette breath and grime, and picked up the handset, my hand shaking like it had when Vince had made me call Raymond. Was that only a day ago? It juddered against my ear, and I took a deep breath and let it out. In and out, in and out. Dead matches and other unidentifiable scraps of rubbish lay on the concrete slab beneath my feet. In and out. An ant travelled along a tiny path that wound through the mess, carrying in its mouth a white egg almost as big as itself. The ant crossed the floor and disappeared into a hole in the dirt on the other side. I took another inhalation, breathed it out, and dialled 999. When I was asked what service I required, I said, calmly, 'Police.'

'I hit my friend,' I told the operator. I was numb with it and these were only words. 'She was going away without me, and I killed her. Something was outside the house, knocking on the windows. She was outside, knocking on the windows, but she's dead.'

'You're saying you've killed someone?'

'She got up.'

'Can you tell me your name?'

'It's Ursula. Ursula Major.'

'Okay, Ursula.'

'And Vince, oh God, Vince. Please send someone.'

'Is anyone hurt?'

'He told me I was mad. He said I was having an episode, but he let it in. And now –'

'All right, Ursula, stay there, someone is on their way.'

'Don't you need to know where I am?'

'We can tell where you are from the phone box you're calling from.'

'Please come quickly.'

'Stay there and someone will be with you shortly.'

'There was an ant.'

'An ant?'

'On the floor of the phone box.'

'Stay there and someone will be with you soon.'

After a few minutes a police car drew up. The two police-men made me sit in the back, where the tang of burgers and cleaning fluid took me back to when I'd been caught skiving. The police then had been brusque – it wasn't their job to discover why I wasn't where I was supposed to be; I was a parcel they'd found on the street, and they were returning it. I shouldn't have expected this time to be different. They asked me to confirm my name, and the man in the passenger seat said, 'What's this about, Ursula?' in a tone that already suggested disbelief and irritation. I broke down as I told them about killing Sue, Vince coming home and the body being gone. I pointed to the Underwood, behind us, down the road, and told them something had come in the night and

Vince had let it in, and this morning he was cowering in the bathroom and there were bites on his arms and legs.

'Right,' said the man behind the wheel, drawing out the word.

'He coughed out a fly,' I said.

They shared a look, and I knew I shouldn't have called them. I was telling it wrong. They didn't believe me. I wanted them to go to the house and find Vince, find the grave, arrest me, put me in a police cell where I'd be safe, where whatever was coming for me next couldn't reach me, where I deserved to be.

'It's Vincent Goldie,' I added, thumbing away my tears. 'In the house.' They shared a more significant look.

Eventually the one behind the wheel decided they'd take me to the station and they'd send someone else to the house. I was so grateful I began to cry again, and they asked where my parents were and who was looking after me and I sobbed out about children's homes and Joy, even though I knew this information would mean they'd assume I was unpredictable, a troublemaker, unreliable.

In the police station I was taken to a bland room where an officer slid the notice on the door to OCCUPIED, brought me a milky tea in a polystyrene cup and two slices of white toast spread with margarine, and left me. Vince's words echoed in my head, and I told myself that now I'd officially confessed there would be procedures and processes. The police would go to the Underwood, they'd find Vince and take him to hospital.

I was starving, and I gobbled the toast and could have eaten the same again. I breathed slowly in and slowly out and tried again to think through what had happened. Vince must have opened the door and let in whatever had been outside. He'd heard and seen it too; it wasn't my imagination or an episode – there had been something. Sue had been out there. But she was dead. But if she was dead, where was her body? Vince had said she was inside him. *Breathe*, I told myself. *Just breathe.* He'd been thirsty like Sue had been, and Raymond, and the car radio had been on, and the record player, and there'd been the awful smell. I was only listing things, not coming to conclusions. I tried to remember the endings of *The Exorcist*, *The Shining*, *The Stepford Wives*, as if that would help. I was holding the cup to my mouth, and I gave a kind of laugh, and I heard it reverberate, hollow and sour. I snapped off a half-moon of polystyrene and crumbled it. Was it my turn next? I crushed the cup and began to sob. Sue was gone, dead, and I had killed her. *Arrest me*, I wanted to shout. *Arrest me!* Questions swirled in my head. The polystyrene cup was a hill of crumbs.

A policewoman sat opposite and smiled. I squinted at her. Was it a true smile, could I trust her? She asked me to explain everything again, and I told her about Sue and the knocking, and the thing at the door, and Vince opening the door. I twisted around and showed her the bump on the back of my head, and she asked me more about Vince and how I'd got the cut on my forehead. I wanted her to take notes, to start a tape recorder, but she sat with her hands on the table. She asked stupid questions about how Vince had known the Underwood was empty, how he'd broken in and what it had been like living with him. She asked me Sue's full name and address, and I knew that they were going to go to her house, and Anita and the children and Raymond would learn what I'd done. I put my head in my hands and wailed.

The policewoman went out for more tea and came back with another polystyrene cup, and Joy.

'What's been going on, Ursula?' she said in her

no-nonsense tone. She sat beside me, lit a cigarette and tapped the ash into a small foil ashtray. 'Do you want one?' She held the packet out.

'Is Anita coming? To the police station?'

Joy looked at the policewoman, who was still standing. 'Suzannah Whelan's mother,' the woman said.

'Her mother?' Joy said to me, surprised. 'I shouldn't think so.'

My hand reached out, I wanted one, but Anita thought smoking was a filthy habit. I rested my elbows on the table and Joy moved the tea out of the way. I rubbed my hands over my face, my face over my hands. My skin was dry and my eyes were stinging. I wasn't sure what time it was, how many days had passed since I'd put Sue in that grave.

'She's been very helpful,' the policewoman said from the doorway. She hadn't sat down again. 'Apart from all this nonsense about ghosts.'

'And the girl is missing?' Joy said to her, as though continuing a conversation they'd been having before they came into the room.

'Seems she's always been a bit flighty, if you know what I mean. Her mother thinks she's gone off, done it before it seems. There was talk of America apparently. We'll be checking airline and boat manifests, but that takes a while.'

'We were going to America together,' I said into my hands.

'What was that?' Joy asked. She stroked my back, and I sat up.

'We were meant to be going to America together. Then she said Vince wanted to come and she wasn't going with me, and that's when I hit her.'

'Vincent –'

'– Goldie,' the policewoman finished.

I looked from one to the other, irritated. I knew they were sharing expressions over the top of my head.

'Did you find him? Was he at the house?' Joy asked. I looked at the policewoman in time to see her shake her head.

My heart ratcheted in my chest, a mechanism working too fast. 'You haven't found him?'

Joy rubbed my back again. 'Did Vince do something?' she asked. 'Something to hurt you or Sue?'

'You don't understand! Vince let Sue into the house, but Sue was dead. He said she was inside him. We started something, Sue started something when she said we had to have a seance.'

'Okay,' Joy said. 'All right.'

After a while she asked if I'd be okay on my own while she made some phone calls to sort out a place for me to stay for a couple of nights.

'I'm not going back to the Underwood,' I said.

She went out with the policewoman, and they stood in the corridor with the door ajar, speaking about a hole in the ground at the property, how it would be a couple of days until I'd be able to get my belongings.

'I can hear you, you know!' I shouted. 'I'm never going back there, never.'

In *Dark Descent* Anita sits on a dining-room chair in the same house Sue had lived in. She is very upright, regal. She takes out a small lipstick mirror that she has tucked under a thigh and looks at herself, wiping below her eyes, which makes no difference to the shadows beneath them. Someone must ask her a question out of range of the microphone because we see her nod, slip the mirror away, and hold up her head.

28

Joy found me an emergency placement with a foster family for three nights in a town up the motorway, on a camp bed in their dining room. The mother and Joy talked on the doorstep while I went into the house, and I heard the mother sighing about the lack of paperwork.

'Anything I should know?' she asked. I didn't wait to hear Joy's answer but looked up the stairs, listening for anyone there, and went through the door to my left into the lounge, where three kids in school uniforms were watching *Blockbusters*. 'Can I have a P, please, Bob?' one of them shouted, and they all laughed. I went into the dining room and the kitchen, and a small utility room, and I crept upstairs while the women were still talking and looked in each bedroom and the bathroom. I waited for the cold rushing feeling, but this bathroom was full of plastic bath toys and smelled of soap. The window was large and looked over the garden. The father came home after work, and we ate in the kitchen and the food was good and there was lots of it. I stayed up as late as I was allowed and when the mother and father had gone upstairs, I moved my camp bed to the middle of the dining room, as far from the windows as possible, lying awake and listening for tapping. I wondered whether the Underwood itself was haunted – John had run away, Joy had been sick. And now that I'd left, perhaps nothing else was going to happen, except that Vince was missing, Sue was dead and it was my turn next. I whimpered into my pillow and drew my knees to my chest. I couldn't explain any of it. I'd killed my only friend, Raymond's sister, and here I was in a foster home and I hadn't been arrested.

On the drive to the foster family, Joy had given me a lecture about my job at the art school, saying she'd arranged some sick leave but that I'd have to go back as soon as possible, and how lucky I was that Alan had agreed to keep my position open for me. I hadn't given a thought to the art school. Joy instructed me that I wasn't to tell the foster family my 'silly stories', they had young children and no one would appreciate me giving them nightmares. Instead, I could talk to the doctor at the appointment she'd made for me.

In the day at the foster parents' house I watched telly, filling my head mindlessly with whatever was on. They didn't have a video player.

'What's this about?' the doctor asked when Joy took me to my appointment. It was hard to look at him because one of his eyes wandered over my shoulder while the other focused on my face. He asked the question in such a kindly way that I only got a few words out before I began to cry, wiping my face and nose with my hands. He held out a box of tissues and didn't ask any questions about what I'd done, only how I was feeling.

On the third morning, a Saturday, I was waiting in the kitchen with the foster mother, eating a pile of toast and jam. The other kids were in the lounge, or the living room as they called it in this house, watching telly. My new bin liner was at my feet. It didn't have much in it: a man's T-shirt to sleep in, clean knickers and what the mother called an emergency kit in a flowery toiletry bag, which included a new tooth-brush and tampons. I'd wondered about asking if I could stay longer, but I knew what the answer would be.

The doorbell went and I jumped. 'Take care,' the mother said. There was something about her, the way she held her head, the fineness of her features, that reminded me of Sadie and how generous she could be, although I didn't always think that at the time: handing out money to beggars in Morocco, giving the food she'd bought for us to a couple of children who she said looked hungrier than me. I was never hungry when I was with Sadie. The mother held her arms out to hug me and I knew if I hugged her back, I wouldn't be able to let go, and so I picked up my bin liner and headed for the door.

I didn't know where Joy was taking me. That's how it usually went. A girl in Doughty House told me once that she'd waited in a social worker's car for three hours while he used a pay phone to make frantic calls to find a place that would take her. I knew too that sometimes they didn't tell you where you'd end up because they didn't want you to kick off and refuse to go to a particular home or town.

'I've got a surprise for you,' Joy said, glancing at me from the driver's seat, smiling.

'Not the Underwood?' I said, frowning.

'No,' she said, tightly. 'Not the Underwood. A colleague of mine went to get your things.' She nodded her head towards the back seat and the suitcase I'd been packing before I ran out.

'Did she get my drawings from the wall? Did she get the pictures of me and Sue from my bedside drawer?' I wanted my sculpture too but knew that was unrealistic.

Joy pinched her lips together. 'She told me you left the place in quite a mess. Overturned furniture in the kitchen, the sofa out on the lawn, curtains torn down.'

'The place was a shithole when we arrived.' A defensive answer.

'But all those things will belong to someone.'

She continued talking while the hard shoulder went by, the bridges and the roundabouts. I closed my eyes and let the sun make kaleidoscopic patterns on the backs of my eyelids. We drove along the motorway and past the houses and the shops, through the town centre and out the other side, and left into the housing estate. I sat up straight.

'No,' I said, looking around. 'Not here. I can't stay here.'

'Anita invited you,' Joy said, pulling up outside Sue's house.

'But I . . .' What was I going to say? *Killed her daughter.*

When I'd come out of the doctor's, Joy had been waiting to take me back to the foster family, and although I was under no obligation to tell her what he'd said, I knew she'd want to know, if only to pass on the details of any medicine I'd been given. I told her the doctor had given me a prescription for antidepressants and had said, if I wanted, I could go and talk to a 'shrink'.

'Psychiatrist,' Joy said, patiently. 'That might not be a bad idea. Get a few things off your chest.'

'They'll put me in the nuthouse.'

'I don't like that term, and they won't.'

'They might. I'm not going to take the pills either.'

'How about you take them for a while and see how you feel? We could call in at the chemist.' She had this smooth-talking voice she put on when she wanted me to do something; I could spot it a mile off. But I could play the game too. 'All right,' I said. 'If you've got the time.'

She glanced at her watch. 'Oh God,' she'd said, and had driven faster.

Outside Anita's, Joy turned off the engine. 'All the family wanted you to come and stay. It won't be for long, just until I find you somewhere more permanent.'

I looked at the house and wondered whether I could pretend to be Sue and fit in without them noticing. 'Have you told them I'm mad?'

'I don't like that term either.' Joy took the keys from the ignition and put her hand on my arm. 'I told Anita that you said Sue had disappeared, gone off suddenly, and that you'd been a little shaken up by it and Vince's behaviour. You need to put all that knocking at the window stuff and the ideas about Vince in his underwear and the teeth marks out of your head. It's nonsense, and Anita won't want to hear it, okay? Sue hasn't turned up yet, but Anita is certain she will, like she did last time.'

'And Vince?'

'And Vince what?'

'Has he turned up yet?'

She looked at her watch and undid her seat belt. 'I don't believe so, no.'

29

Anita opened the front door with Andrew tucked into one arm, welcoming me in with the other.

'Oh, my love,' she said, hugging me, and I smelled the warm security of her, something milky, motherly, and I wanted to stay forever and for everything to be how it was before. Joy put my bin liner and suitcase down beside me.

'Sorry, Anita,' she said. 'Got to dash, but just quickly . . .' She glanced at me, and Anita handed me the baby and I stepped inside. I loved the scent of him too, talc and washing powder. He looked up at me in wonder as though I were a good person and not a murderer. He would never know his big sister. I kissed his cheeks and whispered, 'I'm sorry,' and he raised his little arms, shoving a knuckle into his mouth and sucking it, and I rocked him, overhearing some of what Joy was saying: '. . . doctor's appointment.' She was using her reassuring tone: '. . . nothing I haven't seen before.' Anita's back was to me and I couldn't hear her reply, but it must have been a question about Sue because Joy said, 'I've dealt with runaways before . . . always return . . . a couple of weeks at most. Don't worry.'

I bent over Andrew and let him grip my little finger. Joy tapped her watch. 'Okay, I'm off,' she called to where I stood in the hallway. I waved Andrew's hand at her. 'Bye,' I said for both of us.

'I'll give you a ring in a day or so, see how you're getting on, yeah?' she called to Anita. She was halfway to her car.

'Come in, come in,' Anita said to me as though I were outside. She closed the door and crushed me against her in another hug and took Andrew from me. As usual she got straight to the point. 'Let me say, my love, that I know Sue, and she'll have gone away without telling anyone. That's what she does. I should know – I did it too when I was her age. She'll be back safe and sound in a week. Last time she hitched to Scotland.' Andrew began to whine, and Anita jiggled him. 'He's due a feed. Why don't you go and see Raymond, he's in the kitchen. I'll take your things upstairs. I've put you in Sue's bed.'

'No, not Sue's bed,' I started. How could I sleep in Sue's bed on my first night here, and without her? Andrew began to cry, and Anita picked up my suitcase and the bin liner in one hand and started up the stairs. 'There's nowhere else, love. Telly off in five minutes!' she shouted into the lounge.

I looked in at the twins. 'You're going to sleep in our room,' one of them said.

'Because you haven't got anywhere else to live,' the other added.

In the kitchen Raymond was sitting at the table slicing leeks, and as I came in he looked up at me, his eyes large, his face worried. Perhaps Joy had given him the same story as Anita. I wanted to tell him everything, and I was desperate for him to believe me, although I understood that telling him the truth would mean I'd probably never see him again.

He stood with an effort, and I didn't know whether he was going to slap me or hug me. I braced myself for either.

'Ursula,' he said. 'I've been so worried.'

'About Sue?' I choked on her name.

'About you! I'm sorry I haven't been to the house.' He carried the board with the leeks to the cooker and tipped them into a pan. They hissed and the room filled with their onion smell. I couldn't work out whether I was hungry or not. 'I couldn't face Vince after all that stuff when we were shooting the film.' Raymond glanced over his shoulder and I blushed, thinking about the things he'd learned.

'Raymond, something's happened. I did something –'

He turned to face me, interrupting. 'Joy came round, but you know that. That's why you're here. She wasn't sure about you staying with us, but Mum insisted – you know how much she loves you. I insisted.' I sat at the table. His words were exquisite pain. 'She took me aside and told me what you've been saying, about the hole Vince dug in the garage floor for the film, and stories about ghosts and things knocking on the windows in the night. About – about – claiming that you'd hit Sue on the head. Joy said you'd had a sort of breakdown, but that you'd seen the doctor and she was sure you'd be okay. I said of course we'd be happy to have you here, to look after you. I . . . I want to look after you.'

'It's not a story.'

'No, of course it doesn't seem like a story, not to you. But you'll feel better soon. I know it.' He sat again at the table and began to peel a potato. 'The police came round too, asking about Sue, and Vince.'

'Vince was at the Underwood,' I said, but Raymond didn't listen.

'Sue will have run off. My stupid sister has gone off with that wanker. Scotland or, God, America. Stir the leeks, would you?'

'What?' I looked around.

'Give them a stir so they don't burn.' He nodded towards

the wooden spoon. I stood, picked it up, and put it down again. 'When she went away before, with another idiot, to Scotland that time, she sent postcards saying she was okay and that we shouldn't worry. I'm sure we'll get one any day. She'll have forgotten. I'm just pissed off that she forgot about my car too.' He put the peeled potato in a pan of water. 'The garage phoned and said it had failed its MOT but no one had been in touch to pay for it to be fixed.' He began to peel another potato and then put it down. 'Christ,' he said. 'Do you think they've eloped? Sue wouldn't marry that moron, would she?'

I picked up the wooden spoon, stared at it and stirred the leeks. 'She hasn't done that.' I needed to convince him that Sue was never coming home, that I'd killed her and buried her, and somehow – I had no idea how – her body had got out of its grave and knocked on the windows, hammered on the door, stuck its fingers through the letter box. It sounded mad. I felt a sting in my nose, tears coming.

Raymond looked up at me. 'Oh God,' he said. 'Please don't.' He stood. 'Is it the leeks, or have I made you cry? She'll be back soon.'

He put his arms around me, while mine hung by my side, and he pulled me against him and I let him because I needed it; no matter how much I wasn't worthy or how appalled I was with myself, I wanted this moment of absolution. His jumper smelled of leeks and his neck smelled of soap, and he turned his head and I turned mine so that our lips were softly touching, and his mouth was opening.

'No,' I said, pulling away and stumbling from the room.

30

All day, Anita and Raymond speculated on when Sue's postcard would arrive, and whether she was in Scotland or America or somewhere else with Vince. I wanted to tell them that Vince had been at the house but I knew that would mean I'd have to convince them about all of it. They said it was just like her to leave without thinking about anyone else. I tried to put on an expression of understanding, but I was the cuckoo in the nest, an interloper hiding in plain sight. Anita told us a long story about how she had run away from home when she was a teenager and ended up cold and alone in Norfolk, and Gramps drove across the country to pick her up and didn't speak one word to her on the long trip home.

Raymond cooked and served food and I ate everything he put in front of me and seconds when it was offered, but still I wanted more. I almost came to believe them – that Sue would turn up when she'd had enough of Vince, and that I had imagined everything. On Saturday night I lay awake in a bed that smelled of Sue, as disturbing as it was soothing, jumbled images coming to me of Vince in the bathroom gagging on a fly, the face in the glass, the fingers through the letter box, and it occurred to me that four days had passed since I'd run away, and if Vince hadn't come to find me by now, maybe he never would.

On Sunday, Gran and Gramps and Auntie Julie came for lunch. Raymond cooked roast beef, with Julie and me as his assistants, and he said again how it was just like Sue not to think about calling home to let Anita know she was safe.

Julie stopped making gravy and turned to him. 'If she hasn't sent a card or called by now, I don't think she went anywhere.'

My heart began to beat in my throat. Now was the moment to tell her what had happened. Julie would listen; she would believe me.

Raymond was laying out plates on the kitchen table ready for dishing up. 'She's in Edinburgh or Glasgow having a great time.'

'I've been trying to tell your mother that she needs to take Suzie's disappearance more seriously,' Julie continued. 'But she won't listen. If she doesn't report her missing, I will. And Vince, where's he?' She put her hands on her hips. 'I want to know what his parents think.'

'She's with him. They're together,' Raymond said.

'Christ.' Julie swept her hair from her face. 'It doesn't bear thinking about.'

Raymond shook his head. 'What doesn't bear thinking about?'

'Someone in this family needs to start taking it seriously.' Julie's voice was raised.

'Keep your voice down,' Raymond said. 'Mum will hear you.'

'So she should! That girl, our girl, hasn't been seen or heard of for ten days and no one is doing a damn thing.'

'She's not a girl,' Raymond said. 'She's an adult, and she's done this before, remember?'

'Eight days,' I said, and they stopped talking and looked at me.

'What do you know?' Julie said.

'She doesn't know anything,' Raymond said. 'She thinks she saw things she couldn't have seen.'

'What things?' Julie's hands pressed on the table. 'What things did you see?'

'Things that weren't real,' Raymond said.

'I did it. I did it!' I said, beginning to cry.

'What did you do?' Julie shouted.

'Ursula needs looking after, not yelling at.'

'What happened?' Julie said. 'What do you know?'

'She had a breakdown, she needs our help.'

I put my face in my hands, sobbing.

Gramps came into the kitchen. 'What's all this noise about? Who's doing the dishing-up? Our bellies think our throats are cut.' He bustled about, calming Julie down, putting his hand on my arm in passing, giving me a little squeeze as though I belonged there as much as the rest of them, a touch I wasn't worthy of.

I took a glass of water out to the back step and closed the door behind me. I knew that Raymond would be telling Julie what Joy had told him about the hole in the ground, the knocking on the windows, Sue dead, her body gone. I could see it in Julie's eyes when I went back in, how she looked at me with a mixture of sympathy and derision.

At the dining table, I wolfed down the food while they talked about the weather, about summer holidays and what they'd watched on the telly, when Gran said, 'Anita, I forgot to tell you, I saw Suzie in town.'

The piece of beef in my mouth became a dry lump, and beside me, Raymond stiffened, his cutlery stilled.

'What?' Julie said. 'You saw Suzie? When? Why didn't you tell us?'

'Well, I'm telling you now.'

'When was this, Mum?'

Gran pulled her hand out from under Julie's and waved it in the air dismissively. 'I don't know. Recently.'

'Don't listen to her,' Gramps said. 'She doesn't know what she sees from one day to the next.'

'I saw her, I'm telling you, laughing and carrying on with that young man.'

Raymond cleared his throat, getting ready to speak.

'Which young man?' Anita said. She began to jiggle Andrew although he was sleeping in her arms.

'When, Mum? When?' Julie pressed.

'The one who wears his hair in a bun. Like a girl.'

'Vincent,' Anita said, waking Andrew with her bouncing. He started to grizzle. 'In town?'

Raymond shared a look with Julie that said *What did I tell you?*

'That could have been his name. He looked like a Vincent,' Gran said.

I tried to swallow but the meat was a foreign body, an insect my throat refused.

'Vince,' Raymond said. 'His name's Vince. When did you see them, Gran?'

'Vince? What kind of a name is that?'

'I kept telling her not to hang around with him,' Anita said. 'His sort are troublemakers.' Andrew let out a squawk as though he agreed.

'What sort?' Julie asked.

'Bad seeds,' Gran said.

'Children whose real parents didn't want them,' Anita said.

I stared at Gran and Anita. Andrew's face was turning red, his mother was holding him too tightly. He opened his mouth wide and howled.

'Your children have fathers who didn't want them, Anita,' Gramps said.

'Tell us when you saw them, Mum.' Julie raised her voice above the others.

Anita put Andrew over her shoulder and patted his back smartly. 'But at least I've got them all. I haven't had any taken away.'

'Vince is known to social services?' Julie said, horrified.

I took the piece of meat out of my mouth and put it on the side of my plate. One of the twins made a nauseated face and the other clutched at her throat and stuck out her tongue.

'This isn't important,' Raymond said. 'What's important is when Gran saw them.'

But I thought it was important. All of it was important. I looked around the table at the family that had welcomed me in again and again. Perhaps they wouldn't have if they'd known I didn't know who my father was, and that my mother was dead, if they'd learned my foster family, my own grandparents, hadn't wanted me, if they'd been told I'd grown up in seven different children's homes. My face grew hot, and I looked down at my plate. If Vince was in town it wasn't possible that he was with Sue, because Sue was . . .

'His mother was schizo,' Anita said. 'And he was adopted when he was three.'

I wondered whether she knew as much as she did about Vince because Sue had told her. 'Eight,' I said quietly. 'He was eight.' No one listened.

'When did you see them, Gran?' Raymond asked again. 'When were you in town?'

Gran sliced a potato and put a piece in her mouth while we waited, Julie leaning over her plate. Gran seemed to be considering, enjoying the attention as she chewed, and I remembered the first time I'd met them, when Sue had told them my father had died, and I wondered whether her lie had been to save me from their questions and opinions, or because it'd be easier for her if her new friend came from a background that was more palatable to this family.

'It was when she went to pick up her new glasses,' Gramps said.

'But I took you into town for that!' Julie said.

'That's when I saw them, with my new glasses. He was trying to kiss her. You were in the bakery, and when you came out, they'd gone.'

'But that was weeks ago,' Julie said.

'Was it?' Gran said.

'God, Mum.' Julie shook her head. 'Anita, you need to go to the police and report Suzie as missing. If you don't do it, I'm going to go.'

'She'll be off with that Vince.' Gramps winked.

I didn't look at Raymond. 'Vince was adopted when he was eight, not three,' I said. 'He's a footballer, nearly semi-pro.' Contradictory feelings were swamping me. I wanted to defend Vince in the face of Anita's, Julie's and their mother's prejudices, but I was grappling with my terror of what Vince had looked like in the Underwood's bathroom and what he'd said to me, and the horror of what I'd done. I was also dealing with another emotion that I was only starting to process: grief. I had lost Sue, and in five minutes around the table eating Sunday lunch, I no longer belonged in this family.

After my little speech, I stood and went to the kitchen, put on Sue's raincoat, which was hanging there, and squeezed into her wellies. The dog followed and wouldn't go back in, so I let him come too.

I walked through the afternoon's drizzle to the local shopping precinct, the dog trotting along beside me, and we huddled in a bus shelter. I imagined what they were saying: Raymond defending my strange behaviour; Julie telling them what Raymond had told her. Or maybe they weren't talking about me at all. Whenever a bus came, which wasn't often, I thought about getting on it, wondering whether the dog would be able to find his way home, be able to cross the roads without getting hit by a car. A couple of hours later, I returned to the house. Through the front window, I could see the seething light of the telly and the family sitting around it. I let myself in through the back door, hanging up the coat and taking off the wellies. The dog shook himself from nose to tail, and I was already up the stairs with the bedroom door shut when I heard Raymond call my name.

Thirty-six years on from this day, I watched Ray in *Dark Descent*. He sits at his dining table, upright, confident, facing the camera. Behind him is his glossy kitchen – cupboard doors without handles, and the only things visible a fancy coffee machine, an arching tap with an extendable nozzle and an oversized pepper grinder like the ones you get in old trattorias. Ray pats a breast pocket of his tailored suit, the other, and sweeps his hand back through his hair before he starts to speak.

3I

I'd missed most of the previous week at the art school and I wasn't sure I could face going back, but Joy telephoned on Sunday evening and Raymond called me to the phone. He loitered, as though he wanted to reassure me again, but eventually he went upstairs. Joy said Alan was expecting me in the post room first thing and I just needed to get on with my work and everything would be fine. She said Vince still hadn't been found and neither had Sue been located. *Of course not*, I might have replied.

'Have you found me anywhere else to live yet?' I whispered, looking up the staircase.

Joy's pause, I knew, meant that her patience was running out. 'Are you saying you don't feel safe?'

'No,' I said. 'No, I just –'

'Give things time to settle. You haven't been there for more than a minute.'

In the morning, I tried to avoid Raymond and his misdirected understanding. I didn't want to speak to Anita either. I had fallen in love with this family – their noise and chaos, their Sunday lunches, grandparents, aunt and siblings. I'd thought they were perfect and now I knew they weren't, and it hurt. I got the same bus to work that Sue used to catch, in my washed uniform, with a packed lunch made by Raymond.

In the post room, Alan was too attentive, checking I was

okay and I had everything I needed. I waited for him to say 'Remember, we're all family here', but he didn't. I wondered what Joy had told him and what rumours were going round. Terry, in contrast, was monosyllabic, and I couldn't get anything out of him until I'd packed my trolley and was about to leave for the main building.

'Do you know what they're saying?' he said to my back.

I had a good idea. 'No,' I said, facing the swing doors. 'What are they saying?'

'That Sue is dead, and Vince killed her and buried her somewhere. In the woods or in the garage at the Underwood. The garage we went in, where the hammer was missing.'

I turned and looked at him. 'That's not true.' Most of it wasn't true. I began to explain, but I knew Terry wouldn't believe me either and he too would think I was deluded. What rumours would fly around the art school after that?

'Where are they, then?' he said. He sounded like he was about to cry.

'Honestly? I don't know.' This was some kind of truth.

'They're saying you lost it.' So he already thought I was deluded.

'Do I look like I've lost it?'

His eyes slid away from mine.

'They're saying he murdered Sue!'

I started to push backwards through the swing doors.

'I hardly knew the bloke,' he continued, trying to distance himself from Vince. 'We sometimes went jogging together in Crab Wood, that's all.' The doors swung closed.

In Painting, the studios were transformed. They had been cleared of the half-finished work, the dirty easels, the trestle tables covered in bottles and rags and paint, and the ephemera stuck to the walls. They were white and clean, and the floors had been scraped of their splashes of colour and swept. Stacks of canvases leaned against the walls.

'What's going on?' I said to myself.

A student, packing a toolbox with brushes and spatulas, looked up. 'Sorry, sorry,' she said. 'Just collecting the last of my stuff. I'll be out of your way in a sec.' She stood, clutching her toolbox and two squares of wood, and took in my uniform. 'Oh, you're not a cleaner?' I tugged down the sleeves of my jacket and she smiled, round cheeks lifting. She was wearing paint-splattered dungarees and a loose shirt.

'Post room.' I put my hand on my trolley, ready to push it off.

'It's the Degree Show next week. Us second-years have to clear out.'

I'd heard the words 'Degree Show' mentioned at tea break as a complaint about the extra work, but no one had explained what it was. Perhaps I seemed confused.

'It's when the third-years hang their work? Get their show ready? Get marked.' She seemed to want to chat. 'The Degree Show?' Nearly all her sentences were a question I didn't know if I was supposed to answer. 'It'll be me, this time next year. You should come, to this year's?'

'To the Degree Show?' I couldn't imagine the next hour, let alone the next week; surely I wouldn't still be coming to the art school then. By next week I would have fractured into a million tiny pieces.

'Anyone can look around. Or you could come to the private view. I'll be on the door, I can let you in? A free warm white wine in a plastic cup?' She laughed again and started to leave. 'If I'm not on the door,' she said over her shoulder, 'ask for Georgie Bates.'

I took my trolley to the main office, hesitating, worried Sue's colleague would ask me if I knew where she was. The room smelled of the woman's sweets, but she wasn't at her desk and no one was in front of Sue's ledger. I put the post down and left. In Printmaking, the studios had also been cleared. I went along the corridor to Sculpture, picking out and reading another of Ms Barker's postcards from Canada:

I have put your things from my house in the garden. You had better hope it doesn't rain.

Samuel

I flipped it over as though there might be more information on the front, but there was only a picture of people in canoes on a lake with a mountain behind. MOUNT BURGESS, EMERALD LAKE, NEAR FIELD BC, the inscription read.

I'd turned my back to the swing doors to push through them when I heard shouting from the far end of the corridor and saw three policemen running towards me from the front of the building, and the sound of their boots was the sound of a stampede, unstoppable. *This is it*, I thought. *They're coming. I'm ready.* I stepped out from behind my trolley. The policemen were upon me, panting and holding on to their hats, and I was relieved and terrified that soon everyone would know what I'd done. The one in front huffed out, 'Excuse me, Miss,' and moved me and my trolley aside, and he and the others charged past through the swing doors. Sue's colleague from the main office came on behind, hobbled by her pencil skirt and stilettos. 'It's the second-year studio,' she said, grabbing my arm. Her breath was thick with Winter Mixture. 'Someone called the police from the Sculpture office.' She went to push through the doors, but one of the policemen had returned. 'Clear back, please, clear back,' he said. As the doors swung behind him we heard a woman shouting indistinguishable

225

words, and things crashing about. Beyond the policeman, through the glass doors, I could see the empty noticeboard and Ms Barker's office door, ajar.

Mr Glenmore, the head of the art school, came racing down the back stairs from the first floor, demanding the policeman let him through and asking Winter Mixture what was going on. She told her story again, adding that the police had burst into the main lobby and asked the way to Sculpture. Something about a naked man and a hostage. I began to shake, and I closed my eyes, pressing myself against the wall of the corridor, sure my heart was about to stop. Vince had come.

More questions, and answers guessed at. I didn't join in; I stood at the back of the group that was amassing – early students and staff – and listened. Mr Glenmore tried his best to get past the policeman, saying he believed one of his staff was in there. It was Ms Barker, he said, but the policeman wouldn't let anyone past, and he held his arms out and told us to move back, further up the corridor. We didn't move. 'It's that bloke from maintenance,' someone said, and my stomach turned over. I slotted myself into the crowd; I couldn't leave, I didn't consider it. 'Vince Goldie,' someone else said, and I heard the name 'Sue Whelan'. Winter Mixture told them to stop gossiping and said Sue was in Scotland, in Glasgow, visiting an aunt. A man gave a disbelieving laugh and more police arrived, pushing through the group of about twenty people and telling us to leave the building. We shuffled up the corridor to Printmaking and stopped there. Most of the new police went through the swing doors into Sculpture. The crowd buzzed with anticipation, and a sobbing girl was taken away by a friend. I waited, my arms wrapped around my body, the wall holding me up. I didn't catch anyone's eye; I didn't want them to work out who I was and make the link between me and Vince and Sue.

The swing doors opened and some police came out, herding us back, further up the corridor and into the main lobby – a large atrium where the stairs turned up to the first floor and a sculptural chandelier hung high above. They swept us towards the front door but we separated like a shoal of fish, regrouping at the edges of the room, the entryway to the canteen, up the stairs, against the wall of the main office, and although the police grabbed one student and marched him out of the building, the rest of us evaded them and after that it was too late because we could hear the commotion coming down the corridor.

I hung back behind two women from Finance. I didn't want to see but I couldn't look away. The swearing and shouts of the policemen trying to contain someone preceded them, and when they came around the corner the crowd gasped, and a woman screamed. Five policemen were holding Vince by his arms and legs as though this were a medieval pageant and they were displaying a wild man, a beast, an unholy, through streets lined with people cringing in horror but continuing to watch. Vince's wrists were cuffed behind his back, but he writhed and shrieked, kicking out and spitting. He was thinner than when I'd seen him the week before, each rib defined, hair loose and lank, flipping about as his head twisted. He was still wearing those dirty underpants, feet bare and filthy. But it was what covered his body that made me reel with nausea: more bites on his arms, and long bloody scratches on his lower back, and several that ran down the front of his face.

The police manhandled him as far as the middle of the room, but as he became aware of the crowd hugging the walls he went limp and heavy, and the policemen, surprised, dropped him on his back like a dead body. He quietened and the crowd quietened too, and we heard a tinkling, tinny sound, and at first I couldn't work out what it was, until those beside me looked up and we saw the wires and the metal plates of the chandelier high above our heads moving and clinking like pebbles hitting glass. The police looked up too and moved away, all of us sure it was about to come down. In his sprawled position on the floor, Vince looked around him, rotating his head one way and the other, and I shrank further back, certain it was me he was searching for, but the police took hold of him again and dragged him away. It all happened in less than a minute, but as the door closed behind them, we heard Vince shouting what sounded like 'Your turn next'. The chandelier stilled.

Everyone piled through the front door after the police and Vince. The flashing blue lights of the police cars on the road brought more people to swell the crowd, but I stayed in the foyer, watching through the windows as a wailing ambulance arrived. When the two ambulance men came inside, one of them asked me, 'Which way to Sculpture?'

I led them along the corridor I'd come from. This time no one stopped me going through the swing doors and on into the second-year Sculpture studio. Here, as with Painting and Printmaking, the room had been cleared and whitewashed, and only a few sculptures stood around the sides. Ms Barker was sitting on the floor with a policeman beside her and Mr Glenmore hovering nearby. His secretary was crouching and pressing a handkerchief to Ms Barker's cheek. Between her fingers it was showing red. Ms Barker was shaking, hunched over her drawn-up knees, making small cries. The ambulance men went to her, speaking efficiently, looking at the wound, asking how she was feeling, whether she thought she would faint. I stepped forward to ask her what she'd seen, whether Vince had said he was looking for me. But they kept me back, asked for space as one of them cleaned the gash on Ms Barker's cheek, said how it was likely to need stitches, and applied a dressing. They put a blanket over her shoulders and helped her into a wheelchair one of them had fetched. I stood in the doorway and smelled her citrus perfume, and it wasn't until she was wheeled past that she finally saw me, her eyes huge and jittery, and then she was gone.

I looked down and realized I still held her postcard from Samuel, one corner bent. Running after the small group, I called her name, and they stopped, and I came around to the front and handed it to her, and she gave a little gasp, whether at me or the postcard, I wasn't certain.

32

After the ambulance drove Ms Barker away, I returned to the post room, but as soon as I got there, I began to shake and my teeth to chatter. Alan took me into his cubbyhole behind the counter and brought me a mug of sweet tea. It was the first and last time he made me a hot drink. The members of staff who hadn't known about it before must have heard I was involved with Vince's assault on Ms Barker, and also with Sue's disappearance, but Alan was good enough not to ask questions; he let me sit on his chair with my hands around the mug. I hadn't heard him do it, but I gathered that he had telephoned Joy and filled her in, because she arrived shortly after.

I collected my bag and coat from my locker and, for the second time in less than three days, I sat in Joy's car. As she drove, she lit a cigarette, cracked her window and didn't speak. I was grateful for her lack of questions, but the silence left space for my head to fill with unwanted thoughts. Whatever had happened to Vince, and before him to Sue, was not contained by the Underwood. I remembered the seance and Sue's idea that there was a virus in the house, and wondered whether she, Ray and me sitting around the table with a candle and a glass of water had provided the ideal conditions. But having seen Vince, his bites and his crazed behaviour, I began to think it was more like a parasite: a worm or a fly that burrowed its way through an open wound and laid an egg. And when the egg hatched, the parasite was capable of anything: raising the dead, setting off madness and self-harm, and other things I didn't know about yet. But, I reasoned, Vince had been caught, the police had taken him away. With luck, although I'd need more than luck, this was the end of it.

Joy stubbed out her cigarette and tried to shove the full ashtray closed. 'So, what actually happened at the bungalow, Ursula?' She pushed the ashtray again and it bounced open, spilling butts. What could I say? If I told her the same story as she'd heard in the police station, she wasn't going to believe me any more than the first time, and maybe she could make me take the antidepressants the doctor had pre-scribed, get me sectioned, have me locked up for good if she thought I was crazy and a danger to others. Or I could invent a story about Vince's involvement in Sue's death. But this would need to match whatever he said – if the police managed to get any sense out of him. And I'd be accusing him of a crime I knew he didn't commit, because I had done it. Anyway, he was also a victim.

'I can't remember,' I said to Joy.

She sighed in exasperation and then reined herself in. 'You must be worried about Sue. You can tell me what happened.'

I stared out of the window. 'I can't remember.'

'Think about what Anita's going through.'

'I can't remember.'

It was early afternoon when she dropped me at Anita's. She didn't come in. I rang the doorbell and Raymond opened the door, pulling me inside, to the bottom of the stairs, out of the line of sight of the kitchen. I put my bag and coat over the newel post.

'The police have been again,' he whispered.

My heart began to pound. 'Were they looking for me?'

'You?' he said, surprised. 'No, they have a man in custody. We know it has to be Vince. They said they found Sue's suitcase in the boot of a man's car with her passport in it.' I remembered that morning at the Underwood when Vince had put a suitcase in the boot of his car and Sue had gone to do something with it. 'It's taken them all this time to bloody look in the boot of his car.' Raymond was furious, and I knew only a bad person would put him through this. It'd been easy to carry off my apathy in front of Joy with my *can't remembers*, but faced with Raymond, I was ashamed. 'No one is taken into custody unless a crime's been committed, and Sue wouldn't just leave her passport,' he said. His head was inches from mine, and I was aware of his physical presence as a tremble in my stomach. I heard a baby's soft cry from upstairs. 'If you're scared of Vince, you don't need to be any more.' I thought he was going to hold me, but I couldn't let him do that, I didn't deserve it. I was unlovable. 'I'm scared he did something to her.' He rested his forehead on mine and we stayed like that for a moment.

'I'm so sorry,' I said.

I hadn't seen that Julie had come down the hallway, and that she was watching us, until she spoke. 'You need to come into the kitchen, Ursula,' she said, firmly. 'We have to talk to you.'

Raymond and I jumped away from each other, and I wiped under my eyes. I walked dumbly towards her, and he followed. In the kitchen, Anita was slumped at the table, which was covered in discarded tissues, mugs and glasses, the teapot, a dry sandwich with a single bite taken out of it and a bottle of brandy. Her face was puffy, and her eyes red, and she wore her fluffy dressing gown, matching slippers on her feet. I looked at Raymond for help, but he gazed at the floor.

'What the hell is going on?' Julie closed the door as though I might try to escape.

'Vince was at the art school,' I said. 'He was deranged, crazy, the police had to carry him out. He hurt one of the –'

'The police told us about Vince,' Julie interrupted. 'It's Suzie we want to know about.'

Anita wailed at the name and held a wad of tissue to her open mouth.

'What do you know about what he's done?' Julie asked me.

'I did it,' I said quietly. 'I killed Sue.' My own tears welled and fell down my cheeks, dripping on to the collar of my uniform.

'You didn't,' Raymond jumped in, and I understood he must have told his mother and his aunt that, as bad as this was, I was a good and honest person, and now Vince was no longer a threat, I would want to help them. I wasn't good and I didn't know how to convince them I was being honest.

'That's it, that's what happened.' My voice was rising; I wiped my hand under my nose.

'Then where's her body?' Julie snapped. Anita sobbed louder at the word 'body'.

'If you're protecting him, there's no need,' Raymond said.

'I'm not,' I said, trying to collect myself. 'I don't know where her body is. She was at the door, asking to be let in. She was scared.' As I talked, Anita kept up a steady moaning and rocking. 'But she was dead, she was dead already.'

Julie shook her head, and Raymond closed his eyes. 'She was outside the house and Vince let her in, and he . . .' I trailed off. I could hear what I was saying, and I wouldn't have believed it either.

'And Vince what?' Anita shouted, her voice breaking.

'What? What did that bastard do to my baby?' She started weeping and Julie crouched beside her, and I took my chance: opening the kitchen door and running up to the room I'd shared with the twins for two nights. I grabbed what I could find of my clothes and shoved them in my suitcase. No one followed me. When I was ready, I crept down the stairs, gathered my coat and bag, and then I was through the front door, closing it behind me. I was nearly out of the estate when I heard Raymond calling my name. I didn't stop.

I got the bus into town and went to the tea shop where Sue had asked me to choose who should die, and I ordered a pot of tea and two cheese toasties. I wrote her name over and over on a paper napkin. I ordered a slice of chocolate cake and another pot of tea, staying until the other customers had left and a waitress started wiping the table next to mine. I took my suitcase and sat on a bench beside the cathedral for an hour. The afternoon was warm, and the choristers prac-tising inside sounded like angels. I waited until five thirty and went to the Market Inn and asked for a vermouth and ice and sat at a table to drink it. After a while, when the pub was filling, John came in. I watched him order his drinks at the bar, and when he noticed me, I saw the same terror flash across his face as I'd seen in the hallway of the Underwood. He turned away as though hoping I hadn't seen him.

'John!' I called, and he turned towards me.

'Ursula,' he said, his smile forced. He came across the room. 'How lovely to see you. Do you frequent this estab-lishment every Monday?' He was being polite because we'd once been friends, but I knew he wanted to get away.

'Is it only Monday?'

'A long week?' He sipped his pint, looking off into another

corner of the pub. In a moment he would pretend he'd seen someone he knew.

'I need a place to stay tonight,' I said, and the muscles in his face relaxed, and he sat down, putting his pint and his whisky on the table.

'You've given up on your little house?' he said. 'Quite right. I've never liked bungalows, something too suburban about them.' He was good at faking how he was really feeling.

'The sofa would do.'

'I'm sure we can do better than that.'

John held up his beer and I took my vermouth, and we chinked our glasses together.

33

From that night on, I slept in John's bed in the halfway house. His sheets were an unwashed grey and the pillows had greasy yellow circles. He put a spare pillow between us for modesty and didn't touch me, although the first night I was tensed and waiting for it, ready to fight if I had to. He kept his T-shirt and boxer shorts on, and I changed into my man-sized T-shirt in the dark with my back to him and dressed before he woke. By the third night I barely smelled the dirty sheets, the unemptied bin and the unwashed dishes. Every day I expected the police to arrive to question me again, although I didn't know what I could say except the same old story. When they didn't come, I assumed they believed they'd found their man in Vince, and I wasn't sure how I felt about that. I wondered often where Sue's body was but never came to a satisfactory explanation, only that somehow she was inside Vince.

Each evening, John and I went to a different pub where he bought the drinks. I tried to get drunk, but as soon as my tongue loosened and the floor shifted, I couldn't take another sip. In the daytime I went out, leaving him sleeping, and walked in the opposite direction from the art school and the Underwood, through a nature reserve and across the fields. There was a river out there, clear and wide, and I liked to sit on a bridge and watch the green weed flowing and the trout holding steady against the current. Once, in a village pub, I ordered a ploughman's lunch, and the landlord glared at me from behind the bar as though I might leave with the pickled onion I'd paid for.

One day, when John roused himself and went out before lunchtime – he liked to spend daylight hours in the library reading the newspapers from cover to cover – I pulled off the bedding and took it, together with all the dirty clothes I could find, to the launderette. I sat in the soft and scented air and wondered whether I could mould this life with John into a family. We could rent a flat together, he could find a job, maybe the art school would have me back, our lives would be quiet and normal, and no one would notice us. I picked up a pen and newspaper someone had left in the launderette and doodled in the margin. When the washing was dry, I looked at my strip of drawings and I saw they were of Sue. In John's room, I put the clean bedding back on the bed. When he returned, he didn't notice.

I had a small amount of money in the bank. In the end I'd been at the Underwood for only a month without paying rent, and the electricity meter had eaten coins. There would be no more pay packets from the art school, no one wanted to employ John; we were not going to get a flat together, he wouldn't be my family. I could have searched for work and my own bedsit, but I couldn't summon the energy to put anything in motion, and although I assumed Vince was still detained, and maybe that meant it wouldn't be my turn next, I wasn't ready to be alone at night. Bad dreams woke me in a sweat, and having John in the bed, on the other side of the pillow, was a comfort.

Once or twice I dragged myself out of my self-absorption and asked John about his life before the halfway house, before prison. He'd left his wallet on the table and one morning, while he was sleeping, I pulled out a photograph of a young girl held on the hip of a woman in a flowered dress. The top half of the woman had been torn away.

'Cherry,' John said, awake and watching me from the bed.

'Cherry, as in the fruit?'

'Uh-huh.'

'She's pretty.' He turned on his back, put his hands under his head. 'Do you still see her?' I asked.

'Nope,' he said.

'How old is she?'

'Now? Five and a half.' He got out of bed, picked up his dressing gown and unlocked the door. 'Put it back when you've finished looking,' he said and went out. I heard him climbing the stairs to the bathroom.

In return for the bed and the rent-free room, I cleaned, and I attempted to cook the food John bought. Sometimes I was ravenous, other times I picked at my meal. These duties were a good distraction from my thoughts and made the time pass without me having to work out what I was going to do; without having to think about much. What I couldn't stop myself from doing was drawing. On any piece of paper, I drew faces that all looked like Sue, or I drew John again as I had when I'd lived on my own in the house. I sometimes thought about the sculpture in the Underwood's garden and those murky pictures I'd pinned to the wall of my room, but they seemed disconnected from who I was in the halfway house, as though a different Ursula had made them. I tried again to ask John about Cherry but he shut me down, changed the conversation into a rant about how this country could have been so stupid as to have re-elected Margaret Thatcher, and that I must vote when I was old enough, it was my duty, and if I voted Tory he would never speak to me again.

John returned to the house one day with a box of coloured chalks and a postcard of the *Mona Lisa*. He told me the town centre was full of people with coins making holes in their pockets. I was apprehensive about going into town, worried Anita or Julie would see me and shout at me in the street about being brought up in care, demanding to know where Sue's body was. I didn't let myself think about Raymond. Joy had found me at the halfway house and we'd had a conversation on the doorstep, in which I'd told her I was all right and I was looking for work – untrue. She tried to persuade me to move, to let her find me somewhere else, but we both knew I was no longer on her list. She said Sue still hadn't been found, as though hoping this would draw new information from me, but I didn't reply. I was grateful for her concern, but there was nothing else she could do for me.

On the pedestrianized area of the high street, I put out a trilby John had lent me and got on my knees to draw my best interpretation of the *Mona Lisa*. The shoppers must have given me money for trying because the hat filled. I earned nearly fifteen pounds, and when I stood up, finished for the day, knees sore, and looked at my picture, I realized I'd drawn Sue as the woman with the enigmatic smile.

On the third sunny day of drawing, when I was walking home to the halfway house via a different route, I passed a lamp post stuck with flyers. The one that caught my eye was for the art school's Degree Show, weeks old and coming unstuck. I'd forgotten about the event. I wondered whether Georgie Bates had looked for me at the door. I pulled at a corner of the flyer and underneath was a photograph of Sue and the word MISSING and my breath tripped at seeing her face again. There was more information: her height, eye colour and when she was last seen and Anita's phone number. I thought about Anita waiting for a call that never came, or perhaps she'd received dozens of calls, none of which would have given her the answer she wanted. I thought about Raymond. It was August and he would be going to university soon.

When I got home, John said a man had called in for me. 'He left his number.' He handed me a slip of paper. For a moment I was terrified it'd been Vince, released and coming to find me.

'What did he look like?'

'Nice,' John said. 'Your type.'

The number was Raymond's. I didn't phone, but eventually he found me.

'What happens when it rains?' he asked. He was sitting on a bench in the high street one afternoon, watching me pack up my chalks, and my pulse floundered at that familiar smile, the way he swept his hair from his face.

'It gets washed away and I start again.'

'What's the painting?'

'You don't know it?' I held the postcard out to him, and he looked at it and read the back. 'Lady with an Ermine.' I had moved on from the Mona Lisa.

He compared the picture to my chalk drawing. 'Yours looks like Sue.'

'They all look like Sue.' We stared at it. 'I have nothing new to say.'

'That's not why I'm here.' He held up a paper bag. 'Buns?' He swung it. 'Cathedral grounds?'

We sat on the stone step at the base of the war memorial, and it seemed to me that Raymond had more trouble sitting than the last time I'd seen him, but I didn't think he'd want me to ask if he needed help. He'd brought two buns with pink icing, a lot of which had stuck to the paper.

'I'm going to Scotland for a couple of weeks and then I'm going to university, and I wanted to say goodbye.' He told me about his plans to visit Edinburgh and Glasgow. 'I can send you postcards if you like, paintings of Bonnie Prince Charlie and Mary Queen of Scots, as long as you don't make them look like Sue.'

'I can't promise that.'

We ate the buns. They were doughy and the sugar made my teeth ache. I tore the bag open and we shared the icing.

He talked on, about his driving test that he was taking the next day. As I watched him speak, my mind drifted to our times together at the Underwood: watching films on Vince's bed, eating the food he'd cooked, laughing, and then the seance. The blankness in his eyes. That terrible voice. I still didn't know if I believed him when he seemed not to remember any of what he'd said, how he could have known that I'd been responsible for my mother's death and what I was going to do to Sue. I would have liked to question him, but I realized he'd stopped talking and was waiting for me to speak. I had no idea what he'd been saying.

'Great that you've been learning to drive,' I said.

He laughed. 'You haven't been listening to a word. I've always been able to drive, my dad taught me on some land he owned, I just haven't passed my test yet. I was saying I've bought myself a stick, to walk with.'

'You're not using it now, though?'

'I haven't told Mum. She's weird about it. I'll use it in Scotland and at uni.'

'That's good. You should do whatever you need to do. Sod what anyone else thinks.' He asked me what my plans were, and I thought about Sue and the things she would never do: go to Scotland again, see her brother walk with the stick he needed, eat pink icing in the cathedral grounds. The first time we'd met properly she asked how I was going to get out of this place and yet here I was, still in the same town, drawing on pavements in the rain, clearing up after John, squeezing myself into his life and his bed. She would have told me I was an idiot and I should work out what I wanted to do and go and do it.

'I'm going to art school,' I said to Raymond.

He became excited, asking about which school I was going to go to, whether I'd study Sculpture or Painting, which artists I liked. I told him to slow down, I hadn't got in yet, hadn't applied, I'd probably have to do an A level or two first. I folded the paper bag in half. From his wallet he took a small piece of lined paper, opening it out on his knee. It was the drawing I'd done of Sue the day I'd met him, with the inscription *To Raymond. A nice young man. From Ursula.*

'Do you know what happened to Vince?' I asked.

'You didn't hear?' He folded the drawing with care and put it back in his wallet.

I shook my head.

'Too mentally incapacitated to be questioned and not enough evidence for him to be charged. But if she's dead, he did it.'

'Is he still locked up?'

'Sectioned and held in a secure psychiatric facility. The police won't tell us where.' I folded the bag in half again, and again. 'Ursula –'

'Really, I have nothing new to say.'

'That isn't why I came to find you. I wanted to make sure you were okay.'

'Right,' I said, imagining the posters of Sue he'd be taking with him to paste across the lamp posts of Scotland, just in case. I didn't blame him for his perseverance.

We hugged goodbye in front of the cathedral, holding on to each other a little bit longer than we might have ordinarily.

'Ursula –' he started again, but I interrupted.

'Have a great trip, and a brilliant time at uni,' I said.

I knew he was standing there, looking after me as I walked away.

34

Later that year I began studying A-level Art and working in a shop. I'd found myself a bedsit but I sometimes stayed over at John's, sleeping in his bed, the pillow no longer between us. It'd taken me a long while to be brave enough to let him touch me and to trust he wasn't horrified. But John was neither horrified nor enamoured – we both craved human warmth, and we were there to offer it.

I was asleep in his bed that October when we were woken by a tremendous roaring.

'What is that?' I said, and I felt John reach out to turn on his bedside light, but the room stayed dark.

'It's just the wind. A power cut.'

We got out of bed, and I was relieved that when we looked down on to that scrubby garden the bushes and trees were thrashing back and forth. A plastic chair tumbled across the patio like a cartwheeling child, and an angry bellowing came at the glass and shook it. The metal lids from our row of dustbins clattered up and away over the fence, and at once half-a-dozen carrier bags of rubbish were lifted out, spun round and opened, the contents scattered – pale fragments flying with the leaves and the twigs. Something fell past our window and smashed on the paving: a roof tile. Two more followed. The other tenants were on the landing, whooping and calling to each other, and someone ran up and down the stairs in the way a strong wind will make people go crazy. We got back into bed and waited for the roof to be blown off or for the storm to pass.

'Did the police ever speak to you?' I said quietly. 'About the time you came to the Underwood?'

There was a long pause before John said, 'I don't talk to the police, not if I can help it.' He opened his arm, and I tucked myself into his armpit, my head on his shoulder.

We lay like that for a while longer as the storm roared and crashed around the house. 'What did you see through the kitchen window?' I asked, but he must have been asleep because he never replied.

In the morning, while John slept on, I clambered over him, and from the window I saw that our garden and the neighbours' were decimated. Flattened fence panels and debris were strewn everywhere. I dressed and went out, walking across town, ducking under trees that blocked the roads, passing cars damaged by branches, and crunching over glass from the wall-sized windows of a function room at the back of the Guildhall. I was supposed to be heading for college, but I went wherever my feet took me, down terraced streets and through the park where the Guy Fawkes bonfire would be built in a couple of weeks. Twenty or more trees had come down, and I felt guiltily thrilled by the drama and how the world could be altered by an unseen force.

As I walked through the town, I imagined the eye of the storm, eerily calm and silent while the dustbin lids, branches and small animals flew around it, anticlockwise. Maybe the centre had been the Underwood, a kind of 55 Central Park West where everything started.

I know it is better to face head-on whatever haunts you, but that is often hard to do. The laundry room in the children's home where I'd paid ten pence to watch a girl and a boy have sex was next to my bedroom, and as well as the noises of intercourse, I also sometimes heard children sobbing. But occasionally inexplicable noises woke me: the sound of sawing when the laundry room's light was off, or the repetitive drumming of a small rubber ball as it was thrown against the wall next to my head and then caught and thrown again. My imagination conjured up horrific monsters at these noises, and sometimes I'd be awake all night waiting for the creature to creep into my room. I knew it would be better to force myself out of bed and go into the laundry room to see what was or wasn't there, but I never did it.

My art class was starting, but I found myself for the first time in four months on Barrow Road. If everything was unscathed, I would turn around, I told myself, go back to my bedsit and pack up. I would leave my course, my job, this city, and move elsewhere. I walked down the hill, past the telephone box where a tarpaulin was tangled in a tree, and when I saw the apex of the Underwood's garden I realized something was different, and it took me a moment to understand that the horse chestnut, colossal and mighty, which had once towered over the lawn, had fallen. The hurricane, as I thought of it, had pushed the tree towards the house, lifting its roots, creating a vast mud-and-chalk cavity and leaving a gap in the hedge like a missing front tooth. The trunk on its side was as broad as I was tall and the garden was a mess of branches, twigs and conkers, but the canopy, which had been stripped of leaves by the wind, had crashed through the roof of the house, partially knocking down the end wall of the kitchen and my bedroom. The area near the house was strewn with rubble and glass, as well as household items – the kitchen sink exposed to the sky, a chair upright and in front of the table we'd sat at so often, which was split in two. I looked for Mr and Mrs Andrews but didn't find them.

It was the garage that held my attention, or rather the space the garage had occupied, because the roof and the wooden walls were gone. Only the workbench remained, surrounded by a dozen or so planks. In the earth was a shallow depression.

The new openness of the sky, the birdsong and the smell of the earth after the rain all made the place feel more benign than it ever had before, despite the carnage. I went into the garden, clambering over branches to where I thought my sculpture had been, but I could see nothing of the figure being swallowed by another – it must have been crushed by the falling tree. I was glad. I would start new work as a student at an art school where nobody knew me.

Although the house must have been in danger of collapse, I scrambled over bricks and timber into what was left of my bedroom. The very top of the tree lay across my bed, and the rest of the room was scattered with twigs, plaster, roof tiles and glass. The clothes I'd left behind, the bedding and my drawings were sodden.

I was heading out of the front door – still attached but open, the glass smashed – when I remembered the pictures of me and Sue in the photo booth, pulling silly faces. Back in my bedroom, I opened the drawer of my bedside cabinet and rummaged through the bus tickets, old receipts, scraps of notes and discarded sketches. I cleared a space on the wet carpet with my shoes and tipped out the contents, shuffled through them. They weren't there.

Emma Zahini showed the pictures from the photo booth in *Dark Descent*. I paused the telly on one in particular and examined it, although I remembered it well. I'd looked at the strip of photographs many times, fishing it out of the drawer as I lay in bed. The blue curtain is behind us and I'm looking straight at the camera and smiling, while Sue is in profile with her hands around my head, pulling me towards her as she puckers for a kiss.

It was in my art class, when I was drawing a still life of dried flowers with a bowl of apples, and everyone was talking about the storm and whether they'd been woken by it or had slept right through, that I understood why the Underwood had lost its ability to terrify me: it was because the terror, the parasite, had gone elsewhere.

35

I look for similarities between Sadie and me: that we both left home at sixteen, making things up as we went along but believing we knew how the world worked. It's easier, though, to see the differences: when she was sixteen, she had a baby she decided to keep. When I was sixteen, I murdered my best friend. Sadie died when she was twenty-four – I wish I could have known her when I was an adult; I think we would have been friends.

After my Art A level, I did a foundation course in London and a degree in Sculpture at the same art school. I specialized in wood carving. A traditional method and medium, even if my variation, which is a little off-kilter, wasn't popular in the early 1990s. In those days, it was all about the YBAs, but the fact I was the same age as those young artists – who seemed mostly interested in making money, and art that shocked – and had also graduated from a prestigious school, allowed some refracted light to shine on me. I had my Degree Show, and I would have invited Georgie Bates if I'd known her whereabouts. I got a First.

A woman who was opening a gallery in London came to the show and invited me to participate in her first group exhibition, and I've been with Claudia and her gallery ever since. That makes it sound easy and simple, and it wasn't always, but in general, things have worked out well for me careerwise.

But before all that, in the first term of my third year at art school, I was working in my studio space on a model for a piece that I would go on to call *The Head of the Wind* – a carved wooden head with pursed lips and puffed cheeks and hair that flows in an unseen breeze. When the viewer walks in front of the face, which admittedly looks a lot like Sue, the second of darkness that their shadow casts registers on a photoelectric sensor hidden in the mouth, a mechanism in the plinth is triggered, and a tiny piston blows out a puff of air. Some people find it rather alarming if they're face to face with the piece and not expecting it. But this was also in the future. I was working on a wax maquette for the piece when I became aware of a conversation across the room about a fellow student's work. I recognized the voice asking the questions as Ms Barker's.

We'd been told we'd be having a visiting tutor in the Sculpture department that term, but if we'd also been told who it was going to be, I'd missed it. And I suppose Ms Barker wasn't given a list of students' names. The hairs on my arms lifted as she moved around the studio, going from space to space, asking each student about their work, commenting on it, talking through ideas, until she came to stand beside me and I smelled her perfume, the same lemony one she'd used before. She bent, hands on thighs, to better see the maquette. The model was about the size of my fist and very detailed. Wax is a wonderful material to work with, easily warmed by the fingers to be malleable, but will set to a solid when cold.

'That's beautiful,' she said. 'Are you going to cast it? Lost wax? In bronze?'

'I'm working things out,' I said. 'For a bigger piece.' I waited to see if she would react to my voice, but I didn't notice any change in her.

'In what medium?'

'Wood carving,' I said, as though it were a clue. Still nothing.

'Oak?'

'Whatever I can get my hands on.' We were facing forward, looking at the tiny head, its fine wax hair. 'But lime if I can get it.'

I explained my idea for the mechanism, and she said it sounded fascinating. She said she looked forward to seeing it develop, and she went to leave, but I stopped her with, 'I don't want to make anything that's not specific, not searching, not hungry enough.' And I was aware of her moving back from me, examining my profile, her fingers resting on my bench. She wobbled and her fingertips went red and the joints turned white from the pressure of holding herself upright, and when, finally, I looked at her, she put a hand to her cheek, but not before I saw the tiny scar.

She didn't speak, only hurried from the studio, with the student she hadn't talked to yet staring after her. I followed her out.

Ms Barker was at the end of the corridor with her hands lifted high and flat against the closed door of the Sculpture office, her head hanging between them. Her chest was heaving. I said her name and she straightened and looked at me, her face washed of colour. She had the same sharp haircut with the high straight fringe she'd had when I'd first met her. I thought maybe she'd visited the hairdresser the previous day to get her hair cut for the first day of her new job.

'I need to talk to you,' I said, gently. The wax maquette was in my hand. Behind Ms Barker was the fire exit to the outside. 'I need to know if he said anything to you that day.' Ms Barker's eyes glittered, nervously. 'He did, didn't he?'

'Nothing happened.' Her voice cracked. 'He didn't say anything.'

'I know he did. I know it.'

She made a sound in the back of her throat and took a step away.

'Was he trying to find me?' All the time I spoke I was inching forward, hands behind my back so as not to scare her, to make her stay and talk. 'He's going to get out, one day. They're going to let him out and I think he'll come for me.' My voice was rising and I tried to control it; I had never expressed this out loud before. 'I know he said something to you.'

'No!' she said sharply, as though warning a child moving a finger towards a flame.

'Is he coming? Please.'

Ms Barker moved further back, depressing the bar across the fire exit door, releasing herself backwards.

'Please!' I shouted, but she slipped out as the alarm wailed through the building and students stuck their heads out of the studios, no one hurrying to leave, only Ms Barker running away across the car park. The wax head in my hand had softened to a featureless ball.

Ms Barker didn't return as our visiting tutor, and in the following thirty years I never bumped into her again. I've followed her progress in the art world – she's been doing well with her conceptual pieces, shown and collected around the world. For years, whenever I was invited to exhibit in a group show, I would find out whether she'd be exhibiting too, hopeful we'd meet again and that she might talk to me, but we never have shared an exhibition space, and I can only suppose she does the same checks.

36

If I was aware in my peripheral vision of Ms Barker's success, it was Vince and Raymond I actively looked for. Finding information in the papers or online about the former was almost impossible. All I came across was a paragraph confirming what Raymond had told me: that after Vince had been caught at the art school he'd been sectioned and detained in a secure psychiatric hospital. I knew the authorities wouldn't inform me if he was going to be released – I wasn't his victim and I certainly wasn't a member of the victim's family – and so I was always watchful, always careful. At night I didn't walk home alone, and I was selective about who I gave my address to. I moved from one rented flat to another every year or so, learning about but avoiding my neighbours. My close friends had my mobile number, and I always let it go to voicemail when it rang; my post was delivered to a post-box address; and I rarely called anyone – any social life I had was arranged by email.

Raymond's progress, however, was often in full view. Tracking him became easier when the internet came along: there he was in an old photograph throwing his mortarboard in the air, his name on a list of those called to the bar by his Inn of Court, a picture of him on a flight of steps after winning a high-profile case. It was easy to track his career if not his personal life. I never searched the internet for 'the Bloodworths' or 'the Underwood'.

A few years after I graduated, I had my first solo show in London. Claudia indulged my insistence on privacy – I think she felt it gave her gallery added cachet to have an artist on her list who was a recluse and went by the name of Uschi. Pretentious? Maybe, but it helped me stay below the radar. The anxiety about Vince being let out and coming to find me was fading, but it had not gone.

It took me a long time to build up a big enough body of work for a show – smaller wood carvings and larger pieces that incorporated found or manufactured parts. My drawings were framed and put on the walls: large, expressive faces in charcoal that I'd got on my hands and knees to make, which a reviewer later assumed were of the same woman. Claudia provided the wine, nibbles and the guest list for the private view. I only had to turn up and closet myself in her office, where she would bring the collectors and dealers to meet me, at least the ones she thought were serious.

Through her small office window, I could see that the place was packed. She brought in five people in quick succession to talk about particular pieces of work, and I tried to give them answers that would make Claudia happy. After these there were no more, and for an hour I sat hidden until, bored, I decided to sneak away, but as soon as I was out of the office door, Claudia was there, waving her hands as though herding me back inside. We were almost tussling when a man came up, and Claudia and I stepped apart, disgraced. He wore round wire-rimmed glasses on a symmetrical face, almost too perfect. Claudia had no choice but to introduce us, and the man, Philippe, who was

French, began to gush about how honoured he was to meet me and that he loved everything in the show.

'I hope you don't mind,' he said to Claudia. 'But I brought a friend with me. I know how exclusive the invitations were, but I thought you could squeeze another one in. He says he knows nothing about art, but I am sure he lies.' Philippe turned to me. 'Apparently he does know you, Uschi, from a previous life, when this was not your name.' My smile was stuck to my face, and I was aware of the rictus strain of it. Claudia raised an eyebrow, intrigued that my cover was blown, and Philippe scanned the crowd for his friend. Was there time to run, pack up my life, change my name again, move house?

'There he is!' Philippe waved. 'Over here, Ray!'

I saw him work his way through the people. He was using a stick, and as he came closer I heard its metallic click each time it touched the ground. He was wearing a suit, tie and waistcoat. A goatee covered his chin, and his hair was swept back, receding. I patted my own hair, trying to tame it, and stood up straighter, pulled on the bottom of the jacket I was wearing, and we looked at each other, our smiles widening.

'Uschi,' he said.

'Ray,' I replied.

'How do you two know each other?' Claudia said.

'Old friends,' I said.

'How long has it been?' he asked, and I knew that he knew, maybe to the month or the day.

'More than ten years,' I said, knowing too.

'From school?' Claudia asked.

He shook his head, and a buyer came up wanting to speak and Claudia guided me back into the office. *Wait*, I mouthed at Ray.

After the show a group of us went out for food, and Ray came too. He found a seat at the opposite end of the table to me, and every so often during conversations with our neighbours we'd catch each other's eye, and a churning would start inside me, a need to touch him, squeeze his arm and make sure he was real. I was worried that he still might think me unbalanced, and that he was here to ask what I knew, while of course I wanted, needed, whatever information he had about Vince and whether he was still locked up.

People left the restaurant in dribs and drabs, putting the money for what they'd eaten on the table or paying by card at the bar, until only Ray and Claudia were left. She yawned, stood and kissed me on the cheek.

'It went well tonight. Bravo.'

'Did we sell anything?'

'We sold nearly all of it, and there's definite interest in the other pieces. Back to the studio with you, my girl.' She kissed me again, and whispered in my ear, 'You'll be all right, on your own?'

'Yes,' I said. 'All good.' She blew Ray a kiss, waved her fingers and left.

We sat and smiled at each other for a minute, and using his stick, he stood and gathered the cash. 'I think we made a tidy profit,' he said, stacking it together, sitting next to me.

'Hello, Raymond,' I said.

'Hello, Ursula,' he replied.

We ordered coffee and caught up on each other's lives. He said he was moving chambers to one that specialized more in murder and violent crime. I told him about my degree in Sculpture, the work I'd been making since, Claudia, the gallery. He told me what the twins were up to at school, and what Andrew was into, who was eleven, although I couldn't believe it. Ray said his grandmother had died and his grandfather was in a home. Anita and Julie, he mentioned in passing. I waited for him to ask about Sue, the Underwood and Vince, assuming he'd want to know if my story had changed, but he didn't. I tried to work out if he was married – there was no ring on his finger – or whether he had a partner, children. When we were outside, he gave me a business card and didn't press me when I didn't give him my number in return.

'Call me,' he said.

'I will,' I said, although the thought of picking up the phone made my mouth dry. I needed to flag down a cab and get home, sit behind a locked door.

We went in opposite directions, but when I looked over my shoulder, Ray was looking over his. He turned and walked backwards, and I did the same, and he held his fist to his ear, thumb and little finger pointing out. 'Ring, ring,' he said loudly. We stopped walking, and I lifted my hand to my ear.

'Hello?' I said, looking at him.

'Hello, is that Ursula?'

'It is. Who's this, please?'

'Your old friend Ray.'

'Oh, Ray, great to hear from you.'

'Are you busy tomorrow evening?'

'No,' I said. 'Not really.'

'Can I cook you dinner?'

Ray's apartment was as minimal and clean-lined on that first visit as it was in *Dark Descent*; even the way he cooked was without mess. He opened the door wearing an apron and using his stick, and we kissed on both cheeks, laughing when we went in the same direction. In the kitchen he sang a little as he looked in the oven and declared the involtini would be ready in twenty minutes. They smelled delicious but I was too nervous to think about eating. He poured me a glass of fizzy water and took me on a tour: one big room with the kitchen and an island at one end, dining table for eight and a living area with a balcony and a view of central London in the distance. Down a book-lined hall was an office, window-less bathroom, loo and bedroom. He flung this door open, and we stood looking at his bed and he laughed.

'What?' I said.

'I know you like to get the layout of a place when you first visit,' he said.

Over dinner he told me about Ehlers-Danlos, the connective tissue syndrome he'd been diagnosed with a year or so ago. His mother, he said, still didn't acknowledge it, although it was genetic. He said the worst of it was the chronic pain in his hips and back, sometimes so bad he couldn't get out of bed. He'd been on antidepressants, but they'd dulled his brain and didn't reduce the pain. His elbows sometimes dis-located in his sleep, and he'd wake up screaming, and he'd had to learn how to pop them back in himself. Being in court was the hardest thing because he was expected to stand for hours, days, weeks, and he said he was thinking about using a wheelchair so the clerks and the judges would consider him disabled, and sitting down, he would be in less pain.

'You can leave now, if you want,' he said and laughed.

I half stood and his eyebrows shot up, and I sat down, laughing too.

I was still waiting for him to ask about Sue and the night she had knocked on the windows, stuck her fingers through the letter box. In my own flat beforehand I'd practised my answers in front of a mirror, sounding defensive, angry, defiant, and telling myself that if he did ask, I would leave and not see him again. But the questions didn't come and I relaxed into the evening.

I wanted to ask about Vince, but in the end it was Ray who mentioned him.

'They haven't let him out,' he said. 'I thought you'd want to know. And they never should. He deserves to be locked up for life.' There was bitterness in his voice, anger. 'Don't worry, you'll hear about it if he does get out. I'll make sure it's all over the news. And I'll be the first to ask him where Sue's body is.'

What could I say? Declare Vince's innocence again? If I did, I didn't have an alternative narrative that would satisfy Ray, and I had to admit I also didn't want Vince to be set free.

After coffee, I called a taxi, and Ray didn't press me to stay. I gave him my address and mobile number, telling him that I never answered my phone and that he would have to leave a message. We kissed on the cheek and held each other, and the smell of him, the warmth of his body, was the closest I'd ever felt to coming home.

I switched my phone on more often over the next few days to check whether he'd called, and when he hadn't, that old sick feeling of rejection crept in, and anger, and then I didn't switch my phone on at all. Seeing him had resurrected the questions I'd pushed to the back of my mind for ten years. Where was Sue's body? And was it my turn next? I had bad dreams and sleepless nights; I couldn't work so I stayed at home, pacing and worrying.

A week after our dinner, I looked out of my kitchen window and saw a chalked message on the pavement below:

Ring, ring
2nite, 7.30
The Harp, NW1

I looked up the Harp online and found that it was a boozer in Camden. I thought about the reasons not to go. It would be impossible to ignore the elephant in the room forever, and he would leave me in the end, so there was no point in starting anything.

The bar was crowded and smoky, and I looked for Ray but couldn't see him. At one end was a small platform with a woman standing on it coming to the end of a song. A group of women around her cheered and clapped, and I thought, *Oh God, karaoke*. I pushed my way to the bar and ordered a lime and soda. The chatter of the crowd increased between songs and more music started – a Rhodes piano – and a man began singing about meeting his old lover on the street the previous evening, and the room hushed, and everyone looked towards the stage. Ray's voice was the same as it had been all those years ago, if anything deeper and more mellow. He'd shaved off the goatee, leaving a thick moustache, and he wore a shapeless fedora pulled down low, and as he sang about drinking a beer with his lover he raised his bottle towards the people watching and to me at the bar, and the crowd lifted their glasses and their bottles back to him and sang along to 'Still Crazy After All These Years'. When he'd finished, he put down the mic, but the crowd, who seemed to know him and had maybe come that night to see him, started chanting for more. Ray pinched his fedora to give it back its dimples, clicked his fingers and waggled his head. He sang 'Fly Me to the Moon' without taking his eyes off me, so that in the end people were turning to look. When he finished, the place erupted, and I couldn't stop smiling.

I invited Ray back to my place that night. I'd slept with a couple of men in the intervening decade but neither relationship had been significant, and each time the sex had been with the lights out or most of my clothes on. Ray and I kissed on my doorstep and then halfway up the stairs, and at the top I unbuttoned his shirt and simultaneously tried to unlock my front door. Inside, on my bed with him on top of me, I took his hands, made him pause, suddenly unsure, shy.

'Is it the moustache?' he said, drawing back so he could focus on my face. He stroked it. 'Too much seventies porn star?'

'It's not *your* body hair I'm worried about.'

'I love everything about you, Ursula Major,' he said. 'You are beautiful.'

'We have to promise each other something,' I said.

'What?'

'We have to promise not to hurt each other.'

'I promise.'

'We have a lot of history.'

'We'll work it out.' He lay down with his mouth beside my ear and sang, 'Still Crazy After All These Years'.

Ray flattened my resistance until there was nothing else to do except trust him. I introduced him properly to Claudia and her family and the people I shared studio space with. We went out for drinks and meals with Philippe and his girl-friend, Louisa, and Ray's new colleagues. He stayed at my place, and I stayed at his. He told me over and over that I was beautiful, and while I never quite came to believe it, I did believe he thought it, and that was enough.

I was at my most creative during those months, all my work turning out well even if it still did look like Sue, and I was able to tap into an energy I hadn't felt since that first sculpture and the murky drawings I'd made at the Underwood. I was twenty-eight and Ray was thirty-two.

All Ray's friends seemed to be getting married that summer, and nearly every weekend was taken up with weddings in grand hotels, hearing vows exchanged in flower-swagged barns or attending barefoot ceremonies in the woods. Sometimes I felt Ray was building up to asking me to marry him, but I wasn't ready, and maybe he sensed I would have said *Not yet*, because this question never came.

37

In September it was Philippe's turn to get married to Louisa, with Ray as their best man. The service was in a Dorset church near to where Louisa grew up, famous for its sheela-na-gig and other carvings. The day before the wedding, I went to the church with Louisa and her mother, and while they checked the flowers, I studied the crude sculptures, thinking about the work I was in the middle of and itching to get back to it.

In the evening Louisa's parents hosted a dinner in a local hotel where we were staying. The food kept coming and I kept eating: crab rarebit on a crumpet, roasted halibut with homemade black pudding, creamed leeks and truffle emulsion, a choux bun with spiced pumpkin custard, yogurt sorbet, praline sauce. Food I didn't know existed. When we'd finished, the guests went off to bed until only Ray and me and Philippe and Louisa were left in the lounge for coffee and liqueurs.

'It'll be you two next,' Louisa said. She was tiny, slotting under Philippe's arm where they reclined on the sofa opposite ours.

'I don't know,' I said. 'I'm sure Ray will find someone with fewer hang-ups.' It was self-deprecation, but I was beginning to think maybe we could make this work, convincing myself there was a tacit agreement between us not to talk about Sue and what happened at the Underwood, and that, in some warped way, meant we were being honest with each other.

'Those low-maintenance women,' Ray said. 'They're not all they're cracked up to be.'

'What you see is what you get,' Louisa said. 'How boring is that?'

'I like my women with hidden depths.' He put his arm around me, kissed me hard on the cheek, made me smile, and we settled back into the sofa's cushions.

'You shouldn't keep secrets,' Philippe said to me in his French accent. His eyes behind his round glasses were un-focused, his lips slack. 'Not from the man you're going to marry.' I could hear the alcohol in his voice, and it set my heart thumping, an irregular beat that made me want to outrun it. I looked from Ray to Philippe and back again with a smile on my face, trying to work out what he meant. Ray would, I supposed, have told his old friend about Sue's dis-appearance and her murder, telling it as though Vince was the perpetrator, but surely he wouldn't have said anything about my involvement? Not when he and I hadn't talked about it. Ray's expression gave nothing away.

'What does that mean?' I said, too aggressively.

'Say no more.' Philippe pretended to zip his mouth.

Louisa stiffened, but Philippe was too drunk to notice. 'Have you taken Ray to meet your parents yet?' she asked me, and I appreciated her trying to reroute the conversation, but I also thought that whatever Ray had told Philippe, Philippe would have told Louisa. They knew my history through Ray's filtered view of a mental breakdown, hallucinations, and however else he might have described it, and I hadn't known they knew. Who had Louisa told? Her mother? I'd caught her gazing at me when I was looking at the sculptures in the church, and we'd smiled. I'd thought she liked me.

For a second I considered snapping back that my father had died in a tragic accident and my mother had left me with a bear in Canada, but Louisa was friendly, interested without being nosy. I thought she and I might grow into closer friends.

'They're both dead,' I said. Ray's arm was over my shoulder, and he hugged me. I didn't like telling lies, but I didn't want to make her feel uncomfortable.

'Oh my goodness, I'm so sorry.' She leaned over the low table with the cups and the glasses and the glossy magazines, stretching to touch my knee. She sat back on the sofa, separate from Philippe.

I gave her a quick smile, said, 'It's all right, it was a long time ago.'

'Ray's father is very rich,' Philippe said, as though jumping ahead in a conversation we hadn't had. 'And his mother is very . . .' He paused to consider. 'Forlorn.' He seemed pleased with the word. 'I went home with Ray once and met her and his grandfather and Auntie Julie. They are forlorn.'

'We know.' Louisa spoke firmly without looking at him. 'Do you have any siblings?' she asked me.

Philippe cut in before I could answer. 'Ray has sisters, and a brother, I think.'

'Twin sisters and a brother,' Ray said, and his leg twitched where it touched mine.

'This is correct.' Philippe rubbed his brow with a thumb and forefinger. 'This is correct. And there is your other sister.' He shook his head. 'That is a sad story.'

'Ray doesn't want to talk about this stuff,' Louisa said.

'Maybe not the night before your wedding,' Ray said.

'We should go to bed. I'm tired.' Louisa stood and tugged on Philippe's arm. 'Big day tomorrow.'

'That is a very sad story.' Philippe didn't move. Louisa gave another tug and let him go but remained standing. We knew there would be no stopping Philippe. Ray's leg jigged. We'd promised not to hurt each other, but I didn't know what that meant. He probably thought it was okay to tell his best friend that I'd claimed I killed his sister and then saw her dead body walk around. Or did Ray still think I was holding something back and was waiting for the right moment to drag it out of me? He and I had been seeing each other for more than three months, but instead of having that conversation, we'd been pasting over the past with wedding breakfasts, church services, flower arrangements and fancy dinners until it had become impossible to strip them back and reveal what we each believed had happened at the Underwood. It was too difficult to get to that bottom layer – the smooth pink plaster. If we'd been able to expose the whole wall, naked and vulnerable, we'd have found areas where the plaster had crumbled, where we'd been too rough with the scraper, leaving holes and cracks that would have brought the whole lot down.

'Has Ray told you how sad he is?' Philippe asked me. Ray's leg bounced. 'Ray, did you tell her? You have to tell her if you're going to marry her, your spouse has to know everything. I know' – he surprised us by throwing his torso forward and grabbing Louisa around the thighs – 'everything about my fiancée. Isn't that true?'

'That's true,' she said, and gave an awkward laugh, moving so that he had to let her go. He launched himself back against the sofa.

'Your sister . . . what was her name?' Philippe asked.

'Sue.' Ray's leg seemed to be unhinged from his hip.

'What was that?'

'Sue,' he repeated in a monotone.

'Sue, that's right. She is disappeared, yes? Or dead. Can you imagine what this is like for Ray's mother?' It was unclear who Philippe was addressing or whether he was saying it to remind himself. 'Can you imagine?' He jabbed his finger at me. My face heated up and I wanted to put my hands to my cheeks, but I knew the action would make what I was feeling – shock, shame, a rising anger – more obvious.

'Come on,' Ray said. 'This isn't the time or the place.'

'Not knowing.' Philippe looked like he might cry.

'Philippe!' Louisa said loudly, to make him stop. She gave his arm another tug and he blundered to his feet, almost toppling her. 'I think someone needs to get to bed,' she said as though Philippe were her child. 'I'm so sorry, Ray. You know how he gets when he's drunk. Bloody maudlin Frenchman.' She pushed him and he staggered towards the door, and they left, Louisa apologizing again.

Ray and I remained on the sofa looking ahead, and then we turned towards each other.

'Ursula –' he started.

'You told them,' I said.

He lowered his chin, surprised at my accusation. 'I didn't.'

'You told Philippe about what I saw at the Underwood, and he told Louisa.' I hissed the words, feeling the betrayal like a cloud around my head.

'I told him about Sue. I didn't say anything about you.' Ray pressed on his thigh to stop it moving.

'Then how does he know? He said I shouldn't keep secrets!'

Ray flopped backwards with a sigh. 'He wasn't talking about you. He was talking about Louisa. She had a fling. Last year. He found out. They agreed not to talk about it.'

'He pointed his finger and accused me.'

'He didn't,' Ray said, gently, which made me furious. I wanted him to fight back, I wanted him to be angry. 'Philippe doesn't know. I swear, I didn't say anything. Anyway, it's nothing to be ashamed of. Loads of people have mental health issues.'

'It wasn't a mental health issue.' I spoke through my teeth. 'It happened.' Anger was lighting a fire in my gut, stinging my nose.

'Don't do this, please.'

'It happened to you too, but conveniently, you don't remember.'

'What do you mean?'

'The seance. Sue didn't want me to tell you.'

'Tell me what?' He looked confused.

'During the seance, in the Underwood's kitchen. Before you had the seizure, before you blacked out, something spoke through you.'

'Don't be ridiculous.'

I flung my hands up. 'You see! You won't believe it. But it happened. It all happened. You shouted at us, you didn't recognize your own sister.'

'It was a seizure. I say and do all sorts of things and don't remember them.' He was still calm.

'You think this will work, you and me?' I said. 'When we believe such different things, when we never talk about Sue? You think we can spend the rest of our lives together and never speak about what happened? What's your mum going to think? Julie?' I waved my hand. 'The rest of your family?'

'I don't care what they think.'

He was living a fantasy; I could see that now.

'It's too big. It's too fucking big.' I was shouting and it didn't matter. 'I need you to listen, and you won't let me speak.' Ray shook his head, pleading. 'I know why you haven't told your family that we're seeing each other. I know exactly why. Because they'll want me, the girl who was brought up in care, to tell them where Sue's body is. They won't understand how you can have been with me all this time and not asked. They'll be furious with you, and you won't be able to stand that.'

'Ursula,' he said, reaching for me as I edged away.

I wanted to goad him; it wasn't possible to have an argument with someone who wouldn't argue back. He would leave me at some point; better to make it happen now. His leg was jumping, and his hand continued to pin it.

'I'll tell you again if you'll listen,' I said. 'You can tell Anita again and Julie again, and you can tell Philippe and Louisa and the whole bloody world, if you like.' I stood. 'I killed her.'

He reached for me once more, but I stepped back. 'No, it was Vince,' he said. 'He did it. If the court hadn't thought he was too crazy to stand trial, he'd have been convicted. I don't know why you're still saying this.'

I talked over him. 'I murdered her, and I buried her in the hole we dug for the film, and I don't know where her body went.'

Ray's teeth clamped together. If it was going to end, I wanted it to end immediately.

'For fuck's sake!' he shouted. 'Do you even hear yourself?'

I had him. I had raised him to anger. 'You know what?' I said. 'You're right. This isn't going to work.'

'I never said that.'

I marched around the opposite sofa so he couldn't reach me.

'Give my apologies to Philippe and Louisa, but I don't think I'll be staying for the wedding.'

I was aware that the apology didn't sound like I meant it. Ray struggled out of his seat, grabbing the arm of the sofa, collecting his stick, which swung wildly, knocking a couple of magazines to the floor.

'Wait,' he said. 'You can't end an argument by walking out.'

But I was gone.

Upstairs, I flung my wedding clothes and toiletries into my case. At any moment I expected Ray to come in and try again, and as much as I wanted him to, I was thinking of more arguments I could throw at him. I was almost at the door when I saw his wallet on the bedside table – it was unusual that he hadn't put it in the room's safe. I opened it, and from an inner pocket I pulled out a lined piece of paper, the middle creased with age, the edges brown. It was the picture of Sue I'd drawn the day I'd met him. I had captured her well in a few simple lines: the expression on her face, the tilt of her head. The sister I'd taken from him. I tore it, straight down the middle, and I ripped these two pieces in half, stacked the four quarters on top of his wallet, and left. In reception I rang the bell until a man arrived who found the times of the trains and called me a taxi. I paid for everything I'd eaten and half the room bill, and I stood outside the hotel until the car arrived, glancing over my shoulder and willing the door to open and Ray to emerge. I waited on the station platform for an hour for the night train to London, the late-summer evening cooling my anger. The feeling of victory was seeping away. In the carriage I rested my head against the window and watched the world blur past. I was still hungry.

38

How does a life pass? Twenty-three years since I saw Ray at Philippe and Louisa's wedding. My mind thundering at every private view in case he turned up; disappointment when he didn't. Twenty-three years of making work and avoiding publicity, renting flats and studio spaces, a couple of relationships that didn't last, travel with friends, evening classes to catch up on my education, time spent with Claudia and her family, living through a pandemic, searching for Vince's name online, hours and hours in therapy. I've told my therapists what happened to me, what I did, and most of them didn't try to convince me otherwise. I've found them very accepting once they learn that I have attempted to tell the police. They ask what it's like for me to carry this experience around, how I feel about not being able to speak to people about it. It helps to talk, but it's not a solution.

In 2005, *The Lithopedion* made me, if not a household name, famous in the art world, and the commissions and exhibitions that followed provided enough money for me, at fifty-one, to decide to settle and buy a third-floor flat in a mansion block in West London. I was excited not to have a landlord who might spring a rent increase on me or decide they were going to put my flat up for sale, and not to have a contract that stated I couldn't put a nail in a wall to hang a picture.

*

The flat had good bones, as they say. Lofty rooms with ornate cornices, a large ceiling rose in the sitting room, one enormous bedroom, a bathroom without windows and a kitchen diner which needed ripping out and replacing. The carpets too had to be taken up and the floors sanded and repolished, and the whole lot would have to be redecorated before I could move in. For now, I had only brought over a kettle.

It was the sash windows in the sitting room that sold it to me. They spanned the west and south walls – I had blown the budget on a corner flat – and were floor to ceiling, with wide sills and views beyond the low Juliet balconies to the roofs of the buildings opposite, and in the distance the green of a park.

It was July, late afternoon, and a buttery light came through the glass, spilling across the old carpets and the single dining chair that had been left by the previous owner. I tried to open each window to let in some air, but none of them would budge. Another job to add to the long list of jobs that needed doing.

The doorbell rang and in the small lobby I opened the front door. I was expecting a builder Claudia had recommended, and he was red in the face and sweating, carrying his jacket over his arm.

'Mr Yates?' We got the introductions over with and I let him in.

'I hope that lift is working when we do the job,' he said, following me into the kitchen. 'It'll be a long way up those stairs with a toilet bowl in my arms.'

I explained I wanted the kitchen ripped out and a new one put in. 'Appliances and sink in the same place?' he asked. I hadn't thought. 'It'll cost more if you move them. What about the consumer unit – the fuse box? It'll need upgrading, doesn't look like this place has been touched in, what, thirty years?'

'About that,' I said, feeling more disconsolate as we moved from room to room. He shook his head at everything I showed him but whistled when we stood in the middle of the sitting room. 'Very nice,' he said. 'Very nice.'

'I want the carpets taken up. There are parquet floors underneath.'

He slung his jacket over the back of the chair and groaned as he lowered himself to his knees. He pulled a screwdriver out of a pocket, dug at a corner of the carpet and tutted.

'You've got live woodworm here,' he said. 'Going to have to treat the whole place.'

I got down on the floor beside him and ran a finger over what were clearly ancient holes. I stood up. 'Well,' I said, already decided. 'Thanks for your time.' He stood too and I showed him to the door, and he hung around on the landing at the top of the stairs telling me I shouldn't leave that woodworm for too long and that he'd get a quote to me next week. 'Thanks,' I said twice more and closed the door.

In the sitting room a fly buzzed at the glass and, disgusted, I tried again to open a sash. Three storeys down, the builder was striding along the pavement, speaking on his phone. He wasn't going to get the job; I would find someone else, ask for other quotes, make sure I hired a builder who knew what they were talking about. I still worked in wood, and I knew live woodworm when I saw it. I turned back to the room, pleased again with its proportions, imagining it when it was finished and how beautiful it would be. Mr Yates's leather jacket was on the back of the chair, and I picked it up, irritated that I would have to see him again, and undecided about whether I'd be able to get downstairs and run after him before he disappeared. I turned to the window as though I might be able to bang on it to get his attention. At the same time, I heard a knock on the front door and, pleased, I went again towards the little lobby, but it wasn't the builder. Instead, a different man stood there: leathery-faced, a sore beside his mouth, a patchy beard and black hair streaked with grey, gathered into a low bun.

Vince.

I stepped back, dropping the jacket. Vince – after all these years of wondering if he was ever going to get out, here he was. I'd been beginning to think he must have died in his institution.

He coughed, started to speak, cleared his throat. 'Ursula,' he said, and stepped forward, and I wondered whether Ray knew he was out, or Anita – if she was alive. Vince wore a rumpled suit several sizes too large for his scrawny body, a dirty T-shirt, scuffed trainers. He looked like he'd been clothed by the Salvation Army with whatever was to hand, and he reminded me of some of those men I'd shared the halfway house with. This sad man was Vince, nothing else.

He came forward into the flat and I retreated, laughing at myself for those years of moving houses, hiding my identity, and this is what I'd been afraid of? This grizzled and shrunken man?

'How did you find me?' I said, and put my finger to my nose as I moved backwards, aware of an unwashed smell, sweat and old urine. He walked into the sitting room and I followed.

'Why are you here?' I said to the back of his head. This flat, my own after so long, shouldn't have Vince in it.

'They locked me up,' he said, looking around at the space. 'But you must have known that. And now they've chucked me out. Care in the community. My loony bin was one of the last to go. Not *loony bin*, we're not supposed to say that. Psychiatric hospital.'

He might have been speaking to himself. He was facing the windows, the light silhouetting his gaunt shape, his loose clothes. The fly buzzed at the glass. 'They claimed I did all sorts of things, but I don't remember. None of it.'

Did he not remember his agitation in the bathroom of the Underwood when he told me Sue was inside him, or when he lay on the floor of the art school's lobby, his body emaciated and bitten, the chandelier swaying above him? These images had stayed with me a lifetime. 'You have a beautiful place,' he said. I didn't reply.

He made a noise, and I realized he was humming, a snatch of melody I felt I should recognize, and the hairs rose on the back of my neck. I pressed a hand against the wall to keep myself from falling, as I heard again the sad piano music on the record player. I remembered Sue and me laughing together, and then her dead body on the sofa in the garden, and that thing at the door, humming through the letter box.

'It's hot, isn't it?' Vince said. 'I'm so thirsty.' And I was aware of a pulsing in my throat, a drone inside my head, the taste of soap in my mouth.

'Get out,' I said.

'Surely you'd give an old friend a glass of water.' Vince still had his back to me, and I willed him to turn, and I willed him to stay where he was.

A stomach-churning stink filled the room, shit and decay, and I put my sleeve to my nose. The fly was at the window and in the kitchen the kettle began to rumble.

'She's still inside me, you know,' he said as he turned. The moments were long and terrible.

I stared as he opened his mouth, a dark hole behind bad

teeth, and I remembered him choking in the bathroom of the Underwood, but this time Vince slowly stuck out his tongue. As though called by the smell, the fly came from the window, looping across the room and buzzing around Vince's head before it settled on that slab of pinkish-grey meat. As I watched, he withdrew his tongue, taking the fly into his mouth and closing his lips. He swallowed. I pressed my fingers against my own lips, trying not to gag. He didn't take his eyes off me, but I dragged mine away and noticed, on the back of his hand, a circular red welt. A bite. He began to smile, a slow turning up of the corners, a parting between the sparse beard. And then without warning he charged at the window, moving sideways, head and shoulders first like a bull, crashing through the glass, the window shattering outwards with a tremendous noise.

I ran forward as he toppled backwards over the low balcony, and I caught at a scrap of trouser fabric. One of his hands gripped the rail and the metal creaked and groaned with the strain, and something gave way with a jolt. There was an instant when our eyes met and I thought I saw the young man I'd known in the art school staff room, the one who liked a laugh, who taught me how to breathe.

'I'm sorry,' Vince said and released his fingers, and the cloth of his trousers was snatched from my grasp. I cantilevered in space for a second until I tipped myself back over the sill and into the room.

I didn't hear the thump of Vince's body as it hit the pavement three floors below, but someone on the road began to scream.

Down on the street, I glanced once at his body before I turned away, but it was clear he must have landed headfirst. People came out of their houses and gathered in small groups, and faces stared out of the windows on either side of the road. An ambulance arrived and the paramedics pronounced Vince dead. I sat on the stretcher, shaking, and let them check me over, but I said I didn't need to go to hospital, although my hands and thighs were bruised and my shoulders wrenched. They put plasters on a couple of scratches and let me go.

The police came and looked under the blue blanket covering the body, and one of them closed the road. Out on the street, two officers asked me some questions, and with chattering teeth I told them I'd known Vincent Goldie a long time ago and I believed he'd been in an institution for many years, and I didn't know why he'd come to find me. The police officers came upstairs to see the flat, and when we returned to the street they asked whether they could call anyone for me, and I thought about asking for Ray but I didn't remember his number and no longer had his card, and I knew if he came he would ask more about Vince than I could explain, and so I said no.

I went home and contacted Mr Yates, told him he'd left his jacket and asked him to board up the window when the police had finished. I put the flat back on the market.

39

The police told me that I'd need to go to the station the next day to make a full statement, and I assumed it would be a formality, but when I arrived I was taken into an interview room by a detective. He'd searched for Vince in their database, and it seemed his name and mine had come up in connection with the disappearance of Suzannah Whelan.

It made me clammy, waiting in one of those little rooms again, thinking about Vince and parasites. Had he passed something to me during our encounter, or had he killed himself to save me? I had touched the fabric of his trousers, not the man, but I had no idea how this thing was passed from one person to another. I'd lain awake the previous night thinking again about how parasites move from host to host without discrimination. Some of us might deserve the infestation, but others were just in the wrong place at the wrong time. Collateral damage. Maybe none of this mattered; perhaps Vince's death had put an end to it. This time he hadn't said it was my turn next. Perhaps it was over.

The detective came in and sat opposite me and said I'd been listed as a friend of Suzannah Whelan. He asked whether Vince had mentioned her before he died, and I lied and said he hadn't. The detective wanted me to go over what had happened in the flat, to be clear I supposed about whether Vince had jumped or fallen or been pushed.

I told him Vince had asked for a glass of water and had then become deranged, humming and eating flies, and that he'd charged across the room and smashed through the window. I said I'd tried to grab hold of him, but he'd fallen. I didn't mention the terrible smell, or that he'd said he was sorry. The detective had no other questions; I made a statement, signed it and was allowed to leave.

The police interview room prompted memories of Joy sitting next to me chain-smoking, and when I got home I searched for her online. I found some information about her career and a couple of pictures of her dancing and accepting a prize. I remembered her in the kitchen of the halfway house bringing a bottle of milk out of her handbag, and often biscuits too, and once a head of broccoli. Joy had died of cancer five years before. She'd been one of those people whom I didn't think about from one year to the next, but I'd always assumed she was alive somewhere in the world and that one day I'd have a chance to thank her. It was painful to learn that on an ordinary day, when I was going about my life, she'd died, and it was hard to comprehend how this could have happened without me being aware. I wept a little, for her, for the girl I'd once been, and for Vince.

A day or so later the *Evening Standard* carried a brief piece about a man with mental health issues dying after falling from the window of an empty West London flat.

I thought about Ray often in the following couple of weeks, searching for him online again too. I assumed the police would have updated him or Anita about Vince's death, but I had no idea whether they would have mentioned my involvement and told him I'd said Vince hadn't talked about Sue. I waited for Ray to get in touch. I checked my email more regularly, turned on my mobile and left it on, until I turned it off again. Despondent, unsurprised.

I went online looking for more details of Vince's life and death. Like an itch I cautioned myself not to scratch I was able to leave it for days, and then in a burst of furious clawing I would pass hours scanning news sites and message boards for the name Vincent Goldie. Finally, on a funeral directors' website, I found the date and location of Vince's burial. I had a brief thought of attending before I dismissed the idea, remembering he'd once told me he didn't like funerals, and sure that his parents wouldn't want me there. When the day and the time arrived, I sat on the sofa in my new rented apartment and imagined the service, the coffin in the back of the hearse, his parents beside the grave, heads lowered. I lowered my head too and thought about these rites and rituals that Sue had never had.

The coroner's office got in touch and asked me to write a witness statement, and I gave the same information I'd given to the police. I posted it back and, not long after, I received another letter with a date for me to attend the inquest.

Vince's parents were in the waiting area of the West London Coroner's Court. I knew it had to be them, a couple in their eighties, accompanied by a man of about my age, early fifties. Their nephew, I thought, because Vince hadn't had a brother, only a sister. The woman's thin hair formed a cloud around her pinkish scalp, and she used a tissue to dab under her eyes. The man had a clear tube pressed into each nostril and hooked over his ears, and the wheeze of his oxygen tank came every minute or so and was the only sound in the room. Was this the man who'd said that football was common? The four of us waited without acknowledging each other.

I'd imagined the inquest would take place in a courtroom with the coroner sitting above us, but we were ushered into a meeting room with a long table. Small bottles of water, boxes of tissues and bottles of hand sanitizer were set out in the middle. The coroner, a clean-shaven man with a bald head and dense eyebrows, was seated at one end, and the Goldies did a good deal of fussing about who would sit where and whether coats should be on or off. I selected a seat on the other side of the table. The coroner began by stating that this was an inquest to establish the how, when and where of Vincent Goldie's death. It was not, he said, to decide any question of criminal or civil liability or to apportion guilt or attribute blame. Vince's mother began to silently cry, and the coroner opened the paper file in front of him. There was a knock at the door and we all looked up, my stomach leaping in a learned response, rather than actual fear, that it might somehow be Vince. It was Ray.

Once or twice in the twenty-three years since I'd seen him in person, I'd watched brief interviews with him on television talking about famous court cases. I took in the smart suit and tie, his trimmed white beard, his salt-and-pepper hair cresting backwards, the black-framed glasses and the chair he wheeled himself in with, my heart beating a little harder. I patted my hair, making sure the grips were still pinning it down. Ray apologized to the coroner for being late, saying something about trains and wheelchairs not mixing, and he looked around, taking in Vince's family and me. He nodded and I nodded back, and I had to make myself look away because I could have stared at him forever. He transferred himself from his chair to a seat, one away from Vince's father. I tried to work out why he'd come – surely he didn't think any new information about Sue would come to light – but he sat at the table, looking at his hands, which he held together.

The coroner read out a statement from the woman who'd been on the road outside my flat and had seen Vince fall from the balcony. In it she mentioned seeing me grab at him and nearly fall too. After this, he read out the pathologist's report. This was full of medical jargon, and the most I took from it was that Vince had lower than expected levels of his prescribed medication in his blood and no other legal or illegal substances. Next came a letter from the institution Vince had been in until a week before his death, explaining when and why he'd been released. They'd followed procedures and had assessed that he'd be able to manage independently, but wrote that he'd failed to attend two outpatient appointments and the unit had been unable to get hold of him.

When it was my turn to speak, Ray still didn't look up. The coroner asked me to read out the statement I'd already provided, and asked some points of clarification. When had I first known Vincent Goldie? Had I heard from him in the intervening years? What was I doing in the flat that afternoon? What exactly had we spoken about?

At this last question, Ray lifted his head. His eyes were red-rimmed and I thought about making up a story. I wanted to help him, and he looked at me beseechingly, but although Vince was dead, I still couldn't pretend to blame him for Sue's death. Not even for Ray.

When I gave my answer, it was Ray I looked at. I told the coroner Vince had said, 'I just need a glass of water.' He'd appeared at the door of my flat during that spell of hot weather in the summer. I said he'd started humming, la-la-la-ing a tune, and that he'd eaten a fly. I didn't tell them he'd said he was sorry before he jumped; I knew that Ray, and maybe the coroner too, would think this meant Vince was sorry for taking Sue's life. The coroner said he had no more questions.

'Is there anything you'd like to ask Ms Major?' he asked Vince's parents. The oxygen machine gasped and Vince's mother sniffed, but they shook their heads.

'Well, in that case,' the coroner started, and Ray bowed his head again, 'I am recording an open conclusion.' He turned the final piece of paper in front of him and explained gently to Mrs and Mr Goldie that it was unclear whether their son intended to take his own life or fell by misadventure through the window. The inquest was closed, and we filed out.

Ray and I stayed on opposite sides of the waiting area until the nephew, standing in the way of the exit, had finished helping Vince's parents with their coats and bags, making sure they had everything, checking his phone for their Uber. Ray rolled his eyes and swept his hand through his hair in that old familiar gesture. He tipped his hand in front of his mouth – an invitation to go for a drink. The movement caught the nephew's attention, and perhaps he took it as an exaggerated yawn at how long they were taking, because he left Vince's mother with one arm in her coat, the other flailing, and bent over Ray in his wheelchair, pointing a finger.

'I don't know how you have the audacity to come here today. I know who you are.'

Ray wheeled backwards.

'What's that?' Vince's father asked his wife in a loud voice, and she looked around, confused.

'I know exactly who you are and what your family think,' the nephew said.

'That Vince murdered my sister?' Ray said.

The nephew had turned away.

'We think it because it's true.' Ray was speaking loudly, wheeling himself so he would be in the nephew's line of sight, but the man was hustling the couple out of the door. 'A shame he was too much of a coward to admit it!'

'Ray,' I said to calm him. 'Ray. Leave them. What can they do?'

Out on the pavement, we watched them get into their car.

We went for a coffee in a place overlooking the Thames. It was October and the wind was blowing fiercely off the water, and after a couple of minutes of sitting outside, I took our coffees and we went indoors, where the only free table was in the middle of the room. We ordered cake and had to lean towards each other to be heard over the chatter of mothers, the cries of their babies and work video calls. We got the usual enquiries out of the way: that we were both well, that work was busy, that he was living in the same flat, that I was still renting. He updated me about Anita, frail but very much alive, Julie, the twins and Andrew. We said we hadn't changed, when clearly we had.

He leaned back and I almost didn't hear it when he said softly, 'It's lovely to see you.' He smiled, the same smile he'd had at twenty-one and at thirty-two, and here he was sitting in front of me again at fifty-five, and I smiled too, a grin I couldn't take from my face. I could feel myself blushing and picked up my coffee cup and held it to my mouth. He picked up his spoon and stirred his drink. 'I've written you so many emails over the years and deleted every one.' He tapped his spoon against the cup and put it down, paused. 'Tell me what happened before Vince fell. What you said at the inquest can't have been all of it.'

I pushed my half-eaten cake away. 'Ray –'

He moved forward again, hopeful. What satisfaction would he gain if I told him I'd smelled that terrible stink? Or how every night I double-check my doors and windows are locked, and jump at the sound of cars on the road outside my flat or the lift coming up? In *Rosemary's Baby* there is a scene where the heavily pregnant Rosemary is woken by her husband and Dr Sapirstein, the latter in his suit, waistcoat and tie, who tells her she mustn't say any more crazy stuff or make a fuss or he'll be forced to put her in a mental institution. Rosemary complies.

'There's nothing else,' I said. 'I'm sorry.'

Ray looked down into his coffee as though considering, and then he put his hand out across the table, palm up. I hesitated, looked into his eyes, still beautiful, and put my hand in his.

40

Ray and I started seeing each other again, going out to dinner, meeting in London parks for chilly bench picnics. We walked for miles around the city, looking at public sculptures, me on foot, Ray using his wheelchair or his stick. Beside Elisabeth Frink's sculpture of a horse and naked rider, so familiar to us from our hometown, where in cold weather people would give the second casting a woolly hat and a willy warmer, I bent down to kiss Ray and he pulled me on to his lap.

'I love you, Ursula. Marry me.'

I clung to him. 'I love you too,' I said. I didn't care what Anita, Julie or the rest of them thought; Ray made me feel safe.

Ray had always planned to watch *Dark Descent* at his mother's house. I preferred to watch it alone at my place and he didn't try to persuade me otherwise. The documentary was available at midnight, and ten minutes before, I opened a bottle of wine and took it with a glass to the sofa.

It started with a video: poor sound quality and fuzzy shots of a young man lounging on a sofa, incongruously surrounded by long grass. The person behind the camera asks him something inaudible and, laughing, he rolls over and says he's trying to sleep.

With a clutch of my heart, I realized this was the Under-wood's garden, the man was Vince and the voice was Sue's, even though she wasn't supposed to use the camera. I picked up the remote to pause the documentary, to be able to look at the man who had haunted me for so long, but I put it down again. I couldn't not watch.

The sound on the video is replaced by a voice-over: Emma Zahini. The woman cannot resist the sound of her own voice.

'There are three things you need to know about Vince Goldie,' she says. 'The first is that he had parents who loved him.' She's in a garage or a shed full of shelves stuffed with old pots of paint and cardboard boxes, and is riffling through papers, taking down files and opening them, explaining she's been looking into Vince's involvement in the disappearance of Sue Whelan for more than ten years.

Terry introduces the young Vince: sporty, sociable, a man who liked a drink and a laugh, adopted by a loving family when he was eight.

At least they got that right.

A school photograph shows Vince staring intensely, his features too big for his face. When he was young, he cared for his biological mother, a manic-depressive, Terry says, and corrects himself to 'suffering from bipolar disorder'.

Next, a man who'd been on Vince's football team confirms he was a talented player who could have gone far if only he'd had the right attitude.

And then Sue. A silent snippet of family video of her as a child, staggering as she carries a yellow dog almost as big as she is, and then showing off her biceps in a strongman pose.

A pain in my jaw made me aware I was clamping my teeth, that all my muscles were tensed. *Relax*, I told myself.

Breathe. I could watch this again and again, as much as I wanted, as much as I could stand. I poured a glass of wine and gulped a mouthful, grimaced, coughed, without taking my eyes from the screen.

Anita sits upright on a dining-room chair and talks about Suzie, what fun she could be, how helpful she was with the younger children.

I snorted.

The hair on her head and the mole on her top lip have faded to a pale grey. Once, Sue told me the mole was similar to several her mother had across her chest – vestigial nipples for feeding a litter – and we'd fallen about laughing. At the time it hadn't occurred to me that I was laughing about a woman's body.

Anita says Suzie was a happy teenager. Funny and raging, I thought, but not happy. She says her daughter was a day-dreamer, always imagining other places, America or Scotland, but that she had a steady job as a secretary at the art school.

For the first time, I wondered about visas. Maybe we would have needed one to get to America in 1987. None of us had considered it; maybe we wouldn't even have been let in.

Here again is Sue. Ten seconds of slow-motion footage taken from *The Underwood Possession*, starting with her back to the camera, then turning towards it as though Ray has called to her. She smiles at her brother. Sue, alive again. I might have said her name, cried it, put my hand to my mouth. I wanted to pluck her from the television screen and make her real.

Julie, sitting on a rattan sofa with white cushions, folds her arms and says, 'But you'd never trust Suzie with a secret.'

I laughed. 'Too right,' I said, although there was no one to hear me.

Terry says that Vince could become aggressive and violent when he'd been drinking. Another photograph with his hair down and messy, his expression leering.

Alan in his old people's home introduces *me* to the story by explaining how my mother died in horrific circumstances and that I was brought up in care. They show a photograph of me in my post-room uniform, presumably an old work ID. Me, at sixteen! Not as hefty and awkward as I'd always remembered.

Emma Zahini lets Alan embellish my history as though it might be an explanation for my future behaviour. The selfish mother who lived in a car with her child, dragged her to Morocco and provided no education for her was not the loving, exciting and creative Sadie I remembered.

There is a clip of the real Barrow Road put together with a video snippet of the Underwood as it was in 1987 – the opening shots of Sue's film.

The first reconstruction is of Vince, Sue, Terry and me taking drugs in the bungalow's lounge. Emma Zahini must have recreated it from descriptions that Terry provided, because the set is accurate, full of fussy old-fashioned ornaments, a bag of knitting beside an armchair, a record player. But Terry doesn't run around the outside in his underpants; we don't take the sofa into the garden or go into the garage and scare ourselves. The young woman who plays me is large and ungainly. Terry's voice-over says it was Vince who brought the speed.

Ray next, in his minimal kitchen, looking handsome and calm. 'This is the man I'm going to marry,' I said to myself for the reassurance. We had talked about the documentary before it was broadcast, and he'd told me his mother wanted it made, hoping it would jog someone's memory, reveal a new clue, or that Sue might miraculously appear. He knew I was never going to agree to be interviewed.

He talks earnestly about his love for his sister, the joy she brought him, and how he's missed her every day in the years since she's been gone. One of a kind, he calls her. He contradicts his mother and says he knows Sue would have got to Hollywood and be making films we'd all be watching if she was around today.

Out of shot, hanging on his kitchen wall, was the drawing I'd done of Sue, professionally put back together and framed. The screen blurred and I realized I was crying. I poured more wine, splashing it on to the table and not caring. I didn't drink.

Emma Zahini's voice-over again: 'The second thing you need to know about Vince Goldie is that he was dangerous and manipulative.'

More footage of *The Underwood Possession* with Sue as Mrs Bloodworth, Vince as her husband and me with my mouth open, tongue black.

A journalist from the county newspaper chips in, saying, 'The Underwood had an unsavoury history.' He reads a printout from a Google search. 'The grisly discovery of three bodies at a house in Hampshire is being treated as a triple murder-suicide.'

'Three?' I said.

'Jennifer Bloodworth was found beaten to death in the garden of the property, and it is believed that her husband, Derek Bloodworth, jumped to his death while holding the couple's three-month-old baby, Patricia.'

'No,' I said. 'No, no, no.' I covered my eyes.

In my imagination and in Sue's film, the baby had lived, its cries coming from inside the house even at the very end. The life I'd created for Patricia, of adoption by a loving family who never turn her away, was not true, had never been true. I put my hand over my mouth, unsure whether I was going to throw up. The journalist didn't wait. 'The place was empty for years. Scheduled for demolition. The couple didn't have any relatives, none that anyone could find. Apparently the house was full of their belongings. Who'd want to live in a place like that? I knew Vince Goldie was unhinged, I knew it from the off.'

They show more clips from Sue's film – anything that displays Vince at his worst: shouting at Sue as Mrs Blood-worth, asking for his dinner, demanding sex. It doesn't look like acting. They show the ending, to demonstrate Vince's drinking and aggression I supposed, but which of course also exposes me – the things Vince said about my body and my upbringing, told to whoever was watching.

My phone buzzed and I glanced at the screen. A text from Ray: *I'm so sorry. I had no idea EZ was going to show that. Are you ok?*

I'm ok, I messaged back.

Now Terry again, speaking more quietly. He fiddles with a piece of paper beside him, the size and shape of a bookmark, touching it, straightening it, looking down and back to the camera. He says he got to know Sue through Vince. 'We hit it off, right away. Understood each other. She was a laugh, always up to something, some scheme or idea. We would speak on the phone most days about her plans, the films she was going to make, or the trouble she was having with Vince. I don't know why she stayed with him, but I think she liked his undercurrent of danger. It was Sue who encouraged me to come out. I suppose it was down to her that I did, but that was after she . . .' He pauses. 'Was killed.

'She phoned me on the Saturday morning from the pay phone up the road from the Underwood, not her mum's house. She didn't normally stay over with Vince; in fact, I'd never known her stay the night with him. See, the thing is, I don't think she wanted to.' Terry coughs.

'What?' I said, leaning forward again.

'Yeah, sometimes she could be a tease,' he says. 'Especially with Vince, but that doesn't . . . These days, you know, with consent and all that. "Consent" wasn't a word we used in 1987. So, Sue phoned me, and she said, well, that Vince'd had sex with her in the garden the evening before. That's how she put it, but I knew she hadn't wanted to.'

Off-screen, Emma Zahini says: 'Are you saying Vince raped Sue?'

'She didn't use that word,' Terry says. 'But I suppose, yes. I should have told her to report it, I should have driven round there, but I don't know. In those days we thought rapists were strangers who jumped out of bushes, not your boyfriend.'

I picked up the remote and this time I did press pause. Terry's mouth was open, his eyes mid-blink. I flung myself backwards on the sofa, expelling a blast of air as though I'd been punched in the gut, arms outstretched in horror, surprise, realization. His words sent me back to the evening when Sue and I had been in the kitchen after Vince had gone to his room. I too hadn't helped her, had not understood what had happened, what I'd seen. I'd made it about me. 'Oh God,' I said. I thought about Sadie too and what she'd been through – that my father could have been her boyfriend was not something I'd ever considered. I pressed play.

Terry continues. 'On the phone she said Vince was going to go to America with her. She had this plan, she'd had it for years, to go to America and become a film director. Of horror movies. She told me Vince was insisting he go with her. I told her no way should she let him. Then I said something I'll regret for the rest of my life.' He picks up the strip of paper in front of him and begins to cry. 'I told her,' he says, 'that she had to tell him he couldn't go, but that she must do it in a public place – at the station or the airport – somewhere with other people around. That's what she must have done, gone to the train station and told him, and he killed her. He killed her.' The camera zooms in on his tears, his crumpled face as he covers his eyes with a hand, and to the strip of paper – a column of photographs. Sue and me pulling faces in the photo booth.

Vince's cousin comes on recalling Vince weeping at his grandfather's bedside and talking about football, arriving on his own and staying a couple of nights. Vince was going to sell him his car, and then inexplicably – at the time – changed his mind.

The recording of my panicked 999 call, subtitled because of the poor quality. The horror my sixteen-year-old self expressed was visceral.

Me: 'I hit my friend. She was going away without me, and I killed her. Something was outside the house, knocking on the windows. She was outside, knocking on the windows, but she's dead.'

Operator: 'You're saying you've killed someone?'

Me: 'She got up.'

Operator: 'Can you tell me your name?'

Me: 'It's Ursula. Ursula Major.'

Operator: 'Okay, Ursula.'

Me: 'And Vince, oh God, Vince. Please send someone.'

Operator: 'Is anyone hurt?'

Me: 'He told me I was mad. He said I was having an episode, but he let it in. And now –'

Operator: 'All right, Ursula, stay there, someone is on their way.'

They replay 'He told me I was mad. He said I was having an episode' several times.

I rubbed my hands up and over my face, pulling back my hair as though I could wash away that terror and the realization of what story Emma Zahini was telling.

We see the clip from *The Underwood Possession* where Sue is digging the grave, resting on the spade in between shovelfuls of dirt. And then a reconstruction of me putting a blanket in the hole, flinging the earth about, but in this version I'm not alone: Vince stands in the shadows watching, directing.

'No,' I cried.

The journalist explains who I'm known as now. 'Renowned' is the word he uses. They show a video that circles and zooms in on *The Lithopedion* before I put it in the woods, and a photograph of my fiftyish face. Uschi, the reclusive artist, is outed.

The retired detective describes the hole in the garage floor of the Underwood. He doesn't call it a grave; he says a blanket was found there but it wasn't kept; there's no evidence Sue's body was ever in the hole and 1987 was pre-DNA. He says the team always thought that Vince had got me to make a mess to distract the police from what really happened. That Sue's grave was – is – elsewhere.

He talks about Sue's suitcase, which was found in Vince's car. Packed for a trip to America, with her passport inside. He brings the story back round to me and, holding another piece of paper, reads what he says are brief notes a police officer made at the time – not a statement, not testimony – and never put in the police system. It mentions ghosts and ghouls, and fantastical ideas, including a 'claim' that I'd killed Sue, buried her in the garage, and she had risen up to haunt me.

Buried in a grave that had already been dug for Sue's film, he reminds us. 'Delusional' and 'gullible' are the words he uses. The document says that since I was brought up in children's homes I was therefore susceptible to Vincent Goldie's influence. As if these two things are in any way linked.

Terry returns, explaining that he and Vince would often go jogging in Crab Wood: 'It was unmanaged back then, with secluded areas away from the paths, and Vince knew it well.' He describes Vince, wild and crazy at the art school the day he attacked Ms Barker, although Terry hadn't been there. He implies that Vince was driven insane by what he did, or more insane than he was already. Ms Barker, of course, didn't appear in *Dark Descent*; she would never have agreed to an interview.

The detective explains that Vince, untried, never brought to justice, was held in a secure psychiatric institution for many years.

'The third thing you need to know about Vince Goldie,' Emma Zahini says, 'is that he's dead.'

The detective states that Vince was released last year, and a week later fell from the window of a third-floor flat. 'That flat was owned by Ursula Major, or Uschi as she is also known. The coroner declared an open conclusion.'

I shook my head, sipped my wine, forgetting I didn't like it. I knew what the detective was insinuating – that I might have helped Vince with that fall; payback for all he had done.

Then comes the card Emma Zahini has been keeping up her sleeve. Terry says Vince Goldie was involved in the death of his sister when she was seven and he was twelve.

'She died?' I shouted. 'He never said she died.' But he'd said very little that afternoon on the lawn at the Underwood before he'd pressed the burning tip of the joint on to the back of his hand.

'The official version,' Terry says, 'is that Vince was left by his adoptive parents to babysit his sister – their biological daughter.'

I shouted again. 'For fuck's sake. Are you saying that makes it worse?'

'The official version,' Terry repeats, 'is that he raided the drinks cabinet and locked his sister in her bedroom, where she opened a window, climbed on to the ledge and fell to her death. Sue told me the truth, which Vince had told her. He'd been in his sister's bedroom when she fell, goading her, daring her to climb out, taunting her that she wasn't brave enough. Sue never could keep a secret, we all knew it, Vince knew it too. He would have regretted telling her the truth about his sister as soon as it was out of his mouth, knowing she'd repeat it to whoever she fancied. She told me, after all, so who else might she tell?'

Emma Zahini had drawn a character capable of killing, a motive for Vince to murder Sue and a narrative. Rape. Secrets exposed. Maybe a body in the boot and that body taken to a nearby wood. Manipulating a vulnerable sixteen-year-old so she claimed to have killed her friend, put her in a hole in the ground, seen a ghost. 'Gaslighting', that's the term they throw around these days, although Emma Zahini doesn't use it; she doesn't quite want to let me off the hook.

'It wasn't like that,' I said to the TV, but the documentary rolled on.

Ray, once more. 'What about Uschi's involvement?' Emma Zahini asks off-screen. 'And where is your sister's body?' A long pause before he speaks.

'My sister is dead, and Vince Goldie killed her,' he says.

'But it's over. He's dead too. I don't believe my family will ever get to know where Sue's body is, and I don't need to know the details of how Ursula was misled by Vince. This will be the end of it, and that's fine with me.'

The music starts and text comes up on the screen: *Uschi / Ursula Major declined to be interviewed for this programme.*

41

When the documentary finished, I sat on the sofa, thinking about Ray's words: *I don't need to know the details of how Ursula was misled by Vince. This will be the end of it.* And I realized they were a message for his family and for me. He believes one thing, I believe another; he accepts that and has no more questions for me. I called him and he picked up immediately.

'I'm so sorry,' he said. 'I had no idea Emma was going to show the end of the film. I'm sorry I didn't turn off the damn camera in time.'

I could hear family chatter in the background, maybe someone crying. 'It's not your fault,' I said, although there was a bit of me that thought he was a fool not to realize what kind of woman Emma Zahini was.

'I meant it,' he said. 'The things I said. This will be the end of it. I've wanted to tell you for months, but I also wanted to say it publicly. And I told Anita and Julie and everyone that we're getting married.'

'They're all there?'

'They came to watch. Even the twins. It's up to them if they want to be part of our wedding or not. I can't wait to be your husband.'

I didn't need his family at our wedding, but it made me happy that they knew about me and Ray. We agreed to meet in London a couple of days later to set a date for the wedding.

'I love you,' I said.

Despite Ray's pledge bringing me some solace, I was still troubled that he, Terry and Emma Zahini believed Vince had murdered Sue. I remembered Ray's outburst after the inquest, and I imagined Vince's parents watching *Dark Descent* against the advice of their nephew, the light from a TV flickering over their faces as they held hands, the oxygen machine wheezing. Had they known how their daughter died, or did Terry's revelation come as a shock? It'd been presented as fact, that's what documentaries do, and everyone who watched it would also be sure of Vince's guilt. Vince had – probably – raped Sue, but that didn't make him a murderer.

I went to bed but couldn't sleep, memories looping in my brain, and so I got up, tired of thinking, and put on those old films: *The Stepford Wives, The Shining, Rosemary's Baby.* They still scared me, but it was a soothing sort of terror, fake and familiar, nothing like the real horror I'd once known.

What I hadn't considered was that the same viewers who were sure of Vince's guilt would also be convinced of my involvement. In the morning, after not much sleep, I made myself a coffee, sat at the table and opened my laptop. I don't use social media, but overnight someone must have found my email address and made it public. Hundreds of messages filled my inbox, calling me the name Vince had used, denouncing me as a monster and listing the terrible things they would do to me if I didn't reveal the location of Sue's body.

I deleted the emails as fast as they came in. There were voice messages on my mobile from journalists asking for interviews, offering money for my side of the story. The few concerned and supportive messages from Claudia and other friends made me feel worse. Sue was dead and I'd killed her, but Vince's parents had lost both their children, and their son had been branded a killer with no way to prove his innocence. All I had done for him was sit on my sofa and bow my head when I'd thought he was being buried.

The next day, I stood in a supermarket at Waterloo, wondering which colour tulips Vince would have liked, until, annoyed with myself, I grabbed a hothoused yellow bunch, paid, and ran for my train.

It was pulling out of the station when my mobile rang in my bag. I should have switched it off or not taken it with me. I let it ring out but it rang twice more. It'd be the police wanting to question me again about Vince's death, or Sue's, I thought, or a tabloid journalist, or a crazy person who had got my number. The fourth time, the man sitting opposite me at the table said, 'You'd better get that,' and lifted his chin at the QUIET CARRIAGE sign beside the window, where the rain was running horizontally, blurring the backs of the houses. 'In the vestibule.' He pointed to the end of the carriage and the area beyond the sliding doors. That place had a name? I gave the man a sour smile, dug for the phone, saw it was Ray and answered with a whispered 'Hello?'

'I miss you,' he said. At the doors, I pressed the button and stepped into the vestibule.

I laughed. 'It's only been two days.'

'Why does the idea of seeing family always seem so appealing before I arrive?'

'Count yourself lucky.'

'Yes, I know. Sorry.'

'I hope you're not in the house,' I said.

'I'm at the end of the garden. Where are you? Are you on a train?'

'I'm –'

'Were you leaving me without saying anything? You know I'd have to tell everyone that you jilted me, and what would that do for my social standing?'

'Okay, I'm on a train.'

'You don't really have to tell me where you're going. I'm honestly not the kind of man who keeps tabs on his women. I let the tracker I put on their phones do that.'

I laughed again. 'I'm coming south, down to you.' A pause. 'Oh, but not to see you and your family. I mean, I know that might be a bit soon.'

'Right.' He laughed too. 'It might be a little too soon. But you're coming down? Now I really want to know why, if it's not to see me.'

I took a breath. 'I'm coming to put flowers on Vince's grave.' I waved in the direction of the table, where I'd left the tulips.

'What? Why?'

Because it was the only way I could think of to apologize without making more of a mess of things. I'd considered going to his parents, telling them what had happened, but I knew they too would think I was crazy, or maybe worse, an attention seeker.

'Because . . .' I said. 'Because . . .' I decided to use the words Ray had used. 'Because this will be the end of it.'

'I'll come with you.'

'You don't have to do that. It's just something I need to do.'

'Do you know where he's buried?'

'Magdalen Hill Cemetery.'

'Do you know the plot?'

'No, but I can find it.'

'It'll be dark in a couple of hours, and it's raining. Let me come with you.' I relented and we agreed to meet at the station. 'Love you,' he said.

Ray was waiting for me in the foyer. I saw him before he saw me: he was using his stick to nudge at a leaf stuck to the toe of his polished brogues. When I reached him, he pulled me in close and put a hand behind the back of my head and kissed me for a long time.

'Wow,' I said when he let me go. 'You have missed me.'

He looked hard into my eyes and said, 'You don't have to do this, you know.'

I sighed and took a step back. 'I do. But you don't have to come with me.'

'If you insist on it, then I'm coming too.'

I hadn't been back to the town for over thirty years, and as we drove through it in a taxi, with a driver who wouldn't stop talking, it might have been a different place – more money, more development – and yet it also seemed like nothing had changed and I could have been sixteen again. We went past the city walls, and the art school, which I twisted in my seat to get a glimpse of, past the statue of King Alfred and over the river. It seemed possible we might pass the four of us walking down the street: Sue, Raymond, Vince and me. Except we had never walked together, and two of us were dead.

The driver talked about the local plans for work on the motorway below the bridge we drove over, and then something about the girls' school on the long straight road that rose steadily. The light of the late-January day was fading and he put on his headlights and windscreen wipers and told us about an archaeological dig from a few years ago at the top of the hill, where they had uncovered skeletons from a leper hospital.

I cut through his chatter. 'How's leprosy transmitted? Can you catch it from the dead?'

The man was silent for the first time since we'd got into the car, stumped.

Ray was holding my hand across the middle of the back seat. 'I'm pretty sure it needs a live host,' he said.

The driver turned into the cemetery and pulled into the parking area. I had my hand on the door handle when Ray touched my arm. 'We could still go back.'

'Come on,' I said and got out.

Ray asked the driver to wait, saying we wouldn't be long.

The place was bigger than I'd expected: a sweeping drive and acres of mown grass. Near the entrance, the graves were Victorian and ornate, with statues or railed tombs as though the bodies had their own tiny parks. Along the perimeter, the wind in the tall pines made the noise of waves on shingle.

The rain was heavier, and I opened my little umbrella and Ray squeezed under it too. I was surprised he hadn't brought one, Ray who always planned ahead. But then, I hadn't thought much about how I would find the grave – I'd assumed there would be a map, or I'd look for turned earth.

'Which way do you think?' I said.

'It's pouring.' He stooped further. 'This is crazy.'

'Get back in the car, then.' I was irritated; he didn't have to come.

'This way,' he said and ducked out from under the umbrella. The Victorian-style street lights flickered into life all at once, a yellow daisy chain strung out along the footpaths, and Ray set off. I knew he was irritated with me too from the way he used his stick, as though he'd never used a stick to walk with before, all out of rhythm.

'Wait,' I said, grappling with my umbrella in a gust of

wind. 'How do you know?' Suddenly I wasn't sure it was a good idea to be in a graveyard, even with Ray. I'd never been told where Sadie was buried, it wasn't in my care files, and I understood now why I'd never asked. I looked back at the taxi, where the driver was reading a newspaper under the warm interior light, and for a moment I was tempted to go back, but Ray was already turning off the drive, and I hurried after him.

The rain pattered on my umbrella and dripped off the foreheads of the stone angels, leaving grey teary streaks down their faces, and the tarmac of the path gleamed darkly. I caught up with Ray, linked arms with him and held the umbrella high over our heads, and he gave me a tight smile. After a few minutes of the irregular click of his stick as it touched the ground, I was tempted to ask whether he was in more pain than usual, but he directed us towards a gravelled path to the left that sloped uphill, and here the graves were more modern, clean with sharp edges. The rain became a downpour, and the wind blew in squally gusts, and the path became narrower so that Ray moved in front and I walked behind. I kept my head down, watching the backs of his calves in his jeans, his muddy heels, and I almost ran into him when he stopped.

'Over there,' he said, and I raised the umbrella to see. He must have looked the location up online somehow. The rain was beating down now, but there was still enough light to see that the grass was short, and the graves were evenly spaced with the stones upright. We had stopped at the end of a row, and a half-dozen graves away, at the far end, was a patch of soil.

I went ahead, sensing Ray following, but as I approached, I could see that something wasn't right – the flowers, which must have been left by Vince's parents, were scattered and trodden into the ground. The earth wasn't in a neat mound but strewn about, and the temporary marker – a rough wooden cross with the name VINCENT GOLDIE and his dates – was askew. My blood began to pound in my head.

'What's happened?' I said, turning to Ray and back to the grave. 'What is this?'

'My God. What's happened?' Ray repeated. The wind in the trees was louder here, closer to the edge of the cemetery, and his tone of voice was lost to me.

I stepped forward, moving my umbrella to see better, and the wind caught it, snatching it out of my hand and spinning it across the grass, a black shape, a bat, hurtling over the graves and down the hillside.

Ray put his arm around me. He said something – the word 'terrible' or 'awful' – but the wind and rain whipped it away.

I bent and picked up a flower, its petals crushed. 'Has someone tried to dig him up?' I said, and swayed against Ray, and he moved with me. I saw something on the soil, a long, thin shape, pale against the earth. I let him go and went down on to my knees, not thinking of the mud and the wet, and picked up a shard of polished wood about the length of my forearm. When I turned it over, I saw that a remnant of pale blue satin was attached to the reverse.

'Oh fuck, oh fuck.' I flung it away and bowed forward, panting, gasping.

And I saw again Sue's grave from all those years ago. The dark garage, the earth hurled about, the discarded blanket. And now I imagined hands ripping silky fabric, knocking on the coffin, and then beating, palms flat against the wood, and Vince, or the Vince-thing with its destroyed head, hammering until the wood shattered, and I saw the soil-filled mouth like the one I'd once seen at the door of the Underwood.

Ray stood above me, too shocked, I supposed, to speak, but when I reached for his forearm he held it firm for me to pull myself up. I swiped wet hair from my face with my muddy hands.

'This is Emma Zahini's fault!' I shouted into the wind. 'Stirring things up, inciting hatred. This is desecration. Is that a crime? It must be a crime. We have to report this.' If Ray had managed to work out where the grave was, other people could have too.

'Yes, we have to report it,' Ray said.

The rain was under the collar of my coat, my hair was stuck to my head. Behind us the trees gave out aching creaks as their branches rubbed against each other, and suddenly I had the feeling we weren't alone. If Sue had climbed out of her grave, maybe Vince – or the thing that had once been Vince – could climb out too and be waiting for us, behind a tree or a gravestone, watching. I looked around, but the cemetery seemed empty; no one else would be stupid enough to visit a grave in this weather.

'We should go,' Ray said. 'The taxi's waiting.'

He led me along the path. It was dark now, and I was glad to have him with me.

The taxi driver insisted on putting down plastic bags for us to sit on, but at least he was still there. It was only when I got in that I realized I'd left the yellow tulips on the back seat. Ray gave the driver his old address – Anita's house – and although I thought we should go to the police, I didn't protest.

42

During the short drive from the cemetery to Anita's, I raged; about the people who'd watched the documentary, the emails and messages they'd sent afterwards, and how Emma Zahini was schlocky and sleazy and cheap. The taxi driver was silent, and Ray let me rant, chastened I supposed because he had been part of it. I would have liked to call Emma Zahini right then in the car and tell her what she'd caused, but gradually I calmed, and decided I'd say hello to Anita first, then I would report the desecration, and afterwards I would call the documentary maker.

Many of the houses on the estate had been extended and modernized, and one across the road had been demolished and the house built in its place had windows instead of walls. Anita's looked older, paint peeling from the window frames, a brown stain where the gutter had overflowed and was overflowing now. Ray paid the taxi driver and I followed him to the front door. I'd forgotten Anita would be the old woman from *Dark Descent*; I'd been expecting the pregnant mother who'd first welcomed me in and then dismissed me and all children brought up in care.

'Hello again, love,' she said to Ray. 'You're soaked. Come in, come in. Out of the rain.'

'I brought Ursula with me,' he said.

A cloud passed across her face until politeness took over

and she ushered me in too. I handed her the yellow tulips; the irony that I'd bought them for the man she believed had killed her daughter wasn't lost on me.

'How lovely,' she said. 'You're soaked as well, and muddy. Where have you two been? Take off that coat. Raymond, go upstairs and get a couple of hand towels.'

I hung my coat over the newel post as Ray clomped his way up the stairs, his walk exaggerated as though for Anita's benefit. She went down the hall and into the kitchen and I followed. Nothing had changed here either, it was only more worn: lino torn in front of the cooker, one of the bulbs gone in the ceiling light fitting.

'I hear congratulations are in order,' she said – a way of not congratulating me.

Ray came into the kitchen and handed me a towel, thin from years of use. I wiped my face and hands, patted my hair and the back of my neck, soaking up the worst of it.

'Cup of tea?' Anita asked Ray. She filled the kettle and put it on its base and flicked the switch. It didn't come on, and she flicked it again. She lifted it off, put it down, flicked the switch once more. I thought Ray would offer to help, but he stood silently in the middle of the kitchen, and I realized he didn't have his stick with him.

'Maybe the fuse has gone,' I said.

'Oh dear.' Anita pulled out the plug and looked at it as though she might be able to see the cause. 'It's quite new too.' I examined the plug with her, but it was the type that couldn't be taken apart.

'Ray could check the fuse box, couldn't you, Ray?' I looked at him, and he began to hum, a sad looping tune, and he smiled at me, and his face reminded me of his dead sister.

'I'll just have a glass of water,' he said. 'I'm very thirsty.' I stared at him.

Anita was fussing with the kettle, talking about how much it had cost and how there wasn't anywhere left in town to buy electrical goods. Jess had ordered this one from the internet, and she'd have to ask her to get another, and she always claimed to be so busy.

She filled a glass with water and passed it to Ray. 'Oh,' she said, moving her finger under her nose. 'What's that awful smell? Something must be wrong with the drains. You'll have to look at that for me too.'

Ray took a sip from his glass, and at the same time as his mother, I saw in the water a small dark shape, spinning.

'Wait, love,' she said. 'You've got something in there.'

Ray held up the glass but looked at me, and then he tipped it and drank, the water and the fly.

I ran again from Anita's house. On the main road a bus was leaving, and I waved, and it waited.

I caught a train back to London, shaking in the vestibule and then locking myself in the stinking toilet cubicle. In my apartment I turned out the lights and didn't move any of the curtains. The buzzer rang soon after I'd arrived and I made myself go to see who it was, heart careening, but the monitor showed Claudia, and I didn't answer her insistent buzzing. I lay curled on the sofa, a throw pulled over my head, listening to my own breathing. It was Ray I needed, to hold and console me, to tell me I was safe, that I had nothing to be frightened of. But it was Ray who had drunk the fly.

Eventually, light crept in under the blanket and, using it as a cloak, I ducked and ran to the bathroom, where there were no windows – one of the reasons I chose this apartment – and hunkered on the toilet lid, feet off the floor, body trembling, teeth chattering, and tried to make my brain steady itself and focus. *Breathe*, I told myself. *Breathe*. I felt dried out, desiccated; my eyeballs hurt. I stood up and drank from the basin tap and looked at myself in the mirror.

'He's family; we're all family here,' I said to my reflection.

Behind me on the wall was one of my framed drawings which filled my apartment. In reverse it looked even more like Sue, watching me back, waiting for my next move.

I needed food. Staying away from the windows, I made coffee and three rounds of toast and ate them in quick succession, sitting on the sofa with my laptop on my knees. I searched the internet for Sue's film and found it easily – someone must have got hold of a copy and uploaded it. It'd already been viewed twenty thousand times.

It's not perfect: the camera judders and, unedited, the cuts between scenes don't flow, but I could see the potential of the filmmaker in the composition of each shot and the narrative. A natural storyteller. I stopped before the end, finishing on the moment when Sue as Mrs Bloodworth lies dead in the grass beside her husband, until her eyes flick open.

I closed my laptop and sat in silence. Perhaps I was wrong about Ray. He might simply have been thirsty and hadn't meant to swallow the fly, and he'd been using his stick oddly because he was out of practice. But I remembered the conversation we'd had all those years ago after the seance, and how his pain had disappeared while he appeared to be someone else. I closed my eyes.

Now I hear the beep of the lift button as it's pressed, and Dame Judi's voice saying, 'Doors opening.' My heart beats a little faster, a little harder. I think about the doorbell that rang so insistently at the Underwood that summer night in 1987.

Downstairs, the doors close, metal on metal, and Dame Judi says, 'Going up.' The lift ascends, the echo of the motor sounding in the empty shaft, rising past the first floor. I consider running to the window – I could open it and jump, the ground is far enough away for me to die; or I could run to the bathroom and swallow every pill I can find.

I think about parasites and contagion but don't have answers. I think about reckonings and suddenly I'm calm. I'm not going to run, not again. I've got away with murder for thirty-six years, and now it's time to stop. I stand and walk to the front door to press my palms flat against the wood. The lift is beyond the second floor now, motor whirring. I feel the clunk as it stops. 'Third floor.'

The peephole's fish-eye view of the landing doesn't allow me to see much more than the blank wall across the corridor.

'Doors opening.' The metallic slide reverberates through the surface of the door, the palms of my hands.

I hear hard-soled shoes on the hard floor and wonder if I'm imagining the bad smell coming in under the door. I press my ear to the wood, listening for the regular sound of his stick, the clink as he walks, the humming of the sad piano tune from the Underwood.

And I wait for whatever will come.

Acknowledgements

Thanks to my early readers: Louise Taylor, Judith Heneghan, Richard Stillman, Tim Chapman, Henry Ayling, Chloe Adams, Stephen Fuller and Lucy Atkins. Thanks to Indigo Ayling for reading and commenting about EDS. Thanks also to all my friends in my writing groups who read chapters, sometimes over and over.

Thanks to Jane Finigan and David Forrer. Thanks to all at Fig Tree/Penguin who made this book happen, including Savreet Virk, Karen Whitlock, Ellie Smith, Josie Staveley-Taylor, Annie Underwood, Kayla Fuller, Chloe Davies, Jane Gentle and especially my patient, tenacious and brilliant editor, Helen Garnons-Williams.

Thanks to all at Tin House/Zando for their wonderful work, including Win McCormack, Molly Stern, Nanci McCloskey, Becky Kraemer, Beth Steidle, Alyssa Ogi, Laura Schmitt, Julia Talley, Tiffani Renand, but most importantly, the amazing Masie Cochran.

Thanks to Kate Beal-Blyth and Graham Bartlett for their advice with a couple of areas of research. In addition, I talked to several people who were brought up in care or who have worked in the care system. Without exception, they were all incredibly open and generous in telling me what were sometimes difficult memories. I have invented Ursula's childhood in *Hunger and Thirst* but what I learned from these conversations helped, I hope, give some basis to what I put my fictional character through. I would like to thank Bob, Johnny, Lucie, Dominic, Pawel and Paul.